D1534923

ALCESTIS

ALCESTIS

KATHARINE BEUTNER

SOHO

Published by
Soho Press, Inc.
853 Broadway
New York, NY 10003

Library of Congress Cataloging-in-Publication Data
Beutner, Katharine.
Alcestis / Katharine Beutner.
p. cm.
ISBN 978-1-56947-617-8
1. Alcestis (Greek mythology)—Fiction. 2. Mythology, Greek—
Fiction. 3. Greece—History—Fiction. I. Title
PS3602.E828A75 2010
813'.6—dc22
2009031249

10 9 8 7 6 5 4 3 2 1

IN MEMORY OF MY FATHER.

[ACKNOWLEDGMENTS]

MANY THANKS TO Katie Herman and the staff of Soho Press for all of their hard work and for their commitment to this book; to Diana Fox, my agent, who believed in me from the beginning; and to Elizabeth Harris, Tom Cable, Ana Menendez, and my fellow writing students at the University of Texas at Austin, who improved this book immeasurably. Thanks also to Michael Adams and Lance Bertelsen for the encouragement and practical advice they've given me.

Thanks to Thalia Pandiri, a brilliant purveyor of the classics; to Bill Oram, a fellow lover of science fiction, fantasy, and poetry; and to Paula Varsano, who gave me one of the books that indirectly inspired this novel.

Thanks to Elizabeth Scott, Nephele Tempest, Amy Pascale, Jessica Brearton, Donna Randa-Gomez, Shana Jones, and Molly Sword, who have been invaluable readers and friends for more than ten years.

I could not have written this novel without the tremendous love and support of my parents, Edward Beutner and Betsy Beyer. My father lost his battle with cancer before this book went to print, but neither it nor I would be the same without the benefit of his love (or of his red pen). My mother continues to be my great friend and greater inspiration.

Finally, I offer thanks to Travis Brown, who has taught me—among many other things—how to eat a pomegranate properly.

I have always known
That at last I would
Take this road, but yesterday
I did not know that it would be today.
—NARIHIRA, trans. Kenneth Rexroth

ALCESTIS

THEY KNEW THE child's name only because her mother died cursing it, clutching at the bloodied bedclothes and spitting out the word as if it tasted sour on her tongue. After a few minutes her tongue stilled, and her limbs too, until she lay on the bed gray and cold as stone. The servants stood around the bed in a rough circle, looking down at the tangled mess the queen had made and thinking of the rituals her death would require, the sacrifices, the burning herbs nailed in clusters to the mud-brick walls. The room smelled of copper and sweat, as if a great battle had been fought within it. Anaxibia had warred with death and lost; for the moment, at least, her baby daughter had won.

They'd wiped the babe off, tied the cord, and swaddled her in a blanket. She squalled at first, face purple with incoherent rage, but then she lay quietly in her cradle as her mother's body hardened and cooled. She knew nothing of death. She came into the world as any girl might, unexpected, tolerated. If she hadn't been a royal child, she might have been left alone on a hillside to die nameless beneath the summer sun. As it was, Pelias had no time for the naming of girl children. The king would abandon the palace after hearing of his wife's death, taking a group of his best fighting men to hunt boar for the funeral feast, and would not return until the morning of her burial day. For two days the palace would be empty except for the children and the servants and the slaves and the animals and the body of the dead queen, swelling in the heat. The queen's spirit had already departed, trailing after the god Hermes like a cloak in the dust. The god had looked down at the baby in her cradle, a long, silent look, but she had not seen him—or if she had, she had not cried at the sight.

But now the baby wriggled, bleated like a lamb. The queen's body servant sighed and wiped her bloody hands on her shift. Stirred out of reverie, the other women shook their heads and blinked in the low light.

The women leaned down and rolled Anaxibia's body over so they could strip the linens from the bed. The queen lay slumped on her side, her brown braids mussed and tangled, her face smooth. She was twenty-four years old. The baby girl in the cradle was her fifth child, and the other children had been waiting for hours, clustered outside the bedchamber, to see their mother and new sibling. Their thin voices slipped into the room beneath the closed door. The women looked at each other. "Go on," said the head maid, nodding to two of the others. "They must be told. And the king too."

The chosen messengers left. After a moment, the children began to wail outside the door, their cries fading as the maids hurried them out of the women's quarters. The head maid turned back to the dead queen, then looked at the serious faces of the two other serving women who'd stayed behind, looked over at the baby in the cradle. She bent down to pick up the child and balanced the baby's small damp head against her shoulder. "Alcestis," she said and looked to the others for confirmation. "That what you heard too?"

Dry eyed and solemn, they nodded. They'd seen this bloody struggle too often to weep. "Alcestis," said Anaxibia's body servant, and looked at the baby, who had fallen asleep in the head maid's arms. "Poor thing."

The head maid put the baby down on her back in the crib. She sent a servant to fetch the kitchen maid who'd just borne a son, sent another to call the men to bring oils and cloths. The wet nurse took some time to arrive, but Alcestis did not cry. She lay in the cradle and listened to the skim and slap of the women's hands spreading oil on her mother's flesh, the silky whispers as they combed out and rebraided her mother's hair. She breathed in the smell of the room, the bodily stench of failed combat with the gods, the reek of a thread snipped. The women watched the baby with nervous eyes as they worked. The two who lived to hear of Alcestis' death—if one could call it death—would recall her birth then, and mutter to each other about the way the girl had opened her tiny mouth to suck in the fouled air as if it could replace her mother's milk. Perhaps she'd grown used to death then, they'd say. Perhaps she'd been hungry for it all her life.

I don't remember those moments, those sounds, those smells. But this is what I imagine from what I was told as I grew older. This, said the maids, the servants, my sisters—this was how your story began.

 WHEN I WAS eight years old, I lived with my sisters in the stuffy upper quarters of the palace at Iolcus. We had a small room to ourselves, a chamber that adjoined the female servants' quarters, big enough to hold the bed, a bench, and a small table. It was the room we'd all been born in, the room our mother had died in, though only Pisidice was old enough to remember the disaster of my birth. The room no longer held any traces of our mother. It was a girls' room now, temporary and unembellished, a place for princesses to sleep and grow until we were old enough to be married and carried away.

I slept with Hippothoe and Pisidice, jammed in the middle because I was the smallest. Pisidice came to bed smelling of crushed flowers and wet linen and kicked in her sleep. Hippothoe smelled of garlic and sweat, but it was a warm smell, not unpleasant, and on this night I'd fallen asleep curled up against her bony shoulder with my nose pushed into her skin. The bedchamber was dark and quiet when her writhing woke me. I felt the hot point of her elbow in my chest, quickly withdrawn, and then a light hesitant touch on my arm. I sat up half alert in the darkness and scrubbed at my face with my palms. Hippothoe looked up at me, eyes panic-bright, hands fluttering between us in time with her wheezing breath. She shook her head once and I understood. She was always sorry for waking me, always spent her regained breath on apologies I didn't need. She had these panting fits often, sometimes only nights apart, and I knew we would both be limp and lazy in the morning—but it was my duty to get help, like Hippothoe's own little goddess of health, and I'd grown so used to the role that I almost enjoyed it. I squeezed her hot hand, climbed down from the bed, and stumbled off to wake the servants in the outer room.

The head maid sighed when I touched her, a low, miserable sound, as if she could not bear being dragged from sleep. But she hauled herself out of bed and followed me into the bedchamber to fetch Hippothoe. My sister sat on the edge of the bed, shoulders hunched and heaving, the ends of her hair brushing her hands as they twisted in her lap. She leaned on me to stand, her body shaking as we walked, and I felt strong as a tower beneath her arm.

The head maid led us bleary eyed to the hearth, stepping over slaves sleeping in the halls. We stumbled down the stairs and past our father's empty throne. In the kitchens the head maid boiled water so Hippothoe could breathe the steam and rubbed cut garlic under her nose as she gasped and coughed. The air grew thick and my shift clung to my body, clammy with steam and fear. The head maid and I prayed to Apollo, running through the chant we said so often that I worried the god would tire of our entreaties. I believed then that he listened to me when I prayed. I imagined him stealing silently among us, reaching out to touch Hippothoe's chest with one golden-glowing hand, calming her, fixing her. I held my breath when Hippothoe choked and let it out only when her wheezing smoothed and slowed.

In the bedchamber, Pisidice still slept heavily, only muttering a little when Hippothoe and I collapsed onto the bed and tucked our damp bodies together. I put my cheek against my sister's shuddery chest and my arm along her neck. We looked like one gray-limbed creature, one divine monster, one flesh. I thought we would never be separated.

"Sorry," Hippothoe whispered to me as faintly as if she spoke across a great distance, while I stroked her forehead. "Alcestis, sorry."

⚱

IN THE MORNING Hippothoe's breath smelled faintly sweet, like a baby's, from the honey the head maid had given her for her roughened throat. I lay beside her, my back to Pisidice and my cheek hot on the linens. I had to pee. I'd been thinking of getting up to use the privy by the kitchens before the heat made the smell too terrible. I liked to walk through the quiet palace, to watch the servants and slaves twitch in their dreams like puppies, to watch my sisters snort and toss in the bed. But I waited, for I wanted Hippothoe to wake enough to pet my hair. On some mornings she'd drift into sleep again with a hand curved around my skull while I listened to her heart thud beneath her ribs. Now she stirred, restless and exhausted, and I felt Pisidice bolt into alertness with an allover twitch of her limbs. My eldest sister yawned, rolling, and kneed me in the back. Then she slipped out of bed and went to sit by the narrow window, settling in to watch the shepherds in the distant fields and gaze hungrily at the road as if she expected a visitor. Pisidice did this every morning. She was twelve years old and desperate for marriage.

"No one's coming, you know," Hippothoe said, and coughed hard, jarring me. She rested her thin hand on top of my unruly head.

"No suitors today, Lady Pisidice," I echoed, emboldened by Hippothoe's words. Pisidice did not look away from the window; I wasn't worth her attention. She'd left her comb and jar of oil on the sill and now she rubbed the oil between her palms and smoothed it over her hair, combing it through while she looked out over the royal road. The oil made her braid heavy and sticky; it made her smell like every other woman in the palace. I did not like it.

I began to tell her so, but Hippothoe hushed me and eased me up to sit, levering herself out of bed. "Let her be, Alcestis," she said, only half mocking. "She has to prepare herself."

Hippothoe didn't bother with her hair. It stood out around her head like a cloud, wavy fine and softer than wool. On some mornings she let me braid it and I wove the light brown strands about my fingers like rope. My own hair grew in bristling waves just past my chin. I'd had a bad fever the year before, bad enough that I had prayed to Apollo for my own health, and the head maid had chopped it off. Now I tugged a comb through it a few times before giving up. Pisidice turned her sharp eyes toward me.

"Really, put on a headband," she said. "You look like a boy. No man'll ever want to marry you."

Hippothoe, standing over the basin of water by the door, barked a laugh. "Perhaps she'll have better luck finding a husband if she does look like a boy."

Pisidice pitched the comb at her. Neither of them would tell me what they'd meant, though Hippothoe began snickering again as she yanked her shift over her head.

Our mother's body servant helped us dress. Pisidice was old enough to wear a maid's bodice, though she hardly filled it out. She was lucky she still had time to grow some breasts before she'd have to wear a matron's open bodice. I plucked at the lacings until she whirled around and smacked my fingers. The body servant waited, hands hovering in the air, until we'd settled down, then fixed each lace so they lay in a neat ladder across Pisidice's narrow back. Pisidice turned, cupping the servant's hands in her own, and nodded at her as graciously as a queen. Practicing. I rolled my eyes and chewed on the skin next to my thumbnail while Hippothoe tied back my mess of hair. I had to look presentable for the ritual.

It was the tenth day of the new year, the day of the dead vessel, and Hippothoe and I could not work or eat until we'd done the ritual in honor of our grandparents, Poseidon and the lady Tyro. My stomach already felt hollow. I hung near Hippothoe as we went downstairs, shoving my hand into the crook of her elbow. The skin below her eyes looked purplish gray, stained with weariness, but still she smiled and let me press close.

Pisidice was too busy to help. At twelve she ran the kitchens and supervised the slaves and decided our chores for the day, whether we ought to weave or spin, direct the washing or work in the kitchens. When we married, we would be mistresses of our own palaces, and Pisidice wanted nothing more. I watched her confer with the head maid, Pisidice's dark head tilted up toward the older woman's, her face serious. The slaves had prepared a place for the dead vessel; the omens of the skies had been propitious. It was the right hour for honoring the god of the sea, our grandfather, our household lord—and our absent grandmother. Tyro still lived, but elsewhere; Pelias was not a man who thrived on the care of his mother, and when his father,

Cretheus, had died he'd installed her in a smaller villa in the mountains, given her thirty slaves, and sent my young brothers to see her on days when she would need help to perform the family rituals. I had seen her only once, several years before, and even then she'd been a stooped, gray woman, few signs left of the beauty that had drawn Poseidon to her. She had shouted at Pelias; I remembered that because I had enjoyed it so much. But despite their rancor we celebrated her often in ritual, reminding Poseidon of his love for her and his duty to Iolcus.

"It's ready," Pisidice said to us, distracted. "Go on."

I peered through the kitchen doors to the hall. I had not heard Pelias that morning; he never spoke more quietly than a bellow, and my sisters and I tracked him by sound. If we could, we kept away from him in the mornings, when he shouted at the servants who woke him. We'd retreat to our quarters before he returned to the palace for his midday meal, sit on the bed together, and pick at our haul of cakes and cheese until a slave came to fetch us again. But today was a ritual day, and it would not be easy for us to avoid our father.

Hippothoe waited, silent. Finally Pisidice sighed.

"He's in the stables," she said, and Hippothoe glanced at me and nodded. She took my hand and led me through the hallways to the great hall. A few villagers stood by the doors, awaiting our father; in the afternoons, Pelias sat court here and settled the quarrels of his subjects. He did not yell much. Men would leave with chastened looks, like misbehaving boys called to task, and walk down the broad porch steps speaking of Pelias's fairness, his calm, kingly demeanor. I wanted to roll my eyes whenever I heard them talk of his virtues, but I was convinced that Pelias would appear to catch me before my eyes had made one revolution in my head. Even though I hadn't heard

Pelias's voice, even though Pisidice had said he was elsewhere, I looked for him nervously as we entered the great hall. I saw Hippothoe look too.

The two-handled vessel sat by the round hearth, where Hippothoe had placed it on the first day of the new year after the slaves brought it up from the shore; we girls were forbidden to walk into the water, even for ritual purposes. The seaweed circling the vessel's base had stained the clay white. Hippothoe knelt before the jar, picking the seaweed away and passing it to me as she whispered thanks to the local gods of the shore for giving us their harvest. I wound the crackling black-green strands into a loose coronet and placed it ceremoniously on her bent head. She made a little *ugh* face. We both preferred the laurel garlands of Apollo to our grandfather's brackish crowns.

Most of the seawater in the jar had disappeared into the air, but some still sloshed in the bottom. It smelled like Iolcus concentrated: salt and fish and stagnation. We hefted the vessel between us, but it wobbled as I flexed my pinched fingers, spattering water onto the stone floor. Hippothoe shot me a dark look. The seawater was a gift, and if Pelias saw it slop—but he hadn't. He wasn't there. We hobbled out through the entrance hall and the open doors to the porch and slaves bustled around us as we put down the vessel. One of the kitchen boys brought out a mallet and set it beside Hippothoe, bowing as its head clunked on the floor. She smiled up at him. The rest of the porch was empty, which was only right, for it was our territory in this warm season. Here we sat in warm weather, spinning wool, letting the wind gods stroke our faces. The work of spinning heated the calluses on my fingers and cramped my hands, but on the porch we could whisper to each other without distracting the men inside the hall, without being shouted at for our noisiness or dragged back to our bedchamber by our furious father.

Hippothoe knelt again, facing the sea and the jar. She motioned to me to fix my hair and held out her hand for mine. The creases of her palm sparkled with sweat. I swept hair out of my eyes, knelt, and gripped her hand, my head bent for prayer.

"Earth-shaker, sea-controller, grandfather," she said, her voice still scratchy. "We ask your protection this year, for the house of Tyro's children. For years you have given it, in recognition of your love, and for years we have repaid your protection with honor, for you are mighty and just, Grandfather, and we know it well."

While she spoke I studied the black painting on the sides of the jar, the warriors crouching there, their wedge-shaped beards. They had frightened me when I was younger, but the god my grandfather frightened me more. I imagined him grappling with my faded grandmother on the sands and was struck with a giddy terror that made me sink my teeth into my lip. If I laughed and Pelias heard me—or if Poseidon did—

Hippothoe continued: "We ask your care for the house of Iolcus, for Pelias and Pelias's children. Poseidon, Grandfather, accept this vessel we have made for you, to show how we honor your love. We offer you fealty, lord. For the house of Iolcus, I, Hippothoe, granddaughter of Tyro, second youngest, blessed by your hand, do consecrate this vessel to you."

She let go of my hand, pulled the crown of seaweed from her head, and pushed it through the mouth of the jar, then looked up, almost instinctively, toward the walls and the shore beyond. We drew breath at the same moment and held it, waiting, our chests full of uncertainty. Would he come? Would he be kind to us if he did? Would Pelias be pleased to see his father? Would I be pleased?

I'd seen my grandfather only once that I remembered, though Pisidice said he'd come to the palace after my birth. He had come too for Acastus's growth-day ritual. He had been great and fearsome, more fearsome than my father, and he'd left his trident humming in the corner of the great hall all day. Ever since, the stones in that corner had been swollen and crusted with salt; the kitchen slaves would scrape it off sometimes, those who dared to touch it, but it still crept back, glittery white. Mostly I remembered Poseidon's thick sea-clogged smell, and the way his black hair lay dull and damp against his skull, and the pattern of drips he'd left on the floors, like stories marked out in the stars. I didn't expect him to appear now—there was a reason the words of the prayer contained no specific invitation—but he might. He always might come, always might be submerged offshore, circled with Nereids, waiting to burst from the surf or to drag down some girl careless enough to edge her toes into the water.

We'd waited long enough. Hippothoe stood and ushered me behind her, then bent for the mallet. She swung it over her head and down: the jar shattered, seawater sprayed our ankles, pieces of clay clattered wetly on stone. Hippothoe's skirts were soaked. The silence of the courtyard seemed to swell for a moment, as if we'd been swallowed by some invisible wave, and then the noise of slaves and stable boys broke in upon us. The ritual was done.

Our brothers were watching us from the edge of the courtyard, tall Acastus staring, Pelopia darting sideways glances as if embarrassed. I nudged Hippothoe, who was shaking out her wet clothes. "They're here," I hissed at her, and she nodded—quick, angry jerks of her head.

"I see them," she said. "Behave yourself, Alcestis." It was a fair warning. I was already drifting away from her toward the boys.

Acastus was eight years older than I and Pelopia six—my mother, Anaxibia, had produced a child every two years until my birth, first two boys, then two girls, then me, taking a boy's place.

I saw my brothers at meals and sometimes glimpsed them in the mornings if we got out to the courtyard quickly enough, but I had hardly spoken to them for over three years. Before I turned five I'd been allowed to roam the palace without a sister to escort me; a quiet girl child could move about as freely as a shade. Acastus had been constantly surrounded by a group of young men, boys from the countryside whose fathers had sent them to the palace to earn our father's favor. They lay about in the courtyard, drinking wine and eating the food the servants brought them and talking of shooting contests or women or animals they'd killed, and rarely noticed me fingering the pommels of their swords and tracing the grommets on their leather armor. When Acastus caught me, he used to swing me into his arms and let me pat at his cheek like a baby, feeling the prick of his golden stubble beneath my hands. Acastus looked like none of Anaxibia's other children. He was burnished as a god, blond-brown hair falling to his shoulders, and everyone said then that he was the only child of Pelias in whom Poseidon's blood ran true.

The young men were warriors now. They didn't spend so much time drinking and I wasn't allowed among them. I was little heavier at eight than I'd been at five, but if I stood close to Acastus at dinner, he'd cross his hands behind his back and step away from me. He acted more like a king every day.

Pelopia didn't have Acastus's serious beauty or godlike carriage; he had a crooked nose and a crooked grin, and his hair stuck out funny all over his head, a mass of half-knotted dark curls. I liked his eyes best, for they were coppery in the right light, like ingots set beneath his lashes. They were our mother's eyes, the servants told me, murmuring to me in the kitchens or in the women's quarters late at night when I couldn't sleep, and mine were the same. I'd look like Anaxibia living if I'd only pay attention to my clothing and stop playing in the dirt whenever the mood struck me. My father, the king, would be ashamed, they said, and it was true. Pelias always looked on me with distrust, even before I did anything to earn it.

I was halfway across the courtyard when Hippothoe caught up with me. "Stop it," she said. "You know Pelias is near, and he won't like you bothering them. Come inside and get something to eat. Aren't you hungry?"

"No," I said, lying. I took another step away and Hippothoe's hand curved around my shoulder.

"I'm hungry," she said. I saw how faint she looked, and how gray. Reluctantly, I let her draw me in against her side and guide me back into the palace. We passed the slaves collecting the broken bits of the jar and the splattered seaweed, leaving the saltwater to dry.

I sulked for the rest of the morning.

We wove on the porch that afternoon, until the sun grew low. Then we climbed the stairs to our bedchamber to wait for the evening meal. Pisidice was already sitting by the window, looking for her imaginary suitors, and when she turned to us her eyes shone like the water in the dead vessel. "Did you do it right?" she asked shortly, and turned away when Hippothoe nodded.

Hippothoe fell gratefully onto the bed and propped herself up against the wall, holding her arms out to me. I fell asleep with my head in her lap. Her skirts smelled of the sea. When I woke later, she was still drowsing, her head dangling forward like a slaughtered calf's, her lips open and dry. I sat up.

I heard Pisidice's skirts whispering as she moved about the room, and knew I should wake Hippothoe for the meal, but I didn't want to. I knew what would happen at dinner. Pelias would demand an account of the ritual, but wouldn't notice Hippothoe's faintness or pray for her health. We'd rise from the table when he rose and wait in a silent, trembling line for his ritual kisses: Acastus's fair cheeks, Pelopia's, Pisidice's forehead (his hand skimming her braids), Hippothoe's brow. Then our father would kiss me hard on the crown of my head, never looking at me, while I tried to resemble my mother as much as possible, or as little—and he would leave without speaking to me at all.

※

THAT SUMMER, JUST before my ninth birthday, was hotter than any summer I could remember. The sun dried the land until dust swirled around the palace and strong, salty winds came in from the sea. The slaves hung cloth over the windows, but the dust crept in, reddening our eyes and making each bite of food crunch with grit. My sisters and I sweated terribly in our bed, jamming sticky elbows into sticky ribs.

It had been three weeks since Hippothoe and I had asked Poseidon's blessing, and miserable as the weather made us, the sailing had been calm and profitable. Pelias was in excellent spirits, and summer always made him social. He gave great feasts in the palace, gatherings raucous with wine and shouting and the giggles of local women brought in for entertainment.

On this night he was holding such a feast. The wind gods swept the noise under the cloth hanging in our window and into the bed. Our father's voice was inescapable as a god's, the deep roar of his laugh like a lion's. I lay drowsing with my head on Hippothoe's arm and the sound of Pelias's laugh followed me into sleep.

I dreamed of a creature with a fierce growl and a sad, blank-eyed face, a beast with such a lonely look that I chased after it, trying to pet its mangy ruff. But I could not reach it, and as I ran toward the creature, it spun on me with bared teeth and flashing claws and finally I stopped and let it escape. It called forlornly as it faded into the distance. I thought it cried in the Achaean tongue, but I could not understand it, and I woke teary, half trussed in my shift, afraid.

My head was on the mattress and the cloth beneath my cheek felt damp. I could still hear the growling call of my dream creature. I hitched myself up on my elbows and saw Hippothoe clammy and blue lipped beside me. She barked a cough like a warning growl and convulsed around it with a sound like wet cloth tearing—and then another cough, another, until it all seemed to be one spasm with no breaks to gasp for air.

I scrambled out of the bed and ran into the outer room, screaming for the servants. They came out of the beds so slowly, lumbering like beasts. I had my hands out for the head maid, grabbing for her, pulling her along behind me. She struggled free of my grip. She was saying something about calling the men, but I didn't stop to listen. I ran back to my sister.

In the bedchamber, Pisidice had awakened and was cradling Hippothoe on her lap, tilting Hippothoe's head back over her thigh. The terrible cough had slowed to a hideous dragging noise and Hippothoe's eyes were closed. I pressed up beside them on the bed, put a hand on Hippothoe's chest; I felt my sister's ribs beneath the damp nightdress and something making a thick rattle inside them. I jerked my hand back and stared up at Pisidice, whose face was gray and set.

"Are the others coming?" Pisidice asked me. Hippothoe jerked and moaned in her arms. "They'll have to carry her. Are the men coming? Did you call them?"

"I called," I said thickly. "Is it a curse?"

"Shut your mouth," Pisidice said. "She's ill—it's not a curse. Apollo will heal her."

For the first time that thought did not instantly soothe me. Hippothoe's hair was slicked to her skull with sweat. I smoothed strands away from her eyes, over her fine, hot skin. I couldn't seem to swallow properly, as if her struggle for breath had spread to my own body. "We'll take her to the kitchens," I said. "Once the men get here."

In the outer room there was a commotion, high-pitched chatter and lower voices answering. The head maid rushed into the bedchamber, her shift open at the neck and her heavy breasts swinging beneath it. She bent over Hippothoe, put a hand on my sister's forehead, then felt her fluttering throat and heaving chest. "How long has she been this way?" she demanded, looking at Pisidice.

"Not long," I said. "I just woke. I didn't hear her right away, it was so loud downstairs. I was asleep." I couldn't seem to stop talking.

A distracted nod. The room had filled with people, slaves bearing torches and rubbing at their tired eyes. The mass of their bodies muffled Hippothoe's rattling wheeze. My eyes slipped from one face to another, eyes and mouths and noses I knew, all a blur. Maids and slaves and stable boys, and none of them were doing anything to help Hippothoe.

"Take her," I cried. "You must take her to the hearth, she has to breathe."

There was a long, still moment. Then the head maid stepped

back and wiped her hands on her shift. "Fetch the king," she told one of the servants. "Take a guard with you. You, take her to the great hall. We'll need the royal hearth. The rest of you, call on the lord Apollo at once. Carefully, there!"

The chant began slowly around us, the same words the head maid and I always said. *O, Apollo, golden healer*—

A slave pulled Hippothoe off Pisidice's lap, away from my clutching hands. Hippothoe's mouth hung open and I wished I could reach down her throat to pull out whatever was blocking her breath. Her lips had paled, and when the slave slung her into his arms she gasped and her eyelids fluttered. I grabbed at her wrist.

"Wake up," I called. "Hippothoe, you have to wake up."

The head maid pried my fingers away. "Let go, child," she said softly. "You can follow them down right after. Best you pray to the god your uncle."

I stared at the woman, uncomprehending. The slave carried Hippothoe out of the room.

"Come on," Pisidice hissed, seizing my wrist and yanking me off the bed. I landed hard on my heels and let her pull me into a run. We raced through the women's quarters toward the stairs, the slave ahead of us, Hippothoe's feet dangling over his arm as he walked. He went past the kitchens, past the drinking room, heading for the great hall as the maid had instructed.

"He's not going to the kitchens," I said, panting and desperate. "He's taking her to the royal hearth. Why is he doing that? Pisidice? Are you praying?"

Pisidice didn't answer.

"He has to take her there, like the other times! Boil the water, and—and the garlic—"

Pisidice spun to face me, grabbing at my shoulders hard

and pushing me back against the wall. The rest of the servants passed us by in a rush, faces carefully averted as they chanted. I turned my head to watch them, and Pisidice shook me until my teeth clashed together. I smothered a cry. "This is not like the other times," Pisidice said, her fingers biting into my skin. She bent close. Her hair had come loose from its braid and it swayed in a mass over her shoulders. "It won't work. It won't fix her."

I stilled, staring into her stony eyes. "Why not?"

"Because it's her time to die," Pisidice said, "like it was Mother's time, when you came, and so they couldn't save her then either. Her thread's been cut, Alcestis. The water won't help."

"How do you know?" I pushed Pisidice away. "Only the gods know when she'll die. You're not a god, you don't know!"

"I know," Pisidice said. Each word had a hard punch to it, and I flinched away from her. Pisidice shook her head and reached out. "She's dying. Come on."

We ran again, shoving through the people clustered in the doorway to the great hall. I shook off Pisidice's hand and pushed up close to Hippothoe, hoping to see my sister's chest lift and fall, to see red in her cheeks, to feel her grasp my fingers. My hand fell on Hippothoe's shoulder: her skin warmed my hand, but she did not move. Her face was lax, her eyelids low. She looked like one in a dream. I thought: so the attack has ended; she's fallen asleep. But I leaned in, and I saw that her chest was not rising—there was no cough, no rough wheeze, no breath— but I could not believe it. I bent down and laid my head against her still chest. The world was hushed, the slaves had gone quiet around us, but hard as I listened, I could not hear the rattle of her breath. I would never hear it again.

"No," I whispered, her shift soft on my lips. "You can't go,

Hippothoe. Come back. You have to come back." I pulled back to look at her face again, and now I noticed the blue tinge in her cheeks. Her feathery hair still lay damp with drying sweat. I stroked it, like petting an animal's fur. I could not think.

A hand fell heavily on my shoulder. I looked up and saw my father, or a ghost of him, staring down at Hippothoe. Death was in his face. I recognized it.

My mouth came open, and I seized Hippothoe's cool hand, twined my fingers around hers—I would keep her with me, refuse to let her go—and stared out defiantly at my father and his guests. They stood behind Pelias, insubstantial in the low light, women with white faces and men with dark pools for eyes, their forgotten cups dripping wine on the palace floor. I saw a hint of motion in the darkness behind them, something trailing quietly over the stone—the sound of cloth, the sound of something escaping, the hem of the god Hermes' cloak dragging as he took my sister's spirit away. I had not even seen him come to guide her; I had not even felt her go.

"Move, girl," the king said, voice soft as wind. In the flickering light cast by the torches, I saw his sea-god father in his eyes. My grip slackened, and Hippothoe's hand fell to her side and lay open and unmoving, her fingers curled as if she were still holding mine. Pisidice pulled me back, hard enough to make me stumble.

Pelias bent over Hippothoe's body, her soft hair spilling in tangles over his arm as he lifted her. I could not see my father's face, but the line of his godlike shoulders was heavy with sorrow. He stood for a long time with Hippothoe in his arms, his head bowed, and it was as if the entire room had stopped breathing when Hippothoe did. The servants, the children, the guests, the king: all of us silent and still in the great hall of the palace while the sheets of cloth hanging over the windows swayed in the dusty breeze.

⁂

I WAS NOT allowed to help prepare my sister for burial. Pisidice wasn't either, and I heard her shouting at the head maid the morning after Hippothoe died: Why not, why can't I do it, he isn't even here to see. He'll find out, the maid murmured. Pisidice came stomping back into the room and threw herself onto the bed, knocking me in the arm with her elbow. There was too much space in the bed without Hippothoe and Pisidice seemed to want to fill it.

"He always does this," Pisidice said bitterly, her cheek jammed against the bed. "I hate it."

"Always does what?" I mumbled.

"Goes away to kill beasts when he should be here." She rolled over, away from me, her shoulder jutting up. "It's my job to prepare her. I'm the oldest girl. I should do the rituals."

I didn't know what to say. Pisidice let out a sudden puff of air, a sigh and a sob together. She was trembling, I could see it, her shoulders shaking as she lay there.

"Pisidice?" I whispered. "Are you crying?"

"I want you to be quiet," Pisidice said. "I want you to be quiet right now."

I was quiet. If I reached out, she might pull away and leave me alone in the big bed. I squeezed my hands together until I felt bones grind beneath my skin. The sensation of touching Hippothoe's cold hand came back to me and I shuddered and closed my eyes for a moment.

When I opened my eyes, Pisidice had fallen asleep. I watched her for a while, lifting myself up on one elbow to reach out and

22

feel the warm air slipping between her open lips, to look for the flutter of blood beneath the pale skin inside her wrist. She didn't wake as I curled closer. Her breath was regular and even. Her hair brushed against my nose and the smell of oil and flowers made me want to cry. I had not cried yet. Hippothoe was gone and I had not cried.

Hippothoe was on the other side of life, the world's quiet underbelly. I imagined her standing by the dark river, her chin lifted and her chest still, waiting for the boat to come and looking across the water at the vast, gray line of the dead crowding the opposite shore. All those people, all vanished from some life, leaving gaps behind them, holes like the extra space in our bed. Hippothoe would have to stand among them. Would they frighten her, my brave sister? Would she shrink away from the dead? Or would she open her arms to them, pull another dead child to her side, murmur sweet words in a rough voice until those around her forgot their own fear?

She'd have to wait two more days before crossing the river. Her feet would get tired, I thought, from standing for so long. I wished I were with her, so she could take me in her arms. We would stand together and I would support her as I always had.

But Hippothoe wasn't standing. She was lying dead in the king's chamber with the serving women, who were cleaning her with sweet-smelling oil, wiping away the scents of garlic and dust and sweat, braiding her tangled hair—the hair I'd never get to twist between my fingers again, the smells I'd never again breathe. The grooming would make no difference in the underworld. Hippothoe's feet wouldn't tire, and the river air wouldn't chill her, and nothing could ever make her hair behave, not even death.

I fell asleep and dreamed of running with Hippothoe through

the asphodel fields, following her jagged laugh, timing my pace to her jerky, eager gait, still interrupted by pauses to catch her breath. When I caught her at last she was grinning, joyous, as she folded our hands together.

I woke later to find that the room had grown dim. Pisidice had rolled over while we slept and lay with a hand curled beneath her chin. Her other hand rested on the mattress between us, fingers clasped around my smaller hand.

WE STOOD IN a loose circle around the empty grave. It was near dawn, the sky gray, and my brothers were dark masses beside me, pinning me to the earth. I watched the men lower my sister's body into her coffin. The body, draped in cloth, could've belonged to any girl. The torchlight cast long stripes of shadow over Hippothoe's form, and I could see the point of her nose beneath the bier cloth, the bump of her chin, the twin nubs of her hipbones. Hippothoe's chest was thin and flat as a boy's, as my own. The men had laid lumps of bronze on her breastbone to pay her way across the river. A man would get a dagger, but Hippothoe would have no use for a weapon in the underworld, no need to show the other shades her former strength.

The servant women were crying. They had loved Hippothoe, though not like I had. No one had loved Hippothoe like I had, not Pelias, certainly not Pisidice, who stood now with her hair in an immaculate braid and her eyes perfectly downcast. The women's wailing itched under my skin and I wrapped my fingers into the loose cloth of my skirt to calm myself. Pelopia nudged me with one elbow, a little bump like a mother cow nosing at a calf.

The men put the lid on the coffin, slid ropes beneath it, and lifted. It swayed on the ropes, and I remembered suddenly how much Hippothoe had liked the motion of a ship in the water, how she'd breathed easier in the salt air, how she'd exclaimed over the broken light dancing on the waves. Hippothoe's mouth was closed now, bound shut with a strap of leather to trap her illness inside her dead body. I had a strange urge to yank the strap free, let my sister's lips fall open—but there were no words dammed up behind the leather binding. She'd never call to me again, never sing out the first words of a prayer, never cry a welcome to sea gods or cloud gods, water or air.

Dirt fell on the coffin, making a hollow sound like a gong struck to call shepherds home. I watched the hole fill, the earth spreading in fans on the coffin lid, dry and powdery. Wind blew the dirt into the mourners' faces, where it coated our lips and damp cheeks just as it had all summer. I felt the air gods gather behind us: a hidden ring outside our mortal circle, mourning my sister. They were sorry the wind had sickened her. A sprinkling of salt water fell from the dark sky, dappling the dirt, our clothing, Hippothoe's body. A drop landed on my lip, and I licked it up like a tear, grateful to the local gods for their appearance. None of the Olympians had come.

The men finished shoveling. The grave mounded over the coffin, and I was glad that the wood planks would keep the earth from pressing in around Hippothoe's body. Pelias lifted the libation cup to chest height, above my head, and torchlight flickered on the cup's glazed bowl, which looked fragile in Pelias's large hand. "For you who watch us," he said loudly, as if he could force his voice to carry to Olympus, order his ancestors to care. He thought nothing of the love of the local gods and I hated him for it. I thought I saw the same fury in Pisidice's face. "On this day we honor you, gods. We give you our daughter,

Hippothoe. Accept her among you, and keep her with you forever. Lord Hades, Lady Persephone, give her rest and relief of burdens." He stopped speaking, and the cup wobbled, his hand unsteady. Softly he continued, "I ask you, Father, watch my girl for me."

Pelias tipped the cup and wine spilled out over its round lip onto the smoothed dirt. It soaked in almost at once, leaving a blood-dark stain on the grave, and I imagined it seeping through the soil and the lid of the coffin to stain the bier cloth and Hippothoe's white shift. Pelias righted the cup and raised its empty bowl to the sky.

The air gods melted away like an exhalation. The servant women quieted their cries, and we all stood about, waiting for the king to speak again. Pelias lowered the empty cup. "Cover it before dawn," he said, and walked back to the palace gates. Half the men followed him; the others remained to stand guard over the grave. I stared at the mound of dirt. A hand closed over mine, rough with calluses, male. I looked up the man's arm and saw Acastus, his godly face serious. He pulled me into the funeral procession.

At the door to the palace the men and women separated to wash before the feast. Hippothoe's body had been prepared in the king's chamber, but the women had still set up braziers in the corners of our quarters to chase away illness and bad luck, and the place reeked of juniper smoke, a bitter-sharp scent that stung my nostrils. I rubbed at my eyes and pulled my headband off, pushed damp fingers through my messy hair. Pisidice shoved through the group of servant women and claimed a bowl of water for herself, taking it into the bedchamber. She didn't close the door. I watched her struggle out of her bodice and strip her blouse over her head. Straight shouldered, her muscles flexing around the fine arches of bone in her back as she moved, her heavy braid hanging like a snake behind her. All the women in the room stared, waiting for Pisidice to shudder into sobs, but she pulled the white shift over her head calmly, without a sound.

The head maid frowned and brought me another bowl of water. "Wash your face, child," she said, touching the curve of my cheek. "Your eyes look bad."

I looked at my image, wavering on the surface of the water. I reached down, pulling away from the kind touch of the maid, and put my hands through the middle of my reflected face.

THE FUNERAL FEAST would last until Olympus crumbled, I was sure of it. I was sitting beside Pelopia, and no one remarked upon it when he wrapped his skinny arm around my shoulders and settled me against his side. He smelled more like Hippothoe than Pisidice did, but he was still not right, and I wriggled under the weight of his arm. He looked down at me. His face was solemn, no hint of a joke in his eyes. I hardly recognized him.

"You'll be all right, Alcestis," he murmured. "Eat something now. You don't want to worry anyone."

It was bad luck not to eat at a funeral feast, so I forced a bite of boar into my mouth. The noise in the room was rising, men filling their bellies with wine before they ate, and their voices battered at my ears. I put down the piece of meat and leaned back, slipping out from beneath Pelopia's arm. He turned, startled, and I braced myself against an expected yank, but he didn't grab me. His eyes were sad. "Go on then and be quick about it," he said. I scrambled up from the bench and fled the great hall.

Pelias called after me, but I rushed through the entry hall and down the steps to the courtyard. Through the gate, I could see the men standing around Hippothoe's grave, some leaning on sticks while the others held torches. The night had grown cool, and in their gray-brown woolen cloaks the men looked insubstantial, only outlines against the darkness. Gooseflesh rose on my arms. I took a hesitant step toward the gate, and one of the men looked up, his face a blur beneath his hooded cloak.

I heard footsteps on the stone behind me and shot a glance over my shoulder. Pisidice stood on the porch, eyes hard, hands on her hips.

"Well done," she said. "You've got us both sent upstairs now."

"I'm sorry," I whispered.

"You are not." Pisidice came down the stairs one determined step at a time and reached out to grab me. "Come on, unless you fancy being stuck in the room for a week."

I ducked away from her, toward the gate and Hippothoe's grave. "Don't," I said, suddenly anguished. "Pisidice, don't you—don't you miss her? Don't you?"

"Don't be an idiot. Of course I miss her." Pisidice's voice had gone quiet, but it was not soft.

"I miss her so much," I said under my breath. I wrapped my arms around myself, feeling the stretch of ribs beneath skin. The head maid had told me of a boy who'd died when she was a child, who'd sat by a pool in the woods and stared at his own reflection. He had so loved the beauty of his own face that he couldn't look away from the image, not even to eat or drink, and finally he had withered away to nothing, just some flower petals and a name. Narcissus, the head maid had called him. Now I thought I understood him better. Hippothoe was there in the ground; she would be there for years and years, and if I stood over the grave and looked down long enough, perhaps the earth would open and swallow me, pull me down to the underworld like a sea nymph pulling a pretty sailor over the side of a ship. I could chase Hippothoe, maybe even catch her, and surely the underworld would not be so terrible with my sister by my side.

My eyes were wet. I swiped the heel of my hand across my damp eyelashes and lifted my face.

"Come in," my living sister said, and turned back toward the entry hall without waiting for me to follow. I looked over my shoulder once, but I could hardly see the mound of Hippothoe's grave, the curve of dirt hiding my sister from my sight.

2 THE SHIP FROM Mycenae arrived in the early evening, sails unfurled, skimming in from the horizon with the ease of a dream. Along the rocky shore, watch fires flared bright, sparking as the men threw chunks of salt into the flames. At the window in the women's quarters, I braced my palms on the cool stone sill and arched my back to let the body servant tighten the laces on my blue maiden's bodice. My breath came short, stirring the fine hairs that had escaped my braid, and my cheeks felt fever hot.

I was watching my father marry, surveying the tiny figures on the shore from high above like a god. Pelias was a dark, tall smudge flanked by smaller gray smudges, his bride a white blot surrounded by her brown-robed attendants. The two groups met, shifted in a ripple of bows, moved away again. The dark smudge and the white blot walked to the edge of the gray-green sea and bent down, dipping their hands into the water; I couldn't see the details of the motion from above, but I imagined the slap of the waves against their wrists, the uncertainty of putting one's hands into Poseidon's power and knowing they might be captured in his bronze-hard grip. I couldn't hear the speeches Pelias made, but I knew the pattern of the ritual from villagers' weddings my father had blessed. First he would thank his sea-god father for bringing the woman safely ashore, then the local gods for the gift of good weather, and finally he would ask the permission of Artemis and Zeus and Hera, and they would grant it, or not.

Even Pelias, godlike king, went still as he finished speaking, waiting for an answer from the gods. None of the blots moved. I held my breath, hoping for a lightning strike from the clear sky—but the sea did not stir with snakes, the day remained cloudless, no ravens flew near to croak a warning. The wedding would proceed.

At the window above, I let out a disappointed sigh. The body servant gave my laces one last yank and went to join the group of servants helping Pisidice dress. I dropped my head for a moment and peered down at my chest, the still-surprising mounds of my breasts pushed up high by the bodice. I was twelve years old and just beginning to grow a woman's curves and heaviness. I was glad of the body servant's shy manner; the head maid had a disturbing habit of patting at my chest and telling me I looked just like my mother. I had no memory of my mother, not her breasts or her hair or the tilt of her eyes, and I didn't care to be compared to the woman who had left me alone with Pelias. But I didn't care for this wedding either. Pelopia had told me of Pelias's betrothal and I'd hardly had time to get used to the idea before the woman's ship had arrived.

He'd been leaning against the palace wall, talking at me while I worked the spindle and distaff. Our father was going to be married, he'd said, but he didn't know the woman's name or age, knew only that she came from the south, from the lands held by Mycenae. He'd scowled over my head as he talked, eyes on the horizon.

Acastus had gone to Mycenae less than a year before, bearing tribute to Atreus. Perhaps, I thought, he had gone to fetch our father a woman. I hadn't dared say this to Pelopia; he'd taken a bad fall from his horse in the spring, and the resulting injuries had left him with a tendency to favor his left leg and to snap at comments that would once have amused him. I'd asked instead if the woman Pelias intended to marry was royal.

Pelopia had shrugged. "Suppose not. But that doesn't matter. He's got Acastus."

"And you."

My brother had laughed. "Yes, he's got me to visit his distant holdings and collect a few animals from every poor shepherd I see. Important work."

"Pelopia." My fingers had stilled in the tangle of wool. "Anyone could hear you."

"Calm down, he's not here. Not like it's a secret either."

"Not if you complain so loudly, no."

He'd looked down and given me a grudging smile, nearly hidden by his long hair. It had been growing since he'd hurt his leg, wild curls hanging down in messy ringlets, and sometimes when I saw him out of the corner of my eye I thought he was Hippothoe, grown tall and stiff, walking away from me. "You do talk back, sour mouth."

That was not a warning, not quite. I'd looked down at my distaff, the mess of wool around the smoothed stalk of bone. "Do you think Acastus will bring her? He'll have to come back soon. He must marry in a few years, or at least be betrothed."

"That's for Atreus to decide."

"Atreus meddles."

"He's king of Mycenae, Alcestis." There, a flash of manly disapproval.

"Oh, stop," I'd said. "That doesn't make him less of a meddler, making Acastus wait to marry until he gives permission. Acastus isn't his son. They're all like old women sometimes, I swear it."

"He's already given his permission for Pisidice to wed," Pelopia had said, and nodded unperturbedly when I looked up at him. "She won't be running the household any longer when the new bride comes. You know how well she'll like that. I wager Pelias knows it too."

He'd laughed, and I'd laughed a little then too, at the thought of my imperious sister being displaced. But now, in the women's quarters, I leaned my hips against the windowsill and watched Pisidice snap at the servant who was trying to work one last ribbon into her heavily decorated hair. Her cheeks were flushed with excitement or fury—hard to tell with Pisidice. Hard to tell if I would miss her. Before Hippothoe had died I'd cared little for her, but since then I had grown so used to her presence, her fine features and graceful movements, stylized like a dance. Living with Pisidice was like living with a cranky painting—she was all temper and bright surface. Losing her would make the women's quarters quieter, but darker too.

Before he left the porch that day, Pelopia had stared at me the same way I was staring at Pisidice now, as if I had transformed beneath his gaze. I'd asked him what was wrong, why he looked strange, and he'd said: "Three years, sour mouth. Till it's your turn. If he even waits that long." He'd glanced around the courtyard, darted down to kiss the crown of my head, and wiped his mouth surreptitiously as he'd straightened up. I wore my hair in a heavy oiled braid like Pisidice's, and his lips had come away from my head gleaming. I smiled now, thinking of the look on his face.

Pisidice, who had been watching me, caught my smile and slowly, hesitantly, smiled back.

A shout came up the stairs: the wedding party was approaching the palace. The women made a hasty line at the door, splashing their fingers in the bowl of water there. When I got to it, a sheen of oil slicked the water's surface, a thin gloss of woman. I swirled my fingertips in the water and ran after the others, leaving damp smudges on the stone wall of the stairwell.

Had Pelias been a young and purely mortal man, the marriage would've been celebrated with a great feast held at the house of his father. But Pelias's Olympian father could not host a gathering in his realm under the sea; his mother was estranged and her mortal husband dead. So Pelias hosted his own wedding. The whole household had to be arrayed to meet the Mycenaean bride. I rushed through the great hall to the porch, stumbling among the servants until I found my sister. Pisidice rolled her eyes and grabbed my arm, pulling me down to stand on the lowest step. "I expect you'll be late for your own wedding too," she said. I folded my hands together and tried to look contrite.

The wedding party came over the edge of the hill, the light of the lowering sun striking their faces, flattening their features into beaten gold masks. Pelias towered ruddy as a god above the others. His new wife's eyes were obediently lowered. The woman wore no veil and no bodice, as if she were younger than I, and a murmur went through the Iolcan crowd at that—in the north, brides were always veiled, and the Mycenaean woman's skin was dark as a shepherd's, though even from this distance I could tell that she was beautiful.

Her attendants sang the wedding song as they walked, their mouths like dark caves in their browned faces. I'd hummed that melody as a child, unaware of its meaning, and had wondered at the servants' smiles. At the gate, the attendants halted, and Pelias stepped away from the procession to join his family and subjects by the porch steps. The sun had slipped to the horizon. The palace guards lit torches and passed them to the woman's servants, who hefted them without missing a phrase of the wedding song, and the glow of the torches spread over the courtyard, brushed the faces of the attendants, shadowed their eyes and lips. I hadn't seen such a group of silent men with torches since Hippothoe's funeral. I felt a throb of her absence in my stomach, a flare of the constant mournful ache.

One of the servants did not carry a flame. He stepped forward and held his arm out to the bride as if she needed help to cross the flat courtyard. I frowned, staring at the woman. She was still young, only a few years older than Pisidice, and she had been crying, as if she were going to her grave rather than her marriage bed. Her servants had braided her hair into a thick black crown and had reddened her cheeks and lips, but her eyelids were swollen and sore looking. Her eyes glittered blue-green in the torchlight like sun on the sea.

Pisidice made a soft, scornful noise. Startled, I glanced over at her—I had almost forgotten her presence. She did not look back at me. Her eyes were on Pelias's bride and her mouth had twisted into a knot of bitterness and envy. She could have been married a year before if Pelias had been willing to give her up. Now she would be displaced before a husband had come to claim her.

Pelias held out his hands to his bride. From the side, his expression looked gentle; he was less fearsome when he wasn't speaking. I looked again at the girl's teary face and wondered what my father had said to her during the rituals on the beach. Now, though the wedding ritual did not call for it, he spoke one word: "Phylomache." The crowd flinched again. *Battle lover*: an odd name for a girl, though maybe not so odd considering Atreus's warlike court. The girl stepped forward and put her hands in Pelias's, palms up, as if waiting for an offering.

The wedding song ended abruptly on a high, ringing note that lifted the hairs on the back of my neck. Pelias closed his hands around the girl's and led her through the crowd to the palace. The Mycenaean servants followed them, still carrying their torches, and the rest of the crowd surged up the stairs, girls and boys, palace servants and townsfolk and royalty, pushing me along. My breath caught in my throat, and I hiked my skirts up to my knees and ran with them, following my father and his bride.

We rushed through the great hall and to the doors of the king's bedchamber, and there the group stumbled to a halt, knocking me into the light-haired girl in front of me. Someone kicked me in the ankle and muttered a quick apology. I stood on my toes to look over the girl's shoulder as bodies pressed me forward. Ahead, the bedchamber doors opened, and the boys and girls stared into it, holding their breath, a giant swell of air in their chests, expanding like love. The servants had lit lamps within the room and the large bed seemed to hover in the glow. Light picked out my father's form and the edges of the woman's insubstantial gown, gave her honey skin a sacrificial brilliance. Pelias raised their entwined hands, then turned and led his bride into the bedchamber, and a hoot went up from the crowd, a baying whoop like the call of wolves.

The doors closed, and the boys began to sing, a wave of

sound starting near the chamber and spreading through the crowd. All around me voices leapt into the chorus. I didn't know the words to this song; I didn't want to know them, but I couldn't help hearing, for the village boys and girls pronounced the words clearly, with devotional ease. The boys sang of prowess and protection, the girls of virtue and fruitfulness. Faith and honor till I die, they sang.

The girls began a dance, or perhaps the boys did, a circling pattern of clasped hands and swinging legs. Several of the girls held out their hands as they passed me, forgetting who I was, forgetting that they could not touch. They were giggling, spinning, the words of the song fragmented by mirth. Faith . . . honor . . . I die. One girl managed to grab my wrist, and I yanked it back hard and ran toward the edge of the great hall. I reached the wall panting and leaned my head back against the cool stone.

All my life I had been given warnings: eyes down, voice soft, knees together. You're different, the servants had told me. You are not like us. We are not like you. A royal girl must lie like an undiscovered island, quiet and empty, skin clear and pure as miles of open shore just waiting for that first footprint, the rut of the hull in the sand, the press of discovery.

I'd listened, and I'd believed them, but I had not cared. Purity came easily to me—I was young and alone and untempted. But as I watched the dancers, I thought I saw what the serving maids had meant. I was meant for marriage. I would marry, but I could never reveal to a man what was damp and hungry in me, not like these girls, these laughing children, destined to be shepherds' wives or sailors' mistresses, to die bearing or beaten or old. I leaned against the wall and I felt the skin of my inner thighs brush, the dry slide of hot skin and tiny hairs.

Over the boys' singing, I heard a distinct female cry from within the bedchamber.

I twisted to look back at the closed doors—but there were no more noises, no disruptions in the song. Had I imagined it? I stood on my toes, looking for Pisidice, but couldn't see her in the crowd. Just braided heads and curly heads bent together, all the same, all oblivious—but no, there was a girl with narrowed eyes; there was another who had stopped singing and stood with her head tilted, listening. Their faces were exposed, like unpainted walls. They'd heard the cry too. They knew.

One by one they turned their eyes to me. Their faces were no longer friendly and laughing but cold, sharp, slightly panicked. They were thinking not of the Mycenaean woman but of my father—of what he might be doing to make her cry, of what that sound promised for them. They slipped other faces over his, and they felt other fears, but I had no other faces to conjure. I thought all kings must look as he did and rage as he did, and I, Alcestis, I would marry a king.

I pushed away from the wall and shoved through the crowd, jabbing with my wrists and elbows. The girls turned their faces away, but the boys watched me. Their eyes felt like hands reaching out to stroke me.

I burst through the knot of bodies at the door and into the cooler air of the porch, my breath coming fast and shaky. The porch was empty save for the two guards standing watch at the edge of the steps, hands behind their backs, faces half lit by their torches. I looked over my shoulder toward the glow of laughter and heat within the palace, but no one had followed me. I pressed my fingers hard against the beat of blood in my temples. Sweat was drying on the back of my neck; I told myself that was why I was shivering.

I walked to the top of the stairs, between the guards, and looked out toward the grave circle where my sister's burial mound lay hazy in the faint light of the torches. I was not allowed to visit Hippothoe at night—I wasn't supposed to visit her during the day either, but I woke early enough to leave the palace and return without being caught. Sometimes I whispered stories over her grave, true stories and false ones, whatever words I thought would delight Hippothoe the most. I would crouch by the burial mound until my legs ached and my night shift grew damp with dew. The grave circle was always quiet and empty: just me and the stone markers and the bones. The servants whispered about dark spirits that hung in the air over grave circles, but I had seen no spirits other than the wind gods who licked up curls of the dust from the ground. No spirits and no sister.

The courtyard was empty, the stable boys probably busy drinking in an empty stall, most of the guards sent outside the gates to patrol and watch the guests' belongings. The servants were in the house and I had not seen Pelopia or Pisidice since the wedding song had begun. No one would catch me now.

The two guards shifted, heavy belts clinking. The younger one blinked drowsily, rubbing at his eyes with his free hand. I gave him a sideways look, and he turned his face away: a guard's eyes could not linger on me for too long.

"You," I said and waited for him to look at me again. "Walk with me to the gate."

"The gate, lady?"

"Yes."

"I should not leave my post, lady."

"I know what you should and should not do." I let one foot fall onto the step below. "Ahead of me, please."

He lifted his torch reluctantly and stepped onto the stairs. The torch enveloped us in a small bubble of light. The ground felt unusually rough beneath my feet, as if I had drunk too much wine, and I put out a hand to steady myself and grazed the guard's downy forearm. The shock of it jerked us apart. "Sorry," he mumbled, his blush visible even by torchlight. "I am sorry."

I shook my head. My fingers were tingling. "It was my clumsiness," I said and lifted my head as we stepped beneath the arched gate. "You may stand here and light me." I walked through the gate and into the grave circle, the low wall curving off to either side of me. Shadows lay soft under the encircling stone.

"Lady, where are you going?" the guard asked, suddenly panicked. "Lady? I don't—I don't think you should be in there right now."

I said nothing. I walked among the grave markers until I came to Hippothoe's; it was next to my mother's, though I never visited that stone. The mound of my mother's grave was hardly more than a gentle rise in the soil now, for the wind gods had carried most of the dirt away. Soon the ground would be smooth, and when the circle was full of graves the men would build a round tomb above it, closing my sister in forever. I knelt between the graves, my blue skirts spilling dark against the ground, and put my hands on the soil. "Hello," I whispered. I had not seen this place in full darkness since Hippothoe had been buried. "Hello, Hippothoe."

Only the wind and the distant sound of revels. The woman's shriek was still loud in my head, and I would have given anything to hear my sister's voice drowning it out, anything to have her warm beside me, her head cocked down to let me whisper in her ear. I bent closer to the grave. "Pelias is wed, and his wife cried out in his chambers, and it was terrible," I told Hippothoe. "She's pretty but brown all over like a goatherd's girl. She was crying when they brought her in."

"Lady?" the guard called again from the gate, and I heard the quick, familiar beat of sandals on dirt. I sat back on my heels and waited. The footsteps slowed behind me.

"You aren't going to shout at me?" I asked.

"I'm too tired to shout," Pisidice said. She stood with her arms crossed over her chest, an aggressive habit so old I found it comforting. "Stand up. You're getting your skirts filthy."

I stood.

"You should not have come here tonight," Pisidice began, but stopped when I waved a hand at her. "What?"

"Leave it," I said, and felt pleased when she gaped at me like a fish. "Yes, it's terrible luck to be in a grave circle during a wedding. The grave spirits will eat me. Not every word that comes out of the head maid's mouth is the truth of the gods, you know."

I had hoped to provoke her into yelling, but Pisidice just closed her mouth and smiled a bit. "I know," she said.

"I don't see why I can't come visit her whenever I want."

"On a wedding night?"

"Father's wedding night," I said. "Where else should I be, in the bedchamber with him?"

"Don't be disgusting," Pisidice said, but there was no heat in it. She scrubbed her hands over her bare arms; she was shivering a little, like me. I wondered what she'd been doing in the palace to cause the slick of sweat on her forehead. Had she been tucked into a corner with one of the cheering boys?

"I just wanted to tell her about it," I said. "You know she loved tales."

Pisidice came closer. I could smell the thick flower scent the women had soaked into her clothes. There were creases forming by the edges of her mouth and the firelight deepened them until she looked like an old woman. She bent down, a lock of hair tumbling from her careful braid, and drifted her fingers over the dirt of Hippothoe's grave. Then she rose, and her face was smooth as the gravestone, the line of her mouth straight as the join of two blocks. "You'd have lost her anyway," she said. "In a year or two she'd be married and you'd never see her again."

I lifted my eyes from the grave, coldly angry. "That's not the same. This way—she doesn't miss me. It's better. You don't understand. I'm glad she's dead. She'll never have to be pawed by one of Atreus's stupid sons just because Pelias wants a good match."

"You'll—you'll never see me again."

"You want to be married," I said, though I knew she was right. I didn't like to think of her actually wedded to some distant, unknown man. "Hippothoe didn't."

"Hippothoe was a child," Pisidice said, and there was the bitterness I had expected, the sour grimace. "She never grew up. I want to get out of this house. I want to live somewhere where I can eat food that doesn't crunch with sand in every bite. I want to live in a palace that isn't ruled by a Mycenaean cow." She spat the last word.

"She's not a cow," I said, startled. "She was pretty, I thought."

"She lows like a beast, though."

For a moment we were both silent, equally shocked by the cruelty of Pisidice's words. Then Pisidice snickered, slapped her hand over her mouth, and began to laugh hard against her palm. I stared at her, and then the laughter caught me too, clenched my throat, and tightened my stomach until it felt like crying, like one of Hippothoe's attacks, and I wheezed with each breath.

"Oh, by the gods," Pisidice whimpered. "Oh. I can't stop." She threw out a hand and I caught it reflexively, leaned against her for balance. Then Pisidice pulled her hand away, wiping delicately at her eyes, still trembling with laughter. She looked at me and shook her head to clear it. "Stay still," she said, and reached out to brush tears from my cheeks without ruining the lines of paint around my eyes.

I took a deep, shuddering breath. "I pity her," I said. My voice was rough now, like Hippothoe's. "Don't you?"

"Wait three years," Pisidice said. "See if you pity her then." She turned to look back at the palace. Her arm pressed hot against mine through the slightly damp fabric between us, and then she shifted away just when I would have leaned into the touch. Air sneaked between our bodies again—cool, impermeable space. With Pisidice, I always had to consider what I wanted most: to accept the bits of love she gave or to push her for more, to gain another tiny crumb of affection and then be shoved away.

I remembered what it had felt like to snuggle against Hippothoe's side, to have my sister's skinny arm wrapped around me while I listened to the rhythm of a living heart—but I remembered it distantly, the exact sensations fading, sinking in the honey of nostalgia. Had she really smelled so, and felt so, and made such a murmur in her sleep? I remembered my dead sister's touch as better than any touch I'd had since: better than the casual pats of the servants, the accidental slips of Pisidice's fingers, the occasional furtive brow kiss from my brother. Pelias did not even kiss my forehead at dinner anymore. I'd hated that ritual, until it stopped.

Pisidice looked at me. "We must go in. They'll finish soon."

"They won't finish till dawn."

My sister gave me a sharp look. "And you shouldn't have been outside the palace walls at all. We must go in."

I gave her an ungracious nod and looked back at Hippothoe's grave. My stomach was still shaky with the remnants of laughter, but the sight of the grave caused a heaviness in my belly, a great quiet: the absence of Hippothoe's life. I felt that the best part of me had been cut out like a sacrifice to the gods. I said a small prayer to the gods of the underworld, asking them to care for her. I did not know how well they would listen.

When I lifted my head, Pisidice was watching me. She had her arms crossed over her chest again but her expression was not unkind. "Come on," she said, and turned away. I followed.

The courtyard seemed huge in the darkness. The palace loomed heavy and bright before us, and within it the bedroom song was fading now, voices going ragged with overuse. A breeze stroked my hair like the touch of a ghost. I watched Pisidice's feet on the stairs, the arch of her ankles, the sway of her skirts. I wondered if she would teach me how to walk like a woman— and I felt myself straighten a little, my shoulders going back and my eyelids lowering. We went through the entry hall and through the great hall. All around, boys and girls had paired off to kiss under the watchful eyes of the servants; I heard Pisidice mutter something rude under her breath. We passed a group of boys who stood outside the bedchamber doors, arms linked, shouting out the last boys' verse of the song and grinning at us as we went by.

In the hall beside the kitchens, some boys slept along the walls, and I had to step over their splayed limbs. Their faces were hidden in shadow, but I could guess how old they were by looking at the size of their hands: some nearly twenty, some no more than twelve. The absence of touch was a hollow hurt, but I could not imagine wanting any of those hands on my skin.

I followed Pisidice into the women's quarters and paused to dip my fingers into the bowl of water by the door. The room was empty of servants, the beds smooth and neat. Pisidice stood across the room, arms bent awkwardly as she reached for the ties on the back of her bodice. I wiped my hands on my dirty skirts, walked over, and pushed Pisidice's hands away.

"I can do it."

Pisidice let her hands drop. "Go on then."

I tugged the lacings through each hole in the bodice and listened to the breaths Pisidice let out when the cloth loosened. My sister's skin warmed the fabric, sent out heat to my moving hands. We stood in the women's quarters, removed from the noise and laughter still ringing in the great hall, the fading bursts of merriment. By the time I pulled the last lacing free, we were both holding our breath, silent in the silent room, waiting. Pisidice was waiting for me to finish, waiting for her own wedding, waiting for her life to begin, and I was waiting for her to pull away from my touch.

I will miss you, I thought. But at least you'll be alive.

I SAT ON the porch alone, distaff and spindle lying untouched by my feet, sandals dangling from my toes. It was late afternoon, and the low-angled sun spread out warm over my feet like a sleeping dog. Asteropia was napping upstairs next to Phylomache and the men had gone off to hunt. I put my elbows on my knees, leaned down to rest my chin on my hands, then rubbed at the warm grit of exhaustion under my eyelids. Phylomache hadn't slept well the night before, complaining that the baby she carried was restless, stirred by some night spirit. I'd had to light lamps and place them in the corners of the room, setting up a glow like a tamed sun to chase the ghosts away.

I'd spent nearly three years alone in the big bed, stretched out like a spider in the middle of the mattress. Three months ago I had turned fifteen and Phylomache's daughter, Asteropia, had turned two, and Pelias had sent the child away from her pregnant mother, telling her she was old enough to sleep with me. Asteropia sobbed nightly, writhing in the bed as if she'd been poisoned and smearing her wet face on my bare arms, and I began to fear that her constant crying would keep the god of sleep from both of us. Three weeks later, Pelias had ordered Phylomache out of the royal bedchamber because her constant shifting kept him awake. Asteropia was delighted; Phylomache fumed and took to bed in a sulk as if she could gain revenge through laziness. She would struggle out of bed to go downstairs for the evening meal if she felt well enough, but for the rest of the day and night she would lie on the mattress, stroke her mound of belly, and ask, in a sweet voice, if I'd mind doing just one small thing for her.

She'd give birth in a month at most, and when she performed her daily rituals to Demeter and Eileithyia for a safe and fruitful labor I prayed with her. If she delivered a boy child, even a sickly one, Pelias would take her back. Until then I slept on Pisidice's side of the mattress, crowded to the edge of the bed.

Today the palace was empty of men. Pelias and his steward were away with the hunters again, and Pelopia was collecting tribute from the men of Iolcus. Acastus had still not returned from Mycenae, though Pelias had received word that he was wintering in Corinth to add men to his party, having heard tales of bandits north of Athens. He might be home within a year. He'd stay with every lord or king who invited him to stop and rest, for such hospitality could not be refused, and I'd almost certainly be married and gone by the time he arrived in Iolcus, just a memory to him, a little girl with a messy mop of hair and coppery eyes like our mother's, another sister gone.

I sat up tall on the stool, lifting my arms over my head, pointing my toes toward the gates. My feet were browned from sitting in the sun, paler strips of skin running beneath the straps of my sandals. If I leaned back and twitched my skirts up just enough, the sun god stroked my ankles and calves. I eyed the road beyond the gates, knowing that Pelias would shout at me for baring myself if he saw my skirts bunched up. I was too old to think that the men of the palace did not see me as a grown woman, ready for marriage, ready for bed.

I saw the cloud of dust on the western horizon just as the sentry shouted, and I bolted up from my seat in fright, staring at the dark mass at the center of the swirling dust. My father's men, returning from the hunt, would not stir up so much earth. Once a pack of wild boars had raced toward the palace in just this way, turning aside at the last moment before entering the gates—Artemis had been angry with Pelias over some slight I couldn't even recall—but these were not boars. These were horses, at least thirty, led by a chariot. From this distance they looked like carven toys.

Iolcus had never been attacked while I was alive. I didn't know what to do. Were the horses armored? Were the men? The chariot did not belong to any family I knew, but the whole party was coming down the road at an almost processional pace. It didn't look like an attack. If they knew that Pelias was gone, however, they had no need to rush. They could seize me whenever they liked.

Artemis, I thought frantically, hearing the approaching beat of hooves. Artemis, O goddess of chaste girls, protect me from them!

In a moment they'd reach the gate. I jammed my feet into my sandals and fumbled with the straps, flicking my eyes back up to the road. Men ran from the stables to answer the sentry's call, light glancing off the hilts of their daggers. The chariot was close now, wheels rattling on the packed dirt, the thunder of hooves resolving into the sound of individual horses—jangling tack and air forced through flared nostrils. I stumbled over the distaff and spindle and kicked them under my stool. I could imagine the weight of a dagger in my own hand, the heft of sharp-edged metal, and wondered if I should have prayed to Athena instead.

The sentry stepped into the arch of the gate and held up a hand, nodding when the chariot pulled to a halt. His other hand was curved around his dagger hilt. He said something to the men on the chariot; I couldn't hear the words. But there was a pause, and his hand fell away from the dagger, and I watched in fearful disbelief as he stepped back to let the chariot enter the courtyard.

Two young men rode the chariot, one driving, the other gripping the rails as if he expected to be thrown off at any moment. They were not wearing armor. I had expected them to, and they looked small without it, almost girlish. The driver had golden hair, wavy and shining in the afternoon sun, but I could not see his face. The man beside him looked up as the chariot came to a perfect halt, his eyes skimming over the sentry and finding me where I stood alone on the palace steps. Even at that distance, I saw his smile, a pale flash in his dark beard.

He stepped down from the chariot. My hands ran over my skirt out of habit, smoothed out wrinkles in the fabric. Stupid, I thought, so stupid, he doesn't care what you look like. But it was as if I had been possessed by a god—I couldn't stop the rush of blood to my cheeks as the men approached. And then I could not stop staring, for the man who had stepped down from the chariot, the man leading the others, was beautiful.

It was the kind of beauty that seems unremarkable at a distance but gorgeous in fine detail. The man was slender, only slightly taller than Pelopia, and might have been ten years older than I, but his face was boyish beneath his beard, his straight brow uncreased. His red tunic was as fine as my clothing and just as wrinkled. He stopped a respectful distance from the steps and inclined his head. The charioteer stayed behind, but several of the mounted men came through the gates and stood in a loose phalanx behind their leader. Men now stood behind me too, stable boys and guards, thrumming with nervous energy. I heard them breathing. I heard the rasp of my own breath.

I stared at the handsome young man. He was still smiling, gracious and polite, as if we had just been introduced at the Mycenaean court. He was not a god, that much was clear— I had always thought somehow that if I were to be snatched away, it might be by a god's hands, as my grandmother had been—and he had not come to kill me. Now there were two ways this encounter could turn: toward rape or hospitality.

"May the gods keep you so beautiful, lady," he said. His voice was pleasant as a bard's and he didn't lean toward me as he spoke. His hands stayed open and relaxed at his sides, not twitching toward his dagger or clawing out to grab me. "You are, I expect, the lady Alcestis?"

He was supposed to say, *May the gods keep you well.* "I am," I said, keeping my eyes on the ground. The young man wore well-made sandals, covered in road dust that crept up to his knees. "I regret that my father, the king, is hunting and cannot welcome you now, but if you care to come in, my servants can offer you whatever you may need." The formal words came haltingly to my tongue, like a language I had heard before but never spoken.

"Pelias is away?" the young man asked, startled. He furtively wiped one palm on his hip. Was he nervous? I waited for him to exchange a glance with his men, to command them with his eyes, but he only looked at me, reddened above his beard, and looked away. "I should have thought he would have returned home by such a late hour."

So it would be hospitality. I opened my lips to let out a long thread of air. My chest felt like it might cave in, but I was on surer ground now, the words coming easily, my duty clear. I twined my hands together in front of my belly and looked down as I spoke. "Often he returns past sunset. Please, I bid you come in, and your men as well."

"I thank you." The man knelt quickly before me, his eyes flicking up to make sure I was watching as he bent forward. His hair tumbled into his face. "I am Admetus, king of Pherae," he said. "Your father is my uncle. I am come to earn your hand in marriage."

I looked down at the crown of his royal head. I wanted to put my hand in his hair and curl my fingers over the round of his skull. This was my cousin Admetus, son of Tyro's mortal son, Pheres? This was the first man to court me? The syllables of his name were familiar, but that was all. I'd never seen him. I'd never imagined that he would come to woo me—or that he would be lovely. I took a short breath and the early fall air seemed to ignite in my chest.

Admetus looked up and our eyes met again. I tore my gaze away, my cheeks gone so hot they felt chilled. I could not stare at him in the view of the men. "Welcome, my lord," I said in a rush and retreated into the palace, the group of Iolcan guards parting to let me pass. "Make him wait just a moment," I muttered, my fingers brushing a guard's tunic. When they blocked the door behind me, I broke into a run, dashing among the pillars and beneath the great arch of the entry hall. The great hall was silent, the throne empty, and my voice echoed cold and high pitched off the stone walls as I called for the head maid, the kitchen slaves, Athena, any woman to serve as a chaperone. A male slave burst out from the kitchen hall, his hands pale and grimy with flour, and stopped, breathless, when he saw the shadows of men in the doorway.

"Lady, who are these men?"

"Men from Pherae, with their king. I require a chaperone— the head maid. Where is she? Tell the kitchen there are thirty men outside who'll need food this evening. Good food, the best of what we have. Wine and meat for the sacrifice." I looked toward the entry hall where Admetus now stood, waiting patiently behind two of my father's men. He had a regal stance, though his smile just crested the men's shoulders.

"Go," I said to the slave, not looking toward Admetus, not smiling. "Now." The air beside me moved as the slave bolted into a run.

"Come in, my lord," I called, and, to the guards, "Let him pass. Welcome, Lord Admetus."

Admetus walked into the hall, and as he came forward I heard the slave barking orders in the kitchens and then a shriek—the head maid hearing news of strange men in her palace. Admetus looked toward the kitchens, confused by the sound. I bit down fiercely on the inside of my cheek and stared at the floor until the urge to laugh had passed. I felt dizzy and empty-headed with relief, giddiness bubbling in my belly.

The head maid hurried over, patting at my arm as if to reassure herself that I was still alive, unharmed, unraped. She shot a suspicious look at Admetus, and her protectiveness warmed me, but distantly, like watching a bonfire from my chamber window. Already I was forgetting my own suspicions. I had imagined occasionally what it might be like to have a man court me in my father's palace, and I'd guessed at my own feelings for a suitor, substituted Pisidice's determination or Hippothoe's childish distaste. In my mind the man had always been a vague shape, indistinct at the edges, built from bits of men I'd seen: a stable boy's pretty mouth, a shepherd's broad hands. Dark eyelashes curling against brown cheeks. But now the king of Pherae was here, small and slight, taking hesitant steps into the hall under the head maid's glare, and he blotted out my imagined men.

I waited for him to speak. Admetus took one more step toward me, and the head maid frowned and yanked me back. There was a long, tense silence.

"Is there—is something wrong?" he asked, sounding as uncertain as a child. It was strange to hear that tone in a man's voice; Pelias was never unsure.

I smiled and smoothed my hands over my hips, feeling the cloth move against my skin.

"We must wait for my father," I said. The head maid huffed a breath and gave me a sharp pinch on the soft flesh above my elbow. I twitched my arm away. "He may be some time," I added, looking at the floor.

"I thank you for your hospitality," Admetus said. His dark eyes were soft and entreating, like a hungry calf's. He looked away from me, then looked back, looked away again. It was a pattern; I saw that now. Our eyes could not meet for too long a time, but he could flutter his gaze over me like a bird's wing, and I could watch blood rise above the line of his beard and spread hot down his throat, where the skin stretched silky and fine.

He was waiting for me to say something else, I knew it, but I could think of nothing to say to him, especially with the maid standing beside me. If he were my brother, I could've prodded him for news of Mycenae and the other kingdoms, but I did not know how to speak with a suitor. I was not supposed to know how to speak with a suitor. I did know about the workings of a household, and these days, thanks to Phylomache, I knew a fair amount about the workings of babies, but I didn't think a king would be interested in a discussion of colic. Should we speak of the coming harvest, the god-blessed weather? Silence sprawled between us, broken only by the murmur of our breath.

"Will you not speak?" he asked. "Please?"

Too importunate—the head maid shifted uneasily beside me. I could see lighter lines around the corners of his eyes where the skin had folded when he squinted into the sun, and wondered how it would feel to smooth those creases with my fingers. "I cannot entertain you without my father's consent," I said. "I am sorry I cannot speak to you, but I would not incur his anger. "

"No," Admetus said instantly. "No, lady, I would not have you anger him. You must forgive my insistence. We shall await your father."

We awaited my father for hours, both of us silent, listening to the sounds from the kitchens and the courtyard, the servants talking and his men laughing together outside. I stood until my back began to hurt. When I called the servants to bring in couches, Admetus sat down with an ill-disguised sigh of relief. He reclined on the couch as if he were at a party with my father, propped on one arm, one leg sprawled out along the couch and the other bent. His tunic slid above his knees. The skin there was paler, soft looking, and when he moved a hand to twitch the fabric back into place I stared at the contrast between his sun-darkened hand and his pale thigh, vulnerable as a woman's flesh.

PELIAS CAME THROUGH the gates at twilight with a roar like a wounded beast's. I jumped, startled, and Admetus bolted off the couch. The slaves had their eyes lowered, as always, but I saw one of them fighting back a smile. Pelias stood in the doorway to the great hall, eyes gleaming ferociously. He had a bloodstain on his tunic and a smear of something visceral along one calf.

"Welcome, honored guest," Pelias said, voice booming through the hall, smile knife sharp. "Admetus, son of Pheres, Nephew. I thank you for your visit. What is your purpose here?"

I felt my face go hot. "Father!" I ducked away from the head maid's pinching fingers. "Please."

"I did not ask you to speak, Daughter," Pelias said. He hadn't taken his eyes off my suitor.

Admetus lifted his chin. "To earn your goodwill and request your approval to marry your daughter Alcestis, Uncle."

"Then your mission has already failed," Pelias said. "I have been hunting with my men all day. I want a wash and a meal and my wife. When I return to my home, I do not expect to find suitors lying in wait for me or for my daughter. This behavior is an insult to her virtue and a waste of my time. I will not brook it."

A cold prickle swept over my skin. An insult to my virtue? Admetus could have been a god, could have been a rival lord, and I had greeted him without fear. I'd shown him hospitality and care. I'd been a good host without being a bad woman, but Pelias didn't see. The head maid tugged at my wrist, nodding toward the kitchens, her eyes darting back toward my father. I began to edge away, but Pelias held out a hand and I froze, mural still. "You stay, girl. You've done nothing wrong. You have greeted our guests and made them welcome?"

"Yes, Father," I murmured. Admetus was watching me. I felt his eyes on my face, warmer than the touch of the sun.

"You," Pelias said, turning to Admetus, "king of Pherae, you should not have come here. Alone with my daughter while I was not at home. Unheard of! I grant you a night in my home, but you will leave in the morning at first light."

"My lord," Admetus said, and even I could see how difficult those words were for him. "I was never alone with your daughter. The servants of your house observed us at every moment, both men and women, and your daughter acted with perfect propriety."

"You do not suggest that a child of mine would act in any other way." Pelias folded his arms over his chest. He was at least half a head taller than the king of Pherae, half again as broad through the shoulders.

"No," Admetus said, stumbling over his words. "No, of course not. She is an honor to your house and behaves exactly as a woman should. That is why I wish to marry her, my lord. I will not leave until I have your answer."

"Have it? You've already had it. The answer is no, and you shall leave when I say."

"King Pelias—"

"Quiet," Pelias thundered. "Before I take your impudence as an insult rather than an annoyance. You are a king, Admetus, and I honor you. You are also my guest. You will eat well, you will drink, you will have blankets and couches, and you will cease your talk of marrying my daughter."

Admetus took an involuntary step back, looked from Pelias to me and back again. I watched him from beneath my lowered eyelashes and held my breath. Go, I thought. Go in the morning and do not come back. Then I thought: Come back, and take me away. The idea ran down my spine, crackling like a spark, flaring to life in my belly. I wished he had taken me before my father had returned, taken me when he had the chance, for now I would never be alone with him again.

I began to see what Pisidice had meant, why my father watched me so carefully now. Pelias was right. I was not to be trusted.

"Sir," Admetus said, "I will not cease. I seek her for my wife, and my desire shall not change. But I shall talk of it no more now, not until you agree to hear my case."

Pelias heaved a sigh and settled into his throne. "I will never agree to hear your case, Admetus. It displeases me. See to your men; my servants will assist you."

The young king closed his mouth with a snap. "I shall," he said, sketching a bow with sudden vicious energy. "I thank you for your hospitality, lord, lady." He turned before Pelias could respond and went out of the hall.

I waited for the shouting to begin, but Pelias gave me a tired look and waved a hand toward the stairs. "Up with you," he said, glancing back toward the entry hall. "Take food to the queen. Don't come down until Admetus and his men have gone."

"You're not angry?" I whispered.

"Have you done anything that should anger me?" He turned toward me slowly, and my stomach crawled. I backed away, hands out behind me to feel for the wall before I ran into it.

"No. No, I have not."

"Go upstairs then," Pelias said. I turned and went. The head maid walked ahead of me, uncharacteristically silent. When we came to the kitchen door, she grabbed my elbow and pulled me to a halt, then disappeared inside. She came back with an oatcake and a handful of dried apple slices and pressed them into my hands, anxious, glancing around for my father. I looked past her into the kitchens, where piles of chopped onions lay on a table and slaves bent over to stoke the fire beneath a roasting spit of meat.

"Go on," the head maid said. "Call for me if you need more to eat later. I'll bring something for the queen."

I went, but stopped on the first step of the stairs—if I craned my neck and peered through the pillars, I could just see Admetus's men entering the palace, subdued now that Pelias had returned. The chariot driver was not among them. The head maid hissed at me again, her head sticking out of the kitchen doorway, and I ran up the steps, clutching my sticky dinner in sweaty hands. In the bedchamber, I put the food on the table and went to the window, wiping my hands on my skirt. I braced my palms against the stones that framed the window as I leaned out. The courtyard was bright with torchlight. The chariot driver stood with the horses, holding their reins and murmuring to them, and I held my breath as I watched him, waiting for him to look up. He did not.

"Alcestis?" Phylomache said sleepily. I smiled at her. She pushed herself up, back against the wall behind the bed, and reached out to touch Asteropia's head, a brief glance of her fingers to reassure herself of the girl's presence, the same way the head maid had touched me. "What are you looking at?" she asked me. "Come away from there, you make me nervous hanging out the window like that."

"Admetus of Pherae has come to speak to Pelias," I said. "I'm looking at his horses."

Phylomache took a sharp breath. "When did he come? Just now?"

I pushed away from the window and went to perch on the edge of the mattress. "He came this afternoon while Pelias was hunting. I thought—" I stopped, but Phylomache nodded once, quickly. She knew. "But he was perfectly polite. We just sat, for hours and hours, and then Pelias came home and shouted at him." I rubbed my hands together, the skin of my palms sticking and gliding. "Admetus says he'll have my hand. Pelias refused him. And he didn't do it politely."

"It's not your hand the man wants, love," Phylomache said, and put her own hands on her belly. "You had chaperones, didn't you? The maid at least, surely. You can't have stayed down there with him alone. You would've wakened me."

"I had chaperones and guards. And I prayed to Artemis. He did not dishonor me." I reached over and picked up the cake, breaking off a piece and considering it. My stomach still felt trembly and knotted. "The head maid would've eaten him if he tried anything."

Phylomache's mouth twisted up on one side. "That is not funny, Alcestis."

"I know," I said, and put the piece of cake in my mouth.

"He made a bad mistake, staying while you were alone in the palace."

"So I shouldn't have invited him to stay?"

Phylomache waved a hand. "No, you had to invite him, of course. Your father knows that. He is letting Admetus stay the night, is he not?"

"He is."

"And then?"

"I told you, Pelias refused his suit. He ordered Admetus to leave in the morning and never speak of courting me again."

Phylomache gaped slightly. "He must not like this one."

"It seems that way, does it not?" I looked down at Asteropia, who was still sleeping, sprawled on her side with one fist against her face and her mouth wide open, too exhausted to be awakened by our voices. "She tired herself out today."

"You're so good to watch her," Phylomache said, her voice dropping into the same coo she used on her daughter. "You'll make a good wife, Alcestis."

I picked up the apple slices, slightly damp and flexible now from my touch, and ate one to keep myself quiet. Phylomache didn't notice. She rarely did.

"Tell me," Phylomache said, pulling off another chunk of cake. "Did you like him, this Admetus? Was he handsome or ugly? Did he bring many men?"

"It doesn't matter," I said. "Father won't hear him whether I liked him or not."

"Oh, Alcestis. Have pity on a huge married woman and tell me tales. I'm stuck here all day with nothing to amuse me."

I looked down at the bedsheets tangled around Phylomache's legs. I couldn't tell her what I thought of him. Phylomache wanted me happy in marriage. If she knew I admired my cousin, she'd bother Pelias to accept him, and we'd both suffer for it. "I don't know if I liked him. He's small, much thinner than Pelias or Acastus, and very brown. Looks nothing like them. I suppose he takes after the mortal side. He smiles often. I did like that."

"Not too often, I hope," Phylomache said, leaning in.

"No, not too often. And I suppose he's more handsome when he smiles, though he looks young."

"You shouldn't meet the man first, I think," Phylomache said. "If you meet him before you marry him, then you have time to dislike him. No sense in that. If Pelias chooses him, you'll wed him, and you'll be all right, if the gods bless the match."

"Phylomache, Pelias is not going to choose him."

"Hmm," Phylomache said with the expression that meant she was having a thought she considered very clever. "Does he have a lot of land?"

"He's a king," I said, frustrated. I knew none of the details of Admetus's rule, but that didn't matter—Pelias disliked him because he had come to pursue me, not because of the size of his kingdom. "He must. I don't know. Ask Pelias."

"I will." She smiled. "The boy hasn't lost you yet."

"He's not a boy," I snapped, flushing, and dropped a half-eaten apple chip into my skirt. "And he doesn't have me, Phylomache. You mustn't let Pelias hear you say that. It's not you he'll be angry at."

"Oh, he is a boy," Phylomache said, looking down at her lap where crumbs had landed after bouncing down her belly. She brushed at them ineffectually and spoke again without looking up. "They're all boys, really, even the gods. Hunting and fighting and making babies." She stroked Asteropia's head again, flicking a bit of hair out of the child's eyes. "It's not so bad, though."

I had not seen her look this sad since the wedding. I reached over Asteropia and touched Phylomache's wrist, the skin papery and warm beneath my fingertips. "Are you—are you all right?"

Phylomache heaved a great sigh and looked up, her eyes a little watery. "Yes. Just tired of this. I want the baby out and healthy and grown enough that I can sleep in my bed again."

I want that too, I thought, then bit my lip. "Do you need anything?" I asked. "I can't go downstairs till morning, but I could call one of the servants."

Phylomache shook her head. "No, just help me up. I want to walk around the women's quarters." I slid off the bed and held out my hands, trying not to wince when her fingers clamped around mine. Phylomache hissed when her feet hit the floor and stood slowly, as if she were being lifted by a rope and pulley. She shook off my steadying hands and took a few steps on her own.

"All right?"

A nod. Phylomache lumbered away like an ox. I watched her until she'd gone through the doorway then went to the window again, leaning out to count the torches in the courtyard. Some of them had been doused; Pelias must have decided that the Pheraean men were no threat. The yard was quiet, no talk or laughter carrying on the air. All the men except for the guards must have gone inside to eat and drink wine. Admetus would be sitting in the great hall with my father, suffering Pelias's rude talk or rude silence. I wondered if Admetus was thinking of me—I wondered what Admetus was thinking of me. Did he blush at the thoughts, wipe his sweaty palms against his clothes, look up to see my father staring at him with godlike eyes, furious as a speared boar?

Some light flickered in the courtyard: a lamp, an oil lamp, bright in the body of the Pheraean king's chariot, shining on golden hair. The chariot driver had chosen to stay in the rig rather than enter Pelias's house with his master? I stood at the window staring down at him, lonely in the cool air, and a shiver skimmed my body. I remembered the effortless way he'd managed the horses, the grace of his hands on the reins. He had turned them like a god turns the wind.

The golden head lifted, slow as a sunrise. I drew back so fast I scraped my palms on the stone and stood panting in the dimness of the bedroom. In the courtyard, the light winked out.

"Alcestis," Phylomache called from the outer room of the women's quarters. "Could you come here for a moment?"

I stepped back from the window, scrubbed the heels of my hands over my eyes, and went to help. When I woke in the morning, I crept to the window to look out over the courtyard, but the king, the charioteer, and the men were gone.

TWO WEEKS LATER we had another birth in the little bedchamber. I sat by Phylomache as she panted and cried, giving her sips of cool water and putting a wet cloth over her forehead. Everything went exactly as it had for Asteropia's birth: the labor was short, the afterbirth came out easily, Phylomache tore but did not bleed too badly. The baby was a girl, though healthy.

The servant women wiped her clean and daubed her purple skin with oil, chanting thanks to Eileithyia, Hera's hard daughter, for the mother's health and the baby's life. Phylomache lay limp and triumphant on the bed and watched.

Pelias didn't leave the palace this time, as he had when Asteropia was born, as if he'd thought he could prevent his new wife from dying by allowing her to give birth alone. He came into the women's quarters after the new baby was washed and fed, ignoring the protests of the servant women. The baby was sleeping, but Phylomache handed her up to Pelias without comment, though she frowned when the child began to cry. She smiled when Pelias looked back at her, though, the child held in the crook of his arm. "We shall name her Antinoe," he said, and Phylomache was still smiling, nodding, her dark hair tangled around her ruddy face. No one spoke of sons.

Antinoe was quieter than Asteropia had been, less fussy. Phylomache spent days cradling her with one arm and letting Asteropia snuggle up against her other side, singing softly to the children and calling them sweet names. She stayed in bed far longer than she needed to, and the head maid began coming to me for approval of meals and with requests for trade goods. Pelias didn't notice. He came to fetch Phylomache and the children some days and took them out to the courtyard to sit in the sun. He smiled when he saw Antinoe, and the smile stretched out to include Asteropia and Phylomache.

I had never seen him happy before. I told myself that I was glad of it. Pelias, distracted, had said nothing about suitors for weeks. When he did speak to me, his voice was slightly softer, his fierceness muted. Enjoy it while you can, I told myself. He'll forget this happiness before the baby ever grows to be a girl.

I was right.

Within three weeks of Antinoe's birth, I heard Pelias shouting at Phylomache in the great hall. I was in the kitchens directing the butchering of a lamb, my hands slick with blood. I wiped my hands on a cloth and ran out into the hallway, ducking around slaves carrying food.

The shouting stopped before I reached the hall. Phylomache brushed past me, sobbing, and ran up the stairs. A young servant woman followed, red faced, with Antinoe crying in her arms and Asteropia clutching at her skirt.

I touched the woman's arm. "What is it?" I asked. "What's happened?"

"The queen tried to tell the king whom he ought to choose as your husband," the servant said in a whisper. "The king didn't like it much." She shifted Antinoe on her hip, looking uncomfortable. I held out my arms and the servant gave me the baby with a grateful smile. "Thank you, lady."

I nodded. "I'll take them up. Come, little one," I said to Asteropia, stretching my hand down to splay my fingertips on the girl's head.

Inside the bedchamber, Phylomache lay crumpled on the bed, taking great quavery breaths. I sat down beside her, holding Antinoe against my shoulder and patting her as she quieted. Phylomache looked up with a shuddery gasp then buried her face in her hands again. Asteropia climbed up onto the bed and attached herself to her mother's legs, eyes solemn.

"You were pushing him to accept Admetus, weren't you?" I said, voice quiet so I wouldn't startle the baby braced against my chest.

Phylomache nodded without lifting her head.

"Oh, Phylomache. I could've told you that wouldn't work."

"You saw," Phylomache said, voice rising. "He never listens to me."

"He never listens to anyone," I said. "Don't try to talk to him about me. He's happy with you and the girls. He'll forget about it in a few days."

"I don't know why he won't let Admetus court you. It's not as if the house is full of suitors." A pause, and then Phylomache lifted her teary face, suddenly aware of what she'd said. "I didn't mean—"

I smiled. "They've been waiting until you had the baby. Pelias says he'll have a feast in honor of her and Demeter before the next full moon."

"He will?" She sat up, wiping at her face.

"He'll want to have the wedding after the harvest. The feast must be soon, and now there's a birth to celebrate." I cupped the back of Antinoe's head, feeling the warm, thin skin stretched over the baby's soft skull. The child's eyes had closed, her pink mouth open and slick with saliva. I wiped my thumb across the wet skin beneath her lips and kissed a wisp of feathery hair.

"Oh," Phylomache said, a little exhalation of air. "So there will be others." She held her arms out for her baby.

I laughed, though it sounded sour in my ears, and gave Phylomache the baby. "I'm sure of it."

"And nothing of—"

"Nothing of Admetus."

꧁

PELIAS HELD THE feast two weeks later, on a cool night. Fall had settled in slowly, browning the mountainsides and stirring the gray sea into a pitchy froth. The western wind licked at the coast with his great rough tongue, changing its shape little by little, lap by lap. Pelias had burnt two white goats in the courtyard in the hope that his father would hold back the sea storms for the week of the feast, and Poseidon indulged him. On the day of the feast, the sea lay bright and sparkling, deceptively calm.

I was ordered to wear my finest bodice, the red one with bright yellow stitching, and to let my body servant rub red juice on my cheeks and lips. I didn't ask what the liquid was; it tasted foul, and that told me enough. The body servant yanked my hair into a tight, intricate braid, binding it with bits of yellow linen until I felt like a cow being prepared for a festival sacrifice. Phylomache was allowed to wear a shawl, and I begged for one, complaining of the cold as if I were as delicate as Pisidice had been, but Pelias ordered the head maid to leave me bare armed to show off the whiteness of my skin.

The kings began arriving after noon. Princes, warlords with no palaces or lands—I hardly recognized any of them, though I thought a few of them might have been Acastus's friends as children. Some of them brought entourages of fifty men; some came with only a few attendants. Each tried to anticipate what sort of behavior would best please Pelias: deference or defiance, boldness or restraint. I watched them from the bedchamber window, counting their horses and guards, hoping the kitchens were adequately prepared for this onslaught of stomachs. Pelias would kill thirty cows for sacrifice, and the meat kept for mortals would have to suffice.

I looked for Admetus, looked for his slender brown body and ready smile, but he did not appear. The courtyard filled with men, all slapping at each other in that mock-friendly way, slinging arms around each other's shoulders and shouting out their surprise when they saw old friends. I began to wonder if we should've hidden the wine rather than stockpiling it for this night. Already the courtyard and the palace were thick with the smells of horses and men, sweat and hot urine, oatcakes and burnt oil, road dust floating in the air.

Phylomache and I had been told to stay inside until the slaughtering was done. I couldn't see the bonfire from the bedchamber, but I knew when the sacrifice began—the men quieted as if stoppers had been put in their mouths and the chosen cows began to low as the slaves led them in from the pen beyond the gates. Pelias shouted out an invocation to the gods, dedicating the feast to Demeter for the safe delivery of his child. Distance blurred his words, but I could hear that it was a man's prayer of thanks for birth, not a woman's, and not only because he didn't mention Eileithyia. He never spoke of Phylomache by name. Antinoe he named three times, though he did not mention her sex. I wondered what Demeter thought of being honored for the birth of female children.

The animals' dying gurgles came to us only faintly, but we could hear the thud when each cow fell to the dirt, knees buckling as its blood sprayed over Pelias's hands. I didn't need to see the slaughter to imagine it; I'd watched so many creatures die by the knife that it hardly bothered me anymore. The calves— sometimes they upset me, especially when they called for their mothers. I doubt I ever called for my dead mother as a child—I hadn't known what a mother was until I was old enough to speak and understand my siblings—but the helpless desperation in their animal voices left me unsettled.

"I hate listening to this," Phylomache groaned, shifting on the bed. "I wish they'd do it somewhere else."

"They'd still be killing cows whether you heard it or not." I turned my back on the window.

"If I couldn't hear it, I wouldn't have to think about it," Phylomache said, and put her hands over her ears carefully, so she wouldn't muss her hair. When the sounds stopped, I touched her arm, and she smiled at me, grateful.

"We should go to them," she said, settling her shawl around her shoulders. "Are you ready?" She looked lovelier than she had when she married Pelias, pink with health and still plump from pregnancy, her unbound breasts full above her feast-day bodice. She wore a gold necklace with beads shaped like ivy leaves, a thin glitttering rope across her collarbone. I looked down at my own body, unbreached.

"I'll never be more ready," I said.

The men had become loud again by the time Phylomache and I reached the courtyard. They'd collected the portion for the gods and set it aflame, and the column of smoke drifted into the dusky sky above the palace, reaching up to Olympus. The courtyard smelled of blood and burnt flesh. I coughed into my sleeve then grabbed Phylomache's hand. We walked along the long table until we found the empty places beside Pelias. A skinny man with black tattoos twining around one arm moved down the bench to give us even more room.

Pelias did not announce us, but the men turned to watch us as we sat, a row of eyes following our movements. Phylomache smiled demurely, but I could not; I pressed close to her, our hips jammed together, and stared determinedly at the table. "Move over," Phylomache whispered. "Don't be scared."

"I'm not scared," I said faintly. I moved away, just a little.

Pelias stood and waited for the men to quiet before speaking. The wine in his cup sloshed over his knuckles when he lifted it. "Men of honor, I have called you here to my home to celebrate the birth of my child, Antinoe, and to praise the gods who bless us with this birth. May they live in strength and glory forever and lead us to strength and glory as well, for our children and our children's children."

"May it be!" one of the kings called, thrusting his cup into the air, and the others let out a series of full-throated cheers.

"May it be," Pelias repeated. "I offer you the hospitality of my house. I am glad you have come. You have been invited here not only to celebrate the birth of my child but to compete for the hand of my elder daughter, Alcestis. She is old enough for marriage, and I will find a lord for her before this harvest season ends. I will find the best lord for her." He paused and looked around at the men as if daring them to cheer again. Wisely, they remained silent, though many of them were grinning at me, their teeth flashing in the low light. None of them looked remotely like gods. I felt them watching, and my cheeks heated beneath the red dye. I considered how far I might be able to run from the table before Pelias caught me and dragged me back.

"I know what you must be thinking," my father continued, genial now that the men were behaving themselves. "With such fine men courting her, how will I be able to choose?" Here the men did shout in answer, ribald suggestions about the length of their dicks and the strength of their arms. Pelias laughed, swinging his cup down to take a long drink of wine. "For my part," he said after wiping his mouth on his arm, "I'd have any one of you."

I chanced a look at Phylomache. She was still smiling. Though she had not borne a son, she'd been lucky enough to bear a girl her husband loved, and this feast would secure her place in the household. She wouldn't be displaced by a pretty boy or a village woman. These men would always honor her, would never touch her unless a war turned Achaeans against Achaeans.

Pelias waved an arm, silencing the group again. He glared at a few men who did not stop talking quickly enough. "All of you will stay with us in Iolcus for three days. There will be eating, drinking, contests of sport. I tell you, I will enjoy having such men as my companions. From your skill and your conversation, I will know you, and I will choose the man who will win my daughter in marriage."

I could see chins moving: approving nods, acceptance. Three days, I thought. That will be enough for him, so it must be enough for me. Phylomache turned to me, face bright with firelight and joy, and wrapped my hand in her own. Her palms were warm and smooth. She whispered something, but I could not hear it over the noise of the men muttering together. I knew what Phylomache meant to say. The queen's face was transparent as waxed linen. Isn't this exciting, Alcestis? Phylomache's look said. All these men, here to claim you. Aren't you glad to see them?

I nodded, smiled.

"Now," Pelias said, "let us eat this fine meal." He took the dagger from his belt and poked at the pile of meat stacked before him on the table. I watched carefully to see if he would give the best portion to a particular man; the guests were watching too, and Pelias knew it. He eyed the chunks of meat for a long moment, then stabbed the biggest, best chunk and sawed right through it, cutting it in half. A sound went up from the men, almost a sigh, like Pisidice used to utter when she watched the shepherds. There would be no hero's portion. The meat was passed out among them in equal pieces, running with red juice. I took my piece from the servants with a nod and tried to look only at the meat and bone, tearing bits free with my fingers.

The guests had turned their attention away from Pelias and talked as they ate, gesturing with their pieces of beef. The tattooed man beside me was telling his other seatmate about a new sort of Egyptian bow. I ripped a chunk of meat from the bone with my teeth. Even if I could have run from the table, could have somehow escaped my father, these men would have swarmed to my scent. They'd track me across the sea, I thought. They'd follow me into the sky if a god swooped down and took me.

I heard the noise outside the gates while the men were still eating and talking. It sounded like a rattling at first, as if someone were shaking the table, but none of the guests appeared to notice it. I lifted my head, trying to look over the tall men on the opposite side of the table, but succeeded only in collecting a number of lascivious looks. I turned to Phylomache, opening my mouth to say something, when a horse's whinny cut through the noise of the crowd.

The men looked around at each other, then stood in one clumsy wave, their legs entangled between bench and table. Cups of wine toppled and sent dark streams across the wood. Partially eaten pieces of meat fell to the ground, where the dogs set upon them at once, snarling and whining in the gloom under the table. I looked from the dogs to the men and back again, then turned to see my father marching toward the gate with his dagger in hand.

A chariot came through the gate—a chariot I knew, driven by a golden-haired man. Admetus stood beside the charioteer, wearing a fierce expression and more jewelry than Phylomache owned. He swung down from the chariot as it came to a halt and walked toward Pelias in short, angry strides. Pelias had slipped his dagger back into its sheath. He held his arms out as if to welcome Admetus into them.

"King of Pherae!" he cried. "Welcome. I regret that we have already begun our feast."

Admetus stopped a horse-length away from Pelias. "I see that," he said, and nodded to the men at the table. Some of them returned his greeting. "How strange."

"Strange, no. We began at the expected time, to let the sacrifice burn before the sun set. It was a good slaughter," Pelias said, stroking his beard. "I am sorry that you missed it."

"You did not give me adequate warning," Admetus said through gritted teeth. "You did not give me time. Your messenger arrived only this noon."

"Did he?" Pelias said. His Olympian voice was almost light. "He must have gotten lost on the way. Or ill. Or perhaps he stopped in the village near your palace to sample your women."

Admetus's fingers had been creeping toward the hilt of his dagger, but now they halted, his hand falling loose by his side. He looked right at Pelias, smiling. "You will not speak so of my people in front of these men, Uncle."

"No, you are right, Nephew," Pelias said. "I should not. This is a gathering of equals. And you have arrived late."

Behind Admetus, the chariot driver leapt down from the vehicle. The men's eyes turned to him, but immediately they shifted their gazes away, squinting as if his yellow hair were too bright to look on. Admetus waited for their attention as if he had known that his man would cause such a stir. When he spoke, his words were quiet enough that the guests at the table had to lean forward to hear him. "I am here now, Lord Pelias."

"That's true enough," Pelias said. "But it makes no difference to me whether you are or no. This is a contest, Nephew, and you have already lost. You have forfeited your stake with your disrespectfully late arrival. How can I give my daughter to a man who shows no care for the will of the gods?"

"I took the quickest route here. I drove my fastest horses."

"Indeed you did." Pelias grinned like a wolf. "But how can I entrust this girl to a man who comes so quickly?"

The guests roared with laughter. Admetus colored but held his ground. Pelias didn't give him time to speak again. It was like any scuffle between men—knee in the stomach, sharp teeth, and bared bellies—and my father used his voice like a bludgeon.

"Enough, enough," he said, holding up a hand. "Admetus, I tire of this. I have refused your suit once before. I had thought that you understood me, but it seems that you require a more forceful rebuke." He paused and looked at the gates, at the dark road Admetus had traveled. "Or perhaps it is a challenge you require, to show me your true nature so that I may understand why I should even consider giving my daughter to you. It is a challenge you shall have then. I will give you my daughter—"

I closed my eyes and waited for him to finish.

"I will give you my daughter if you come to claim her riding a chariot pulled by a lion and a boar."

My eyes opened. Around me, men's voices bubbled and hissed. I watched Admetus's face shift, his brow smoothing and the corners of his mouth sagging, humiliation draining away to be replaced by despair. His dagger hand twitched by his side. But then another hand slipped around it, and his chariot driver stepped up beside him, bending his head slightly to murmur in Admetus's ear. A slow smile grew on Admetus's face, nothing like the quick, broad grins I had seen when he visited before. This smile had cruelty in it, and joy, and it made something in the pit of my stomach turn over like a stone rolled by the tide.

The golden-haired man turned back to the chariot, stepping onto it to loose the reins from their knot on the frame. Admetus looked up at Pelias and said calmly, "Do I have your word on that, Uncle, as a king of the Achaeans?"

"Do you have my—of course you have my word. Do you think I would make such a statement if I did not intend to honor it?"

"You will honor it," Admetus said. "But for now I will leave you to your feasting. Honorable men, Lord Pelias, Lady Phylomache. Lady Alcestis." He nodded to each of us then spun on his heel and walked back to the chariot, taking the blond man's hand to be pulled up. With a flicker of the whip on their backs, the horses startled and bolted into a tightly controlled circle, whirling the chariot in a spray of dust. When it settled, Admetus had vanished.

Pelias stared after the departed chariot, silent, beginning to realize what he had done. It was not wise to ask spectacular things of young men in this age, only a generation or two removed from the gods who had fathered us. All strangers were shown hospitality because any stranger could be a favorite of the gods—any stranger, and any king. Pelias had set my fate in motion—and his own.

The men had gone quiet. The dogs still tussled for bits of meat. Phylomache sat next to me with her pink mouth open. Pale, they were all pale with sudden worry, and I was the only one at the table with any color left in my cheeks. I licked my lips. The bitter paint was sweet on my tongue, and when I took a deep, triumphant breath I caught the smell of fate that hung around the courtyard, stronger than the reek of smoke.

ADMETUS RETURNED LESS than two months later, at dusk, when everything seemed to happen. This time I didn't see him arrive, didn't see the cloud of dust or the chariot careening up the road, but I heard the sentries at the gate shout, calling for men to help them close the heavy wooden door, then the thunder of feet on dirt as slaves ran from the palace and stables to obey—and I knew he had come back for me.

I did not pray to Artemis or Athena. I bolted down the stairs, one hand skimming the wall to steady me, and flew through the great hall and out to the porch, catching myself on one of the columns when I skidded. Pelias stood at the bottom of the steps, yelling at the men to open the gate. "Let him in," he roared. "Let the boy in! Do not block this gate as if I am afraid of him. Let him come!"

The slaves hauled the gate door open, and there were the boar and the lion, there was Admetus's chariot, rocking and shuddering as the beasts pulled at their harnesses. Their muscles slipped and bunched beneath their hides, teeth snapping, paws and hooves digging ridges in the road. The boar tried to dance sideways and gore the lion with one tusk, but the lion avoided him, ruff shaking as he snarled, and the chariot driver called out to them in a language I did not recognize. His arms were taut with the effort of holding the creatures. The beasts subsided, panting. Admetus looked at Pelias, teeth bright in his dark face as he smiled.

"I had your word, Uncle."

Pelias took several steps toward the chariot but stopped when the lion growled. "You did," he said heavily. "I do not know what god assisted you, but I will honor my promise."

"Good," Admetus said. He did not step down from the chariot. "Then you agree to give me your daughter Alcestis in marriage."

"I do."

"Wonderful." His voice was sharp, but he looked at me where I stood on the steps and I thought his smile softened. "Lady Alcestis, if you will." He held out one hand to beckon me closer. I took a step toward him, imagining what it would be like to put my hand in his, to stand on the juddering chariot, pressed close to his body.

Pelias seized my arm, his grip bruise firm. "You cannot take her now. You must give us time to prepare. A proper wedding, a proper celebration. A month at least, Admetus."

Admetus shook his head, though he had to tighten his grip on the rail of the chariot when the motion made it rock. "I will have her, Uncle. I won't wait a month to see what other tricks you can conjure. I have won your contest."

"Several days then. A week. We will bring her to your palace in Pherae to marry you before seven days have passed."

Admetus considered. "On the seventh day. I will expect you. And I will expect her dowry." He nodded to the chariot driver, who called out to the beasts again in a low, clear voice, and they turned and jolted away. As they reached the bend at the bottom of the hill the chariot sped up, whipping around the curve fast as a lightning bolt thrown from Zeus's hand. The men at the gates stood and gaped. To have harnessed such animals without injuring himself, to have a servant who had driven the animals from Pherae to Iolcus, to speak so calmly when the beasts were snarling only an arm's length away—they thought he must be a god. They shot uneasy glances at my father, a mixture of awe and resentment, for if Admetus were a god and chose to punish Iolcus for Pelias's bad behavior, the entire house would fall.

"Back to your work, fools," my father said, as if disgusted. "He's not a god, though he's had the help of one. His father is as mortal as any of you, and his mother too."

The slaves hurried away from the gate. I turned to go back to the house, hoping Pelias would forget my presence, but he marched up the steps behind me, and my skin went tight with fear.

"You, inside," Pelias barked, grabbing my arm again and shoving me into the entry hall ahead of him. I tried to struggle free but he spun on me and pinned me against the brick wall, hands pressing hard on my shoulders. His eyes shone white rimmed like a statue's.

"Father," I gasped, hating the weak sound of my voice, hating him for forcing it out of me. I saw him tense when I spoke, and I knew then that he would hurt me; I just didn't know how.

"What did you do? What did you do to him when he came here before?"

"I did nothing!"

One of his hands left my shoulder and crashed into my

cheek, knocking my head back against the wall. "You will not talk back! Always talking back, just like your mother."

The side of my face throbbed hot and bright, and the back of my head stung. I swallowed against the thick, sniffling feeling that followed being hit, the sparkles in my eyes like coming tears. Not so bad, I was thinking, if that's all I get. "I did nothing," I whispered. "I tried to be good."

"Did you help him?" Each word was punctuated with a shake, his fingers pincers in my flesh. I gritted my teeth so that I would not bite my tongue, but it was clear that he wanted an answer. My voice came out in a spiraling cry.

"No, how could I have?"

"Calling a god to aid him with the beasts," he hissed. "Giving yourself to a god to get the husband you want. You women can't help it. None of you can."

Something clicked in my head like two wooden beads meeting on a string. I braced my hands on the wall behind me and pushed against his grip. "I did not help him," I said clearly. "I don't know how he did it. A god must have helped him, but I know nothing of it. Take your hands off me. I'm not your mother. I don't consort with gods."

Pelias drew a hand back to hit me again.

"Will you deliver me to my husband with a broken face?" I said, low and fierce. "He'll like that, Father."

He released me and took a step back, startled. Then the surprise broke into a laugh, bitter as ashes. "You have grown, girl," he said, spitting the last word. "Go up to your quarters and don't come down until the day you go to be wed." He stalked off through the great hall, shouting at the servants to get out of his way.

I sagged against the wall. One of the servants stopped,

concerned, but I waved her away. She continued on, but looked back at me twice before she left the hall, her eyes round with worry.

I climbed the stairs to the women's quarters slowly and walked through the empty main room into my bedchamber. Phylomache was bent over a basin in the corner, her back bowed as she threw up. The sickness had started again the week before and we had both known what it meant. There was no thrill in her eyes this time, no flushed joy. She was too tired for joy.

Phylomache stood, wiping her mouth and dipping her hands in the bowl of water by the bed. She flicked hair out of her face and saw me standing in the doorway. Then she saw the bruise.

"Alcestis," she whispered, crossing the room in a moment to examine my face. "Child, are you all right?" Phylomache touched the edge of the swollen place with hesitant fingers, pulling her hand away when I winced. "What's happened? Did Pelias do this?"

I nodded. "Because of Admetus."

"Admetus? Why did he hit you because of Admetus?"

"He came back. He won the contest—he won me. He did what Pelias asked."

"He didn't," Phylomache breathed.

"He harnessed the lion and the boar and drove them here. To fetch me. But Father told him we needed time to prepare, and Admetus said he'd give him a week. And then Father hit me because he thought I'd helped Admetus somehow. He said I must have given myself to a god to get the husband I wanted. I don't care whom I marry! He's the only one who cares, and he hit me because of it, because he was too stupid to think before he talked."

The world seemed too loud, too dizzying. I was growing

hysterical. I shut my mouth abruptly and waited for Phylomache to chide me, to tell me I shouldn't speak of my father that way, but she just pulled me closer and wrapped an arm around me, squeezing my shoulders hard. I took a long breath and calmed myself, pulled out of Phylomache's embrace and wiped roughly at my eyes. "I think the chariot driver did it," I said. "I think he's—" But something stopped me there, the word freezing in my throat.

"It doesn't matter how he did it," Phylomache said, as if she hadn't heard. "Point is that he did. How long did you say he gave Pelias?"

"A week."

Phylomache laughed a little, the sound rusty in her throat. "Impatient. Well. You'll need all your clothes washed and mended, and we'll have to pack them for the road."

"I can't help with much. I'm sorry. I have to stay here. He told me to keep out of his sight."

"It's all right, Alcestis. If you watch the girls, I can do it. You mustn't worry." She reached out, rubbed her clammy palms up and down my arms. "We'll have you out of here in a week. He'll forget about it, you know he will."

"I don't know," I said. "I made him furious."

Phylomache smiled, lips curving in a line I had never seen. "He'll forget," she said. "No man wants to remember being bested by his daughter." But the smile was gone as quickly as it had appeared, and she pulled away suddenly, dropping heavily onto the bed.

"You all right?" I sat beside her, put a tentative hand on her knee.

"Yes. I just feel sick. It'll go away in a month or so, praise Demeter."

"You should rest."

"No, I can't," Phylomache said, but weakly as I stood and pulled a blanket over her. She settled beneath it with a pale smile and patted the edge of the bed. "Sit, sit again."

I sat, curling my hands in my lap.

"You know—about men and women, don't you? About the wedding night?"

Anguished, I said, "Phylomache—"

"Don't make that face at me. Do you or don't you?"

"The servants talk of it all the time," I said. "And I've seen the animals bred. I don't need lessons, please." Pisidice had tried to tell me of wedding nights too, and I had not let her. I remembered her dreamy tales of men when we were children, and Hippothoe's grimaces in response.

"Lessons," Phylomache said, laughing again. "I'm not the one to ask. Pray to Aphrodite for that if you must. She's the only woman I know who enjoys it."

"Some of the serving women do, I think."

"Oh, well, serving women. Alcestis! You're marrying a king. You'll be taking advice from the slaves next." Phylomache shifted up onto one elbow, propping her cheek on her hand. "Don't look so sour. It isn't that awful. Just let him do what he wants as long as it doesn't hurt too much. If you're lucky you'll conceive right away, and then you won't have to worry about it for most of a year."

I flopped down and pushed my hot face into the musty mattress. "I'm not listening to you," I said, my voice muffled, but I was listening, and I was shivering, and I was thinking of Admetus: just let him do what he wants. I'd always thought of marriage as a distant necessity, a blurry destiny, awaiting me as I grew, but I'd dreamed in ideal domestic terms: a few boy children to keep me safe, girls to love me, obedient servants, health, and quiet. I'd fantasized only of being out of my father's house and mistress of my own.

Phylomache petted my back as if I were one of her own daughters. "Hush, now," she said. "Come, we'll sort through your clothing. Call up one of the serving girls."

Within an hour she had me half buried beneath a pile of clothing and was chattering contentedly about how we would fit everything on the packhorses. I let her talk—once I was married, I would probably never hear her voice again—but I kept imagining my sisters' voices murmuring beside me. Hippothoe tried to comfort me with calm words from her rough throat, saying, *Admetus will treat you kindly, Alcestis. You've seen that he cares for you. He'll honor you. It will be a good life.* But she kept repeating herself, as if she could think of nothing else to say, and my imaginary Pisidice just crossed her arms and said: *Now it's your turn.*

⁂

FOR THE NEXT week everything made me think of my wedding: the weight of a child on my hip, the sway of my skirt around my ankles, the stroke of my hair over the bared skin of my back as I dressed. How would my husband's hands feel on my flesh? I knew only the touch of sisters and servants and stepmothers. Would he touch like a woman did, gently and confidently, or like a man—like my father, with force just contained? What kind of touch did I want?

By the sixth night I had tired myself out thoroughly enough with anxiety to sleep well. Phylomache had to shake me awake in midmorning, hissing at me to get up, get up, did I want to be late to my own wedding? Yawning, I obeyed, and found myself surrounded with servants bearing food and clothing and jewelry.

"Phylomache," I said in sleepy protest.

"What?"

"Can I piss first at least?" I shot a look toward the chamber pot. The servants, laughing, went back into the main room. Phylomache crossed her arms over her chest and watched me as I used the pot. She was trying hard to look disapproving.

"It couldn't wait," I said when I was done, and giggled nervously, then put my hand over my mouth. "Oh. I can't laugh during the ceremony."

"You will not laugh during the ceremony," Phylomache said, half helpful, half threatening.

"I will not laugh during the ceremony," I echoed, and took a deep breath. "All right. What must I do first?"

I ate while the servants slicked my legs with oil and then skimmed it off. They did the same to my belly, my back. The strigil bumped across my rib cage, tickling as it went. Phylomache lifted my hair off my neck as they worked. "You'll have the ritual bath before the ceremony," she said. "It should be just your hands, but watch what Admetus does. Just for that part, of course. For the rest of it you'll have different duties."

"Yes, I understand that," I murmured.

Phylomache yanked at my hair a little. "Shush. You can't talk back to his family like you do here, Alcestis. They'll throw you out."

"Maybe Admetus likes women who speak up."

"No man likes women who speak up." The servants had finished oiling me. Phylomache let my hair drop and took the clothes from the servant who had brought them. "Now, dress."

I wore a red bodice, a gold and red skirt with ornamental

patches, red smudges on my lips and cheeks again. The body servant had painted a line along my eyelashes with charcoal ground in oil and warned me not to rub my eyes; the stuff lay thick on my eyelids. My hair was tied in a tight braid laced through with ribbons. It felt like I was dressing for any other festival. I wondered when I would begin to feel different, like a grown woman and a wife.

Phylomache waved the servant away and gave the laces of my bodice one last tug.

"Ow."

"Be glad I let you eat before the bodice went on."

The process took hours. Finally, when my hair was finished and I only needed to put on jewelry, some of the servants left to serve the noon meal. When they were out of the room, Phylomache turned serious, cupping my shoulders in her hands and looking into my eyes. "Don't be nervous," she said. "Use your best manners. Be polite to his parents. Be polite to his servants; they'll listen better if they like you. Don't make unreasonable demands."

"Not until I know them well at least," I said, earning a glare. "I'm teasing, Phylomache. I'll be too petrified to make any sort of demands."

"You, petrified?" Phylomache grinned at me and took my face in both hands, leaning in to kiss my nose—one of the only places she could safely touch without ruining my paint. I made myself sit still for the kiss. "I doubt it."

"The men are in the courtyard," one of the servants called from the main quarters.

"Oh," Phylomache said, pulling back. "Are you ready? Everything must be packed by now. Come on, say goodbye to the girls."

I kissed the children carefully, Asteropia trying to wriggle away, Antinoe's blue eyes blinking in confusion. "Goodbye, goodbye," I said gaily, and then I felt it: the sudden tightening in my belly, a chill traveling beneath my skin. "Phylomache, here," I said, and we embraced quickly. I laughed as I pulled away, a high, tremulous sound. "Do I have to go?"

"Yes," Phylomache said, eyelashes damp and sparkling. "You'll be late. Go, go with them. Goodbye!"

The servants hurried me out of the room. I looked back from the main quarters and saw Phylomache leaning against the frame of the bedchamber door, Antinoe on her hip, Asteropia clutching at her skirt with one hand and waving with the other, a solitary motion, slow and final. I felt with bitter surprise how much I loved them, and wished I could turn and bolt back to the little room where I had been born. But I had been promised elsewhere. I waved once, touched my hand to my lips, and followed the servants down the stairs.

Pelias stood in the doorway to the courtyard, a hulking shadow in a brown tunic. He should have been wearing a bright color, something celebratory. I stopped beside him. "I don't suppose you've forgiven me yet," I said softly.

He did not move or acknowledge me.

"Well, you'll be rid of me soon enough." I walked past him to join the group of guards and servants milling about in the courtyard, wondering with each step if he would stop me, seize my arm, or shout. He did nothing. That stung just as badly, and I paused for a moment, as if to give him a chance to haul me back inside. Finally he walked down the steps and brushed past me, going to the stallion tethered by the gate and barking at a slave to help him mount.

"Goodbye, Father," I whispered. It felt superfluous to say

it then. We had no connection to sever. When should I have bid him farewell? In the moment between my birth and my mother's death? The day when I first began to bleed between my legs like a woman, or the day before Admetus came, when I had no suitors and no desire for them?

I would play my part in the wedding ceremony and serve Admetus honorably, and when I was wed it would not matter what my father thought. He would possess me no longer.

The men brought out the rest of the horses and donkeys, several of them laden with my belongings. For all the noise Phylomache had made about packing, I had few possessions. There were only twelve men accompanying us; the rest would stay in Iolcus to guard the palace, Phylomache, and the children.

We rode through the gate with no wailing or crying to send us off. From the middle of the procession, I turned back and saw the women of the household lined up on the steps, leaning against each other as if they needed support. I imagined my sisters standing in front of them: Hippothoe would've been near Phylomache, and would perhaps have wrapped a wiry arm about her rounder waist; Pisidice would have stood to the side, alone. But their images vanished like shades, slipping away to death and marriage. The head maid raised a hand and waved as silently as Asteropia had. I did not dare wave back.

I rode one of the quiet mares, my horse's bridle tethered to a guard's saddle, my legs on one side of the horse's back and my rear on the other. My buttocks fell asleep almost at once, but I didn't care—I was watching the sea pass by, and the juts of rock, and the way plants grew spidery in the cracks of cliffs. These things had always been here, only leagues from the palace, though I had never seen them, and they would still be here, along this road, when I had grown old in Pherae, worn out by childbearing and worry.

We turned inland from the coast, the afternoon sun bathing my left side in warmth. I listened to the clanking of the men's gear and the horses' bridles and tried not to think about the wedding or the ceremony or my husband. I thought instead of my sister's grave, the mound of dirt slowly wearing down to nothingness, the wind gods smoothing her absence away. But oh, I couldn't cry—Pelias would hit me if I arrived in Pherae tear soaked and swollen. I prayed silently to Hera the white armed, asking her for calm.

We rode first to Pheres' house, a villa nearly as grand as the Iolcan palace. The courtyard bloomed with torches, lit even during the early evening hours, that gave off trails of pungent smoke. Light-headed, I clutched at my horse's withers as the convoy came to a stop. The old king of Pherae stood on the steps of his villa with his wife, the servants of the house behind them, their faces indistinct in the dim interior. Beside them: Admetus. He was dressed all in gold and red just as I was, his skin glowing like warm earth and his wide mouth smiling. Heat spread up my throat to my cheeks and the prayer in my head faltered and stopped.

The guard helped me down from the horse, hands strong around my waist, but I still landed with a jarring thump and had to stomp my numb feet so the blood would flow. Pelias turned to glare at me, holding his arm out for me to take. I hurried to his side.

I was beginning to shake a little, tremors starting in my chest and radiating out to my fingertips and toes. The air was not cold, but I couldn't seem to stop trembling. My teeth chattered, just faintly, and I clenched my jaw shut and tried to smile. Pelias walked in long strides toward the house, dragging me along. He stopped at the foot of the stairs, looking up at the king and queen and my husband.

"Lord Pheres, brother," Pelias said stiffly, "I give you my daughter in marriage to your son, King Admetus. He has won her by right. May he have much joy of her."

Pheres held out his hands. "I bid you come in, King Pelias, brother, Lady Alcestis. Be welcome here. We will have the ritual bath and then the sacrifice. Pelias, your men may wait outside."

Pelias dropped my arm and walked up the stairs ahead of me. I lifted my skirts to my ankles and took the stairs slowly, watching my feet. The touch of a hand on my arm startled me, and I looked up to see Pheres leaning toward me, a smile beneath his bristly gray beard. There were deep lines etched at the corners of his eyes, like writing inscribed on a tablet. "Welcome, child," he said, his voice quavery, and folded his hand around mine.

A dip of my hands in the water, Admetus's fingers brushing mine beneath the rippling surface. Smiles all around, except on Pelias's face. I felt breathless, light enough to float away. Time slipped by quickly, the sun setting earlier than I expected, as if Helios were conspiring with the men to hurry the ceremony. We stood in the courtyard, staring up at the fading sky, and I listened as Pheres called upon Zeus and Hera. Strange, I thought suddenly, to ask the blessing of the god who slept with every woman he could find and the goddess who had to allow it. Admetus echoed Pheres, his voice a low murmur under his father's chant.

My hand did not seem to fit in Admetus's, but he didn't let me go when I wriggled my fingers, just glanced over at me and smiled. Distracted. His palms were cool and sweaty too, still damp from the ritual bath. Was he frightened? I hoped he was.

Pheres had stopped speaking. I lifted my head and found them all watching me, waiting for Admetus to lead me to the palace. He was smiling down at me again—though he was not tall, he still topped me by a few finger-widths—and he reached out to touch my face, thumb soft on my cheek. "Come with me, wife," he said. Around us: the torches, the servants, the expectant faces. Pelias had remained in the house. He would not accompany me on this part of the journey; I had passed out of his control and become a woman of Pherae.

The attendants sang as we went, the song I remembered from Pelias's wedding, and Admetus walked at my pace. His parents followed behind us, though the old king leaned heavily on his walking stick and wheezed when the road sloped up. We came to the Pheraean palace in full dark. Pit fires burned around the edges of the building, casting light up its sides so that it seemed too large and bright to be real, a house for a sun god rather than a mortal palace. I gasped as we came through the gate and clutched at Admetus's hand. He led me to the center of the courtyard, the center of the waiting crowd, and stopped there, lit all around by the wavering flames, his eyes bright.

"Here we stop," he said, "so that I may honor the gods who helped bring this day to pass. The goddess Demeter, who delivered my wife from a dangerous birth. The goddess Aphrodite, who instructed Eros to fire his darts when first I saw her. The god Poseidon, protector of her father's house. The god Apollo, who brings light and healing, who has always aided me. I give you my thanks, deathless gods, for this woman, my wife."

He twisted to address the crowd, calling out, "Welcome your queen, Alcestis of Pherae!"

They startled me with their cheers, for I'd been watching Admetus speak like a king. I tried to smile again, and this time I found that I could, for there were honest smiles on the faces around me. I'd never been celebrated or welcomed like this. Pheres' wife stepped up and touched Admetus's arm, whispering to him. He let go of my hand and stepped back, letting his mother take his place. She slipped her hand through the crook of my elbow and led me across the courtyard and into the grand palace, Admetus right behind us. The great hall was dim, the round hearth burning low and the light of the bonfires flickering through narrow windows, and the room was lined with boys and girls who looked no different from the children of my own village. They stared at me as I entered, their eyes hungry and glittery, just like their king's. They were waiting for the bedchamber door to close behind me so that they could sing and dance and taste wine on each other's lips. The bedchamber doors were closed now. I walked up to them and stopped, not sure what to do.

Pheres' wife leaned in and kissed my cheek gently. "You're a good girl," she said. Then Admetus was beside me, arm around my waist, beckoning the servants with his other hand. Two men swung the doors open, and the crowd's chatter grew until it felt like a wall of noise behind us, pushing us into the room. Admetus looked over his shoulder, gave the crowd a lighthearted wave, and pulled me through the open doors.

I DIDN'T KNOW what I had expected to see—chains on the wall perhaps, or an altar stained with the blood of virgin girls? The bedchamber looked just like Pelias's had, better appointed than my own but no more frightening. The thud of wood on wood, the sound of the children raising their voices in song, Admetus's body warm and solid against me—those things frightened me. But Admetus pulled away almost at once, smiling at me and sitting down on the bed with a heavy sigh. I stared at his feet for a moment, my heart thrumming, trying to think of what to say. Why had he not seized me? What should I do?

"I'm glad that's over," he said.

Over? My eyes snapped up to his face. "Is it?" I asked after a long moment. "I believe the people outside the door think otherwise."

Admetus smiled, that quick grin like a crease of sunlight on water. I didn't know if I could trust his smile; I didn't know what it meant. He held out one hand to me and I saw his fingers tremble. "There's time enough for that, Alcestis. As long as the bedclothes are dirty in the morning, no one cares what goes on in the bedchamber. Here, sit. You must be exhausted."

Hesitantly, I sat.

"Did you think I'd leap on you as soon as the doors were closed?"

I looked up at him sideways.

"You did," he said. "Oh."

"I believe that's how it's usually done," I said stiffly. "Not that I'd know."

"Me either," Admetus said absently, then blushed, color shading up over his cheekbones. "I mean, I've never been married before."

"I hope not."

He made a frustrated sound in the back of his throat, a noise I'd never heard before. Soon I would learn all of his noises, his private language, the way I'd learned my sisters'. Or would I listen for him as I'd listened for Pelias, breath held and heart stopped? "You mustn't be frightened," he said, though he didn't sound confident. "I won't force you. I'd never do that."

"It wouldn't matter if you did," I said, thinking of Phylomache's wedding night. "No one would know."

"I won't." He reached over and picked up my hand, folding it between his. "Alcestis. Wife."

He sounded like a king beginning a speech, but I was the only audience and he didn't have to make pretty speeches to get my clothes off. He'd earned that right, even if he was reluctant to take it. "Admetus," I said. "What is it?"

"I'm glad I won you," he said, leaning closer, his thigh warm against mine. He smelled like a man, the hot tang of oil and leather, but beneath those scents was a hint of herbs and sweetness, as if his tunic had been pressed and stored with flowers. I had not realized that men could smell different, had never been this close to a man who wasn't a father or brother.

"I'm glad too," I said, then softly, "but I don't see why you did."

He pulled back, squinting. "What do you mean?"

"Why you were so determined to win me," I said. "Pelias was cruel when you came. I did not think you'd come back."

"He was not any kinder to you." His warm fingers curved more tightly around mine. "I was told of your worthiness—and I saw it was true. I loved you when first I saw you. Pelias did not treat you well, Alcestis. Everyone knows he blames you for his wife's death." He watched to see if I would flinch at that, but I did not; I knew it too.

"Will you treat me well then?" I whispered.

"I will." His fingertip brushed against the curve between my thumb and wrist. Outside the door the boys were singing their chorus, shouting out the last few words of each line. I looked up, and Admetus was watching me through lowered eyelashes, shy as a girl. I still felt quivery and strange, as if I had left a part of myself behind in Iolcus and its absence had made my body light.

"I don't know what to do," I whispered, and closed my eyes.

He settled my hand on his knee carefully, like releasing a stunned bird. His skin felt hot and dry, furred with small, crinkly hairs, softer than those between my legs. I rubbed my thumb across the round bump of his knee, the long line of sinew on the side of his thigh, and the muscle beneath the skin trembled at my touch. I jerked my hand away, my eyes flying open, and gasped to see Admetus's face only inches away. His eyes were closed too, though they fluttered open now. Flecks of green in the brown of his irises, like sparks sinking beneath his heavy eyelids. "Shhh," he said, leaning in. "I said I wouldn't hurt you."

A hand curved around my thigh, hot through the cloth of my skirt, then Admetus's mouth grazed my jaw, my cheekbone. He skimmed his knuckles across the plane of my cheek. I sat still, breathing shallowly through my mouth. I sound like Hippothoe, I thought. This is silly. I picked up my hand and put it back on his leg with the same sort of determination I would have used to touch a spider.

My husband pulled back, smiling, and I could tell that he meant the smile to be reassuring. He kicked his sandals off, and I did the same; Phylomache had said I should mimic him. He murmured, "Come here," and stretched a hand out to pull me farther up on the bed. We lay down in the middle of the mattress, knees bumping, a hand-width of space between our bodies. I felt like I was leaning out through the window of my bedchamber, safe only because of my fingers gripping the frame.

"Admetus," I said, but he hushed me with a finger over my lips then leaned in to kiss me. He had a warm, clinging touch, his lips soft and undemanding. I opened my mouth a little and stroked my tongue over his lips. Let him do what he wants, Phylomache had said, but I was never going to bear him children if all he wanted to do was kiss me chastely as a girl.

He made another interesting noise somewhere in his chest and slid his arm over my hip, yanking me closer and deepening the kiss. There, I thought, and then I thought: Oh. He was so warm and close, our hips pressed together and legs entwined. I felt a smooth touch on my foot, sliding up past my ankle. I laughed involuntarily into the kiss and pulled my foot away. "That tickles, you know," I whispered against his cheek.

"What tickles?"

"My foot."

He looked confused.

"Didn't you just—"

There was an odd sound, a hiss like concentrated wind.

We leapt into a frightened upright tangle, standing pressed together in the middle of the mattress. Admetus had an arm around my shoulders and he crushed me against him, his nose against my cheek, muttering, "Don't move, don't move."

Snakes lay in twisting knots across the bottom of the mattress. Not just there—I could see scales glinting in the lamplight, piles of long bodies littering the floor between the bed and the doors. Tens of them, hundreds? I couldn't tell, couldn't even count them, all the tangled skeins of flesh. Which god had done this? My heart thudded in my chest and I couldn't catch my breath. O Artemis, I thought. O Athena, O Hera, O Aphrodite. O Poseidon, Grandfather, call them away!

The snake that had touched my foot slid across the mattress: a pale brown viper with darker patches, its body as thick as my calf, mouth open as if it were scenting us. Its eyes looked like small gray jewels set in its wedge-shaped head, sparkling and opaque. It had touched me—touched me, and I'd thought it was Admetus. Revulsion shook me, knotted me up under Admetus's hard hands.

"Don't move," he said again. "It'll bite you."

"I know," I said, and the words came out calm but squeaky. The snake twisted its head away. "We have to get out. Admetus. There has to be a way out. I can get around it—"

His breath was coming in little puffs against my ear. "Don't," he said, "just don't touch it, let it keep going."

Oh no, I thought, it won't keep going, not if we've angered a god—but it did, skimming over the mattress and skating down off the bed, joining the mass of writhing bodies on the floor. The other snakes on the bed followed it, like cows trailing after the leader of their herd. I'd never seen snakes behave like that. I'd never seen so many snakes. Admetus clutched me harder, and we were both trembling, passing a shudder back and forth. I tried to struggle out of his arms, and he let me go with a shake that made me bite down sharply on my tongue. I stared at him, shocked, but he wasn't looking at me.

"You stay here," he said, and edged toward the side of the bed, peering at the snakes on the floor. The motion attracted them, and some of them began to sway up, hissing and flicking their tongues toward the bed. My chest froze, and my fingers went numb, as if I were turning into a statue.

"They'll kill you," I said, grabbing at his arm. "Call for help."

"They won't hear over the singing." His face had gone white and his eyes wild. He bent and blew out the lamp beside the bed, darkening the room further, and hefted it as a weapon. Several of the snakes let out violent hisses. "I have to go."

I looked down at the blanket of vipers, untameable creatures. "Who helped you with the lion and boar?" I asked, talking so fast my words ran together.

"What?"

"What god helped you? You're a brave man, but you didn't harness those animals yourself."

He stared at me, the warm brown of his eyes a thin ring around his dark pupils. His nostrils were flared in fear like a horse's. "Apollo," he said finally, stumbling over the name. "Apollo caught them and trained them to the whip."

So the god who'd let my sister die would save my husband now. It was the kind of poetry the gods liked. But I had no choice. "Call on him to banish the snakes," I said urgently. "If a god led them here, another god can drive them off. Call on him now."

"But I can't," he said, child simple. "He isn't here."

"He'll hear you." I clasped a hand around his elbow and shook it a little, the way I might have done to reassure Asteropia. "Admetus, come, please call him."

"You can't listen," he said, pleading suddenly, his voice gone low and rough.

I put my hands over my ears, which at least kept out the hissing of the snakes. I could still hear the low rumble of the revelers in the great hall, oblivious to the danger within the bedroom. Shadows sculpted Admetus's face, and I turned away too, but not so far that I couldn't watch his mouth move. Most of the words blurred into incoherence, but I caught a few things: help and please and honor and love, Apollo, please, please. My heart pounded harder. I squeezed my eyes shut and thought of the chariot driver, always standing beside Admetus or behind him, murmuring in his ear. He would come. He had to come.

Something bumped against the back of my heel and I let out a shriek. Admetus stopped midword and caught me as I stumbled toward him. The snake hissed and lunged just as he swung me up into his arms, and he did a strange frantic dance, kicking the thing and jumping on it until he crushed its head beneath his heel. His face was twisted up and for a long, horrible moment I thought he'd been bitten.

"It's dead," he said, breathless. "It didn't get me—"

The doors crashed open. Admetus's breath rushed out, a snakelike hiss by my ear. I squirmed in his grip and turned to see Apollo standing in the doorway and, behind him, the startled faces of the children, frozen in their dance. He looked like the chariot driver and yet unlike him, as if the form of the chariot driver were a set of clothes he'd only half finished putting on. His skin absorbed the torchlight and magnified it. The doors slammed shut again behind him, and that light began to flare, a brilliant pure white brighter than the sun. Admetus's hand wrapped over my eyes, but the light crept through his fingers, stabbing at my eyes until I cried out. All around I could hear the snakes hissing—and then suddenly the hissing cut off and the light winked out like a snuffed torch. The room was quiet. The entire palace was quiet—no noise from the children outside, from guards or servants running to their aid. I could hear Admetus panting.

I reached up and pried Admetus's hand off my face. I tried to look at Apollo, but he was still too bright, a halo lingering around the edges of his body. Then I saw the snakes, or what was left of them. Their bodies remained, but Apollo had altered them, hardening them into long brown shapes that I recognized after a moment as boughs of wood. He had saved us.

The god sighed. When I glanced at him this time, his skin did not burn my eyes, but I saw sun in every crease of it, every neat strand of his hair. He gave Admetus a look that I did not understand, a look that made my stomach grow hot. "Admetus," Apollo said, and his voice was like weary music, holy and disappointed. "This was unexpected. I did not think you would call so soon."

Admetus set me down slowly, slipping his arm from beneath my knees. I flexed my toes on the mattress and kicked a wooden snake off the bed. My heart was still rabbiting in my chest.

"I'm sorry," my husband said. "I'm so sorry, I don't know why they came. I must have done something wrong." He sounded like a woman apologizing to her husband, but he didn't move toward Apollo, and Apollo's expression did not change.

"To whom did you sacrifice when you married her?" the god asked calmly.

"You. Demeter. Aphrodite. Poseidon. Zeus and Hera, in the ritual at my father's house."

"You forgot Artemis."

My husband's mouth moved, but he said nothing. I bit the inside of my lower lip to keep quiet and stared down at the bed. How had I not noticed that my husband had not thanked the goddess for giving up a girl to marriage? Had I been so terrified? Now I stood in the bedchamber with my husband and a god, married but not bedded, the thump of my heart quieting in my ears, and my cheeks went hot with shame. I should have noticed. How the goddess must have laughed when I prayed to her for deliverance. How she must have smiled in triumph!

"Admetus," Apollo said. "You must be careful. More careful than this. I heard you this time, but I cannot always protect you." I'd lifted my gaze when he spoke. He looked at me, his eyes as bright as his skin, and did not smile. His stare had a weight that a mortal's could not possess, almost palpable, like a heavy blanket draped over my body. I gazed at his beautiful face, unsure what to do—I'd seen Hermes and my grandfather, Poseidon, but nothing in my training had extended to the proper greeting of gods when met in the bedchamber. Was I even supposed to look at him? He was my cousin, after all, and my husband's friend, as well as Hippothoe's betrayer. Would he even know her name if I asked him?

I didn't realize I had been holding my breath until the god looked away.

"I'll be careful," Admetus said.

"You will do more than that. You will burn this wood and make sacrifices and hope that she forgives you, Admetus, for if she does not, your life will be unpleasant. Burn the wood in the morning. Make it a good ceremony."

"Don't be angry," Admetus whispered. One of his hands twitched by his side, brushing against my hip, half a caress—but he was staring at Apollo with longing and fear.

Apollo shook his head, pushed a hand through his shining hair, a startlingly human gesture. "I am not angry," he said, but even I did not believe him. There were words in the air unspoken, like the lines of text painted around the borders of murals, writing I didn't know how to read. Apollo stared back at my husband, and his face reflected like polished bronze: longing and fear, longing and fear. It was like nothing I had seen before.

"Thank you," I said softly, "Lord Apollo."

The god turned to me once more. "I'm glad you are not harmed, lady," he said, and his voice sounded like a choir of mourners all crying out the same sorrow.

I felt Admetus's eyes on my face and flushed.

"Now, King Admetus, I'll speak to your people," Apollo said, some of his glow slipping away, and turned around to push the wide doors open again. Admetus stirred, ready to follow him, but I clamped my fingers around his forearm, as if I could keep his people from seeing what I had seen. To my surprise, he obeyed me, standing quietly as the doors swung open.

The crowd, it seemed, had been milling around uncertainly, unsettled by Apollo's arrival but not aware of any danger. They turned toward the bedchamber now in small groups, girls grabbing at each other's hands, a few boys stepping forward as if to challenge the visitor. They chattered to each other, muttering questions and squeaking in surprise when they saw the wood spread out on the bedchamber floor.

Apollo waved a hand at them and they quieted instantly. "Why have you stopped singing?" he called, echoing against the stone walls. "You celebrate this marriage, do you not? Yet you only sing their happiness for the space of an hour? This is no kind of wedding ceremony!"

He lifted a hand over his head and flicked his fingers. The torches flared brighter, setting off pleased gasps throughout the room. "Return to your celebration!" he cried, and one by one the revelers turned away, slinging arms around each other's shoulders or sidling up close at the hips. The god turned away and lowered his hand, closing the doors without touching them, and looked at Admetus and me. Each gesture was careful and restrained, movement made formal, action given structure and meaning. I realized that we were still standing on the mattress, balancing like sailors on a raft. I didn't want to let my husband go.

"Come here," Apollo said to Admetus. "Speak to me a moment and then I must go."

Admetus went at once, the boughs cracking under his bare feet. I sat down abruptly on the mattress, folding my knees up to my chest and rubbing my ankles. Admetus stood close to Apollo, his hand on the god's arm, his fingers curled hard against Apollo's smooth flesh. He spoke in an urgent whisper, but I could not distinguish words—and I was too distracted to listen, my eyes caught by the possessive push of each one of his fingertips, points of heat and contact, familiar touch.

Finally Apollo shook his head once, twice. He spoke quietly, but I heard him.

"I will speak to the Fates," he said, and I didn't understand what he meant. Speak to the Fates? But the danger had passed, and we lived—the Fates had allowed it. They kissed once, the god's lips brisk on my husband's cheek, and then Apollo went to the window and leapt out with feet so light that the brittle wood strewn on the floor did not crack beneath his weight.

I put my chin on my knees and watched Admetus. He didn't move for several minutes, stood staring down at the wood-scattered floor as if he expected the boughs to become snakes again and strike at him. As if he wished they would. "Sit, husband," I said. He looked up, eyes blurry and confused. "It's all right, I promise. Come sit."

Admetus walked back toward me and sat on the edge of the bed, his shoulders hunched up and his back rounded like a dejected child's. I didn't know what to say to him.

"We are safe," I tried. "They're gone. It was an oversight, that's all. The sacrifice will please Artemis and she'll forgive us. She was only sending a warning."

He gave me a watery smile but didn't look any happier. I touched his arm, frowned when he shifted away. "I should collect the wood," he said dully. "To burn in the morning. She'll know if I don't do it myself."

"I know. Just wait a moment, please. I'll help you. In a moment." I crawled around to sit behind him and slid my hands over his shoulders where the muscles bunched. What would he do if he left the bedchamber now? Was Apollo waiting for him in the courtyard, standing below the window like a shepherd come calling for a village girl? If he left, I couldn't follow him. I had to keep him here, to make him see me again, to make the ritual of the wedding matter.

"All right," he said, but he didn't relax under my touch. I cursed silently, thinking of how easy Phylomache had made it sound—just lie back and take it and my duty would be done—and bent down to kiss the curve of his shoulder, pushed my nose against the tight muscle.

"Don't worry about it, just for a little while," I whispered, lips moving against his soft tunic. "Please."

"I can't."

"You can." I pressed up against his side, slipping an arm around his back. I trusted now that he would not hurt me. I just wanted him to touch me, look at me, promise he wouldn't cast me out in favor of the god. Where would I go as a rejected bride? Pelias would not take me back.

"I can't stop thinking about it," he said with a sharp laugh. "He must think I'm a child."

I sat back on my heels, hovering behind him, thinking. "What did Apollo say?" I asked. "Before he left."

"You didn't hear?"

"Not all of it," I said. "His voice does carry, though."

"It doesn't matter what he said," Admetus said, dropping his head forward into his hands. "He only said it to cheer me up because he knows I feel like an idiot and a coward."

"You were brave," I said steadily. "You killed that viper. Apollo answered when you called, Admetus. Do you think a god would do that for any man who happened to ask for help? He favors you, that's clear enough."

"You think so?" He lifted his face. "Zeus forced him to serve me. Can you imagine a god obedient to a man, even a king of the Achaeans? But I was kind to him before I knew his nature. That's the reason he shows me favor. I'm a good host."

"He likes you. He honors you, Admetus. He didn't come here out of mere loyalty. He saved you. He saved us."

Admetus sighed and rubbed at his temple. "He said he'd intercede with the Fates, convince them to spare me once from death, whenever my appointed day comes. They'll give me a second chance. It's his wedding gift." He laughed again bitterly. "Though I don't think he intended to give it to me on my wedding night."

"That's a kingly gift, husband."

"I know it. I don't deserve it."

"You do. And you have another gift waiting, you know," I said quietly. "A gift it is my duty to give on this night."

He lifted his head, stared at me with dark, reflecting eyes. For a moment I wondered if he had even heard me, but then he reached out with one trembling hand and touched the smooth slopes of my breasts, the bound plane of my belly.

"Here." I took his hand in mine, pulled it around my waist to the laces of my bodice. "Help me with these. I can't get them undone alone." I could have, of course. But I could not do the rest myself.

"I thought—I thought you wouldn't want to. After the snakes."

I laughed. The sound came out sharp, and I worked to soften my voice. "You'll spoil me with kindness," I said. "Come here, please, kiss me." I moved up on the bed, spread out like I had been when the snake had skimmed across my foot, and pulled at his shoulders, urging him to lie beside me, atop me, whatever he wanted.

I rose to catch his lips and he kissed me with bruising pressure, bending my head back on my neck. My teeth cut the inside of my lip, and I whimpered into his mouth, clutching at his shoulders as he leaned into me, body fever hot now and smelling of fear sweat, his hip bones knocking against mine. Another kiss, and another, hard and unyielding, as if I had done something to anger him. Hera, I thought, suddenly panicked, Aphrodite, you got me into this, and now you must help me through it, you must tell me what to do. But the goddesses did not intervene. I could still hear the occasional shout or laugh from the great hall, but the bedchamber was silent except for the wet slide of our tongues and Admetus's breath on my face when he pulled away from me. With the only lamps in the room behind him, his face was blank and unreadable, a flat gray blur.

"I can't, I can't," he said, a breathless rush of words, and jerked away from me as if I had struck him. I pushed myself up, half sitting, and stared at him with a sick, cold knot in my belly and not even the faintest idea of what to say.

"Tomorrow," Admetus said, looking away from me. He swallowed, spoke again in a distant voice. "After the sacrifice. Not before then. I can't. I have to burn the branches."

"All right," I said, shaken. "It's all right. I'll help you. Let me help." I sat up and crawled toward the edge of the bed, but he put a hand out blindly to hold me back.

"No," he said. "You stay here where you'll be safe." He got up and took off his belt, his embroidered overtunic. His sheathed dagger thunked heavily on the small table by the bed. He stood there, breathing hard, looking at me. I turned my face away.

"Alcestis," he said.

"Yes?"

"Don't tell anyone," he muttered, and went to the doors. The hinges sang as he opened them.

I had no one in Pherae to tell.

I put my hands up to my face. My hair hung in tangles, pulled free of its tight braids, and I prized out the pins and the ribbons until it fell onto my shoulders in a heavy, oil-scented mass. My scalp burned. My mouth stung, scored by my own teeth. I felt filled up with words, things I was aching to say, a torrent in a dry canyon. I missed Hippothoe. I missed Phylomache. I missed the head maid.

I heard the hinge cry again and scrambled for the other side of the bed as the door swung slowly open. By the time my husband had come in with the slaves I had swaddled myself in bedclothes like a corpse, my back to the door and my body perfectly still. I listened as he whispered directions, listened to the hollow scraping sounds as they gathered the dry wood into bundles and carried it out of the room. The celebration in the great hall had changed; Admetus must have told them of the goddess's anger, for the village children were singing a song of hunting for deer in the forest, of bathing alone among quiet trees, of skin unsullied and solitude true.

The doors closed. The room was dark without the slaves' lamps, but someone—Admetus—had not left. I heard him moving about, his clothes rustling. Shocking how loud one man could be, when trying to be silent. More scraping on the floor, a faint curse when he dropped an armful of boughs, a long silence. Was he looking at me, at my shape under the covers? He took a gulping breath, another, and then he began to weep.

I felt Artemis' arrow in my chest. I wanted to go to him, but I could not. I knew it as suddenly and certainly as I had known Hippothoe was dead. If he knew I was awake to hear him, he would never forgive me. I closed my eyes in the darkness and listened to my husband cry.

The tears lasted only a matter of moments. He drew a shuddering breath, the branches creaked as he lifted them, and the door opened and closed as he left. But still I waited, my body sore with the effort of stillness, until I knew he was gone. Then I sat up and rubbed my hands over my face, pushed my hair behind my ears, and rolled up one sleeve of my blouse. I clambered across the bed, keeping watch on the door, and slid my husband's dagger out of its leather sheath.

I ran the blade over the soft flesh behind my elbow. It bit easily into my skin, and I flinched, pulling it away and cupping my hand below the shallow, stinging cut. It gave me the blood I needed. I wiped the knife on my red bodice, slipped it back into its sheath, and pushed my bloody hand between the sheets where it would be sure to leave a stain.

ANOTHER SLIDE, A slip, a choked-off cry. His teeth in my shoulder. I was shaking again, trembling as he pushed into me, a long, slow shove that stopped my breath. I arched against him, overwhelmed by the feeling, rough as sand and glorious bright like the sun on a cresting wave. It had been too long, and it hurt, and still I didn't care. I moaned and closed my eyes when the echo of my voice came back to me, the low, wounded sound of a sacrifice.

"Oh," he panted against my skin, "oh, oh, yes." A frenzy of pushes, and then he seized up and shouted and thrust into me once, twice, a third time before slumping to lie with his cheek on my shoulder. The warmth in my belly faded, a hot, receding tide. I put a hand up to cup the back of his head, to stroke the curls stained darker with sweat. The air in the bedchamber did not move, heavy with the smell of sex and scorched dirt, draped over our bodies like a hot cloth. Admetus stirred against me, dragged in a long breath, and settled with a drowsy noise. The back of his neck was slick, my fingers slipping as I stroked him quiet. "Alcestis," he murmured, and I whispered back: "Yes."

Sometimes my husband called on Apollo while he moved

within me. The first time he had tried to apologize, awkwardly, but I'd stopped his mouth with a kiss to quiet him. The next time he had said nothing afterward. Even after a year we hadn't learned how to speak of the god, but with every tongue-slip Admetus grew sweeter to me, reaching out to touch my hip when I walked by or stroking hair back from my face as I fell asleep. I learned to feel thankful for these touches. And I prayed for children to come.

But they had not come yet. A year had passed, studded with nights when I had rubbed up against Admetus's side, slipped a hand beneath his tunic, let him bend me over onto my elbows so he did not have to watch my face. I liked to watch his face when I could, to see the pleasure sweep through him like a wave of riders across a plain, drumming the earth like thunder. I liked the way his eyes squinted tight, as if he were looking at the true form of a god, finding, somehow, a little of Apollo's brightness hidden inside me.

I liked this time too, this quiet, when I did not have to listen to him talk about brigands on the borders of Pherae, about the poor olive harvest, or the likely-looking crop of young men who would soon join his guard. I didn't mind listening—I was thankful, in fact, that he told me anything about the state of my village—but it could grow tiresome after a while, for I was rarely allowed to answer back. Admetus liked me receptive and quiet. I would nod when he wanted a response, smile, let him talk through the decisions he'd already made. I'd once heard him telling his steward that he'd been lucky to find such an intelligent wife, one who could advise him and help him rule wisely.

This is how I help him, I thought, folding my palm over the bump of his shoulder blade. It was the same thing, really. Receiving him. Letting him do what he wanted, like

Phylomache had told me before my wedding night. Not making trouble.

After a few minutes he pushed up and rolled off me, dropping a kiss on my shoulder as he went. I didn't move. It was too hot to move, and sweat funneled through every crease of my body. I watched him dress, a pattern I knew by heart, the tunic and the belt and the sandals, the scrape of fingers through his messy hair.

"Maybe the anniversary will bring us luck," I said, half hopeful. "Maybe Demeter will bless us."

"Maybe." He glanced back over his shoulder, smiled. "You needn't worry, Alcestis. A child will come in time. You're still fresh and young."

"I'm sure you're right."

"I am," he said. "Come, we can't miss dinner."

"You can miss dinner whenever you like, my lord," I said. He shook his head, but he was smiling as he straightened his tunic and slipped his dagger into his belt. I waved him away when he looked at me again. "The maids tell me I shouldn't stand up for a while after. It doesn't help if it all runs down my leg."

He blushed. Today I found it endearing. "Alcestis," he said, drawing out my name, "you talk like a man."

"I talk like a maid," I said. "You should be glad they watch their tongues around you, my lord. They're good girls, but they do go on."

"You'd know if they were not behaving well, wouldn't you?" he asked, the question utterly casual.

The liquid sweetness in my muscles vanished, and I propped myself up on my elbows, watched him carefully as I answered to make sure I chose the correct words to please him. "My lord, they are pious women who do good service to your house. I wouldn't keep them on if their behavior disappointed me or dishonored you."

He nodded, flashed me another bright look. "Of course. You know I wouldn't doubt it."

"Mmm," I said, and lay back on the mattress. Admetus walked over to the bed and stood with his hands on his hips, looking down at me. I closed my eyes and smiled, knowing my smile would please him, convince him that he could leave me alone for a while.

"Stay here if you prefer," he said. "I can send a maid with some food. Would that suit you?"

"It would, husband."

He bent down to kiss me, a quick friendly pressure on my forehead, where the sweat had dried. I opened my eyes to watch him leave, closed them again once he was gone. Later we would have to talk about the plans for the anniversary feast, the food and the guests and the sacrifices. Apollo had made Admetus swear that he would hold the feast in Artemis' honor, to soothe her again for the slight we had dealt her on our wedding night. I had not been Artemis' creature since the night a week after the bonfire of wooden snakes, when I'd pulled Admetus down onto the bed and told him he was shirking his duty to me as a husband. I worried over her anger, but distantly. More often I worried that Admetus would tire of me and find some village woman capable of pushing out sons for the honor of Pherae. I understood why Phylomache had looked so tired and nervous during her first year in Iolcus. In the long waits, the weeks when Admetus ignored me in favor of a visiting group of hunters or a promising guard in training, I collected herbs and built tiny fires in honor of the goddesses of childbearing in the corner of the bedchamber, watching the stack of leaves and sticks sputter and melt into ash. I bled every month and swore as I wrung out the cloths.

Admetus was unbothered by the wait for children, or so he told me. I wondered what he told the men in the drinking room. I'd thought Pelias entertained often, but Admetus had a group of constant companions who spent nearly every night in the palace. Like all men, he was most comfortable among his own kind. He usually brought me in to make a brief appearance in the evenings, kissed me in front of the men, and kept a possessive hand on my hip while the guests shouted advice or made muttered offers. It was a ritual, like slitting a beast's throat or burning grain: they reached out for me, Admetus glared, and I smiled demurely at the floor. Once the ritual had been observed, I was allowed and expected to leave. I spent my nights in the empty bedchamber, watching the striations of light from the courtyard torches wriggle on the star-painted ceiling. Supervising the kitchens occupied me for part of the evening, but the servants knew how to handle Admetus's guests and grew frustrated if I lingered there for too long.

I could have begged the maids for tales about the men, but they knew little more than I did, and I would not weaken my position by relying on them for gossip. The maids liked me well enough; the girls made irritating sympathetic noises about my monthly bleeding, but some of the older women would snap at them and say that I was young enough to wait a few years and would be glad of the reprieve when my babies came. The slaves gave me no trouble. I had an enviable position, Phylomache would've said. The gods had given me a kind husband and a comfortable life.

Apollo had visited eight times during the year.

Once I had come back to the bedchamber in the middle of

the day and overheard them arguing, Admetus shouting and Apollo responding in low, measured tones that sounded no less angry. Admetus was saying something about a nymph, about a loss of dignity. I heard Apollo say, "What do you know of dignity?" before the room went silent—a heavy, muffled silence, like movement beneath blankets. I thought they were in our bed together, and my throat closed. But when I pressed my face to the just-open door and peered through the crack, they were standing upright in the middle of the room, Admetus's head on Apollo's shoulder, Apollo's hand glowing pale against my husband's dark curls.

I'd stood and watched them for a long time. My husband's face, turned toward me, was calm and smooth, his eyes closed and one corner of his mouth curled up, a child's expression he wore in sleep. I leaned against the door frame with a hand on my stomach, unable to pull my eyes away. I knew Apollo must have been aware of my presence, but the god's eyes had been closed as well, their brilliance shuttered.

Lying on the bed alone, I looked over at the spot where I had seen my husband and the god. I was sweating again. I sat up, making a face at the inevitable liquid dribble, and reached out for the cloth on the bedside table, wiping down my forehead and neck before I swiped between my legs. "I hope that was long enough, Mother," I muttered to Demeter. "I can't sit here and soak in it all day."

The goddess, predictably enough, did not answer.

I got out of bed and smoothed down my skirt. I went to the window and hitched one hip up on the sill, ignoring the twinges in my thighs. The stark hills of Pherae rose up around the palace, furred with browned grass and marked with juts of gray rock. I didn't love it the way I had loved Iolcus; I didn't stare out at the lines of the hills and dream about walking them alone, stealing a horse and racing down the road to the beach. The ocean was too far away to see from my window in Pherae, and the sky capped the edges of the hills like a lid on a jar.

Men would come over those hills in the morning, three days hence, to begin the feast. Admetus had sent messengers to invite the lesser kings of neighboring villages, his parents, his friend Creon. I had met Creon only once, though the servants said that he had been a regular visitor before Apollo came. He reminded me of Acastus, a handsome and serious man with a passing resemblance to a deity. Admetus had sent no messenger to Iolcus, though he had instructed the others to invite my brothers if they ran across them. Acastus, still traveling home from Mycenae, would not come, and Pelias would never let Pelopia spend the time away. The palace would once again fill with men I did not know, Achaeans gathered to celebrate our marriage and to honor Artemis, to placate her, to keep her distant and benevolent.

It might work, it might not. Gods did as they liked, and mortals struck or kissed or killed each other without knowing why then sat in the dust of battle and talked until they were hoarse, trying to explain the actions of Olympians. Misunderstand the meaning of a bird's flight or the shape of a cow's intestines and you could lose immortal favor; walk in the woods or by a river and you might be stolen away.

I lived as we all did, with a constant edge of fright. Caring for strangers improved your chances; having children worsened them, though children were needed to uphold the glory of the Achaeans, to carry our ways over the mountains and seas. Children would succor you when you grew old, if you were lucky enough to grow old, if they hadn't knifed you first. Snakes became wood, wood became snakes, girls became trees. A sea or a river might rear up as a dripping god and seize a girl in watery arms, as my grandmother had been seized. Only a year or so ago I had heard of a giant swan that had seized a woman from the ground and coupled with her in the sky in full view of her people, the woman screaming and the swan's wings buffeting the air. The woman had birthed a monstrous egg from which two small children had stepped, perfect in every way. They were beautiful children, yes, and they were hers. And yet they were the swan's, and they would make the woman think of the swan, of Zeus, every time she saw them. Always she would think of the egg pushing out of her body, the inexorable, smooth force of it. The thought made me shiver in horror and envy. I was right to be afraid.

The feast of Artemis would begin with games held on a plain not far from the palace, and the men would return covered in sweat and oil, calling for wine. Then would come the libations, the sacrifices, beasts slaughtered, and bonfires lit. The celebration would go on until the sky paled in the east, and I would spend nearly all of it in this room, just where I was now—looking out across the courtyard to the hills, the walls of my world, and hoping I never had to cross them again.

ON THE DAY of the feast, I did not rise in time to watch the sacrifice. Admetus liked to have me with him, despite custom, and on some days he would call me out from the palace before the killing was done. But on this day he left me in bed, too eager to greet the visiting men to wait for his wife. I slept until half the day had passed; there were some privileges, at least, reserved for the mistress of a house run by slaves who didn't need or care for my instruction.

When I stood up from the bed, I felt so dizzy that I staggered like a drunken man. I put a hand to my forehead and took a deep breath through my nose. My stomach cramped in a sudden sick wave, and I squeezed my eyes shut hard, panting a little. The slave girl who had just come in with the oil and strigil rushed to support me. Her hand was cool on my arm.

"Lady?" she said.

"I'm fine," I told her, aware that my words might seem more truthful if I could wrench my eyes open. I did: she was staring at me round eyed, her duties forgotten. I tried to smile. "I'm only tired. I'll be fine."

Unconvinced, she made me rest my hands on her shoulders as

she stripped off my shift, tugging it one handed down my arms and over my hips. Her eyes swept appraisingly over my belly, and I could see that she wanted to ask me about my sickness, wanted some bit of knowledge to hold over the other girls. But the stretch between my hip bones was still flat and hard, and I wouldn't let myself hope until my belly grew.

She oiled her hands and rubbed them over my skin, then scraped me clean with the strigil, the dull blade bumping over my bones. Her hands slowed on my stomach; so much hope these women had for me, who might hold the future of the house of Pherae in my womb. I touched her shoulder, just lightly, and her eyes fluttered up to my face. I shook my head. She flushed immediately and ducked back to her work, her hands brisk on my legs, almost harsh. I stood and listened to the men calling to each other in the courtyard, their words too distant to be heard, only the tone audible. I could hear my husband among them, shouting directions to the slaves and greetings to his friends.

When the slave girl had finished, I called for my older body servants, the Cretan women who knew how to twist my mess of hair into a respectable braid. They worked in silence, too wise or too tired to twitter about my nausea, and when they had finished I was wrapped in red and gold, the colors I'd worn to be wed. They dressed me like a virgin again, my breasts bound up tight in the high-cut bodice. They daubed rose oil into the short, wavy strands of hair at my temples and pulled the rest back, threading heavy locks of it together. The weight of the hair made my head wobble on my neck and I nodded with each pull and slip. I was hot, even with the chill late fall air slipping around our feet, and I could feel sweat mixing with the oil on my body, long, slow drips sliding down my spine.

I sat down heavily on the bed when the women finished pinning my braids. My hair murmured like a nest of metallic snakes. I reached up to touch it and then pulled my hand away, pinching at the bridge of my nose. The subtle thump of a headache was growing brighter and sharper.

"You should rest, lady," one of the slave women said, and her tone was perfectly even, like the flat of a sword.

I shook my head gingerly, the beads singing. "Tomorrow," I said.

In the kitchens I did not eat. I could smell the sacrifice burning in the courtyard and it turned my nervous stomach. Admetus had not yet sent a slave to bring me to the feast. He'd promised that I could accompany him, muttered it into my hair in the night, but he had forgotten. I had expected him to forget.

I heard Admetus and the men make their way from the courtyard into the palace, the crowd of bodies moving up the stairs, entering the megaron. I stayed in the kitchens with the slaves and watched their hands, the practiced movements of cleaning and cooking, the clever dance of fingers around bronze blades. I should've been waiting in the hall beside the megaron, ears open to my husband's voice, but I felt cold and quivery and didn't want to share that hall with the little wind gods who swept along it. I leaned against the kitchen wall, where the air felt thick with grease and the smell of char. Like the smell of the god on my husband's skin. It hung there for days after Apollo visited, the scent of sunlight on his shoulders, the tang of laurel in the soft hair behind his ears.

In the megaron, my husband called out my name. I could hear the slave's feet slap on the stone as he hurried to fetch me, but I waited until he came through the kitchen door before stepping away from the wall.

"Will you come, lady?" he asked. I followed him.

The men in the hall were whooping and shouting to each other, no different from the men who'd attended my father's feasts. They sat in lines on each side of the long wooden table, picking meat from the platters in front of them, pitching bones across the table with bursts of laughter or cursing. They were gaily dressed and flushed with drink. I stepped between the slave girls who surrounded the table, their arms full of platters and jugs and their hips probably sore from pinches, and wondered how many of those girls would no longer be devotees of Artemis after this feast night.

The men did not quiet when I appeared, which suited me, for I didn't want their attention. My husband's attention, as always, was elsewhere. Admetus slipped an arm around my waist when I slid onto the bench beside him, but did not look away from the brown-haired man to his left. Some neighboring king? Half the faces at the table were unfamiliar. The half-Olympian Heracles had not come; Admetus had received word weeks ago that he was in Egypt and would not reach Pherae in time for the feast. Creon nodded to me when I sat, but he was the only visitor I recognized well. He had arrived dusty and tired the previous day and had earned only a few moments with Admetus before my husband had abandoned him to return to planning the layout of the visitors' tents. Godlike in looks he was, but not a god, and even he could not rely on Admetus's love. As on the day before, we looked on one another with cold sympathy.

I glanced over the men once more and calmed a little. Apollo had not come to the feast. I had been certain that he would. For the last several days I'd waited for the signs of his arrival: the scent of burnt air rising from his heels, the way the palace grew hot with my husband's joy. Lust is as pungent as a roasting sacrifice. It tightens the throat and roils the stomach, makes you ravenous until you remember that the flesh does not burn for you.

My husband's father, seated across the broad expanse of the table, gave me a wavering smile, the droop of his right cheek half hidden by his beard. He'd spilled something on his tunic and his wife was rubbing at it tenderly with a wet thumb.

The men had been drinking for hours, even before the sacrifice; the table was sticky with wine, and they'd progressed to the stage of toasting when any phrase seemed worthy of a drink. While I sat, they had toasted to the favorable wind given by the sea god, to a peaceful winter (though it was still autumn), to the first hard frost, and to Admetus's well-trained servants.

"To your lady wife!" cried a red-haired man at the far end of the table, hoisting his goblet above his head. The men turned to look at me and I fought the urge to put my hands over my face.

"To my lady wife," Admetus agreed, and drank, then kissed my forehead hard just as my father used to do. When he glanced my way again, I forced myself to smile. The wine made his dark face soft and ruddy, as if he were a wax figurine set too close to the fire. His full mouth looked sweet as a boy's when it was stretched wide around a laugh or round in amazement at some tale of a great beast or a fine plunder. Sometimes I was still struck by his beauty, hollowed out by it until I went weak and pliable in his arms.

Now his arm dropped from my waist: he'd turned back to the brown-haired man. I picked at the meat set out before me and sipped my watered wine, willing my stomach to settle. Artemis would be pleased by this celebration. The feast would end without another plague of snakes, and I would spend one more night lying on my back alone in the middle of the bed, staring up at the patterns of distant torchlight on the painted ceiling of our bedchamber.

I looked up at the ceiling of the megaron as I thought this. That is why I saw him first.

The god came through the palace roof, soundless and slow. He didn't look like Apollo or like my sea-god grandfather. He was Hermes of the winged heels and gentle smile, and his cheeks were smooth, as if rubbed sleek by the rush of air against his skin. He lit on the ground with a murmur of cloth and came to stand at the head of the feasting table. The hall seemed airless, the torches flickering as all the mortals drew in giant breaths, as if we could hold in that air, hold in life against the will of the Fates. The roomful of kings went faint like maidens at the sight of the quiet god. I choked on air and clutched at the table just as the rest of them did. Still, for a moment I was glad—glad that Hermes had come rather than Apollo, glad that I would suffer loss instead of betrayal. Loss was as familiar to me as the god's worn gray cloak. I was close enough to see the hem of it swirl around his feet. There were ragged threads along its edge, threads I had not been quick enough to see when Hippothoe died.

Hermes looked over the guests, his eyes resting above their heads as if he saw some marker floating there, some blot on a soul that might indicate which man should die—which man or which woman. The knowledge seemed to echo in him as in a quiet hall of fitted stone or a grove of wintry trees standing bare against the cold. I let out a long breath and waited.

The god pulled his moon-horned wand from beneath his cloak, lifted it, pointed. "Admetus," Hermes said. "Come."

Someone shrieked, and I pressed my hand to my mouth but

found my lips closed—I hadn't made that sound. I looked to my husband and saw the terror in his face.

Admetus, the god had said.

My husband's mouth was open, soft as a baby's, still wet with wine. He'd gone white around the lips and sweat darkened his beard and dampened his curls. I touched his arm and felt it twitch beneath the layer of fine cloth. I'd picked out his tunic the morning before—he'd wanted to try it on before the feast—and sat squinting from the bed as his body servants had laced it along the sides of his ribs. He'd seen me looking and smiled at me, that tender crooked curl to his lips, and I'd remembered how I had looked on him with wonder on the day we were wed. I couldn't stop thinking of it as the god stood waiting—the tunic, the shape of his body beneath it, that flash of memory tinted with happiness.

He was staring at the god. "Apollo told me I would not die," he said, and he sounded uncertain, like a child who's just been given a frightening truth and told to swallow it as easily as a sip of wine. "He swore that someone else could go in my place." He had never told me of that requirement; under the froth of my fear, I felt a stab of surprise and resentment.

Hermes nodded, a little flicker of agreement. "It is true." The wand did not waver. "I honor the word of Apollo. But you must find a sacrifice to go in your place. A life for yours."

Panic tightened my husband's face. "I must choose?"

The god inclined his head and blinked his round, dark eyes. He stood impassive and tall, remote and solid as a mountain. He was utterly without human restlessness. Only the little wings at his heels fluttered, stirring the heavy cloth of his cloak, as if at any moment he might burst from stasis into flight. "A death for a death," he said softly.

Admetus had turned away, eyes sweeping over the people at the table. His hands flexed on the edge of it. I watched his fingers instead of his face; I couldn't bear to see whom he would choose. "Creon," he said, voice rising, and a little more air leaked into the room. The faces of the other kings lightened. Creon would die for him, surely; it was the stuff of youthful oaths and sworn blood brotherhood. They didn't know, then, what it was like between Admetus and Creon, what it was like between Admetus and me. Admetus said, "Creon, you—"

Creon's pretty head dipped slightly, the smallest movement of chin toward chest. He didn't shake his head or look away, but I felt Admetus flinch. He wanted immediate love, immediate sacrifice, or he would not be satisfied, even with Hermes waiting there only an arm's length away. I felt the god's presence beside me like the whir of a hummingbird's wings.

One of Admetus's hands had risen from the table, reaching out to his friend, but now he flung that hand toward the other side of the table and pointed, trembling, to his parents. I thought he must have been mistaken—he must have meant to point to Theomenos or the redheaded man—but his hand did not shift. "My lord Pheres," he said quickly, "my lady Melanira." His voice was unsteady. I suppose that was to his credit.

I was shaking my head and I couldn't seem to stop. This was not my husband; this was some other man, some shepherd, some slave. This was unworthy.

"You will take my place," my husband said to his aged parents, and now his voice grew edged. Even his face looked sharper, the bones standing out beneath his skin as if he had already died. "You've had good lives. The gods will bless you for this. You must save me. You cannot let me die."

Pheres lifted his head, the left side of his mouth quivering.

Melanira's hand was tucked into the crook of his elbow, her other arm around his bent back. She too was shaking her head, slow motions back and forth, like the rub of her fingers on her husband's tunic. "No," Admetus's father said finally, the sound garbled but harsh. "No, my lord."

Admetus gasped. It was a weak little noise, the sound made by a slapped child. If this went on much longer, it would not matter if he did go with Hermes in the end—he would be remembered only as the king who'd tried to use a god's favor to cheat death, and I would be the cowardly woman who whimpered over his body. His shame would doom me to starve. His parents might house me out of pity, but when they died I would be cast out of Pherae, and Pelias would never take me back, not when my husband had brought dishonor to all of Tyro's children. I might rely on the hospitality of strangers, but no Achaean man would wed me, stained as I would be by Admetus's weakness. I'd wander aimless and alone; it would be a death on earth.

I stood, tangled in my skirts, the bench pressing against the backs of my knees. It took the men a moment to notice me. It took Admetus a moment longer than that. I was watching him, to see how long it would take; I had never learned to look away when I should. "I will go," I said.

Admetus's mouth worked silently. I waited to hear his words. My blood was thrumming in my ears like discordant lute strings, wild as a wine dance.

"You cannot. I forbid it," he said. "Alcestis, sit down."

I looked away from him to the quiet face of the god, who had lowered his wand when I spoke, as if I had truly surprised him. Now he lifted it again and flicked it once. The bench slid backward and I stepped away from the table. Admetus made a grab for my arm, but his hand slid off me, as if Hades already possessed me and I were fading from the world. My husband was seated and I was standing—it was wrong, and I had to resist the urge to sit again, to bow my head and study my hands like a good wife. I was a good wife. My hands were trembling, but I didn't feel the fear that made them shake. He grabbed for me again. I stepped back, and a pin slid from my hair and rattled against the floor, loud in the silence.

I reached out for the god. Hermes' palm was smooth and cool, and his fingers folded around mine. He pulled me close, his cloak brushing my ankles, and his arms settled heavily around my ribs. His body was warm all along my back. I'd never been held like that before, nor had I ever been so close to a god, not even my sea-god grandfather. He smelled like the pale green of new growth, like spring flowers still folded in their leaves. Like the fresh sweat of young girls. Like Hippothoe. I began to shiver.

"The woman shall go down to the dwelling of Hades," the god said, stirring the air by my ear. So they breathed; I had wondered. "Her death for yours, Admetus."

"No! I said I forbid it! She is my wife, mine to command, and I say she will not go."

"No longer." Hermes tightened his arms until I thought my bones would crack. I did not make a noise. I was not braver than my husband, but I'd had more practice at staying silent. "She belongs to death."

"Alcestis," my husband cried, "why have you done this? Do not go in my place. I will go. I will honor the Fates. At least take me with you! Do not leave me here alone."

Alone in this great palace, I thought, as he would leave me if he died. His voice was full of a new terror; he had not considered the idea of being left. I was a little gratified that it frightened him.

"Do you not love me? Alcestis!"

I could not speak. Hermes bent his mouth to my ear and said, soft as air, "Bid farewell to your husband, Lady Alcestis."

I lifted my head from Hermes' shoulder. It was growing heavy on the soft stalk of my neck. I looked over the assembled lords, the echoing megaron, the palace that had never really become my home, the husband who had never really become my own.

Admetus's face shifted, the corners of his mouth moving up toward the corners of his eyes, terror shifting into a mask of grief. Tears shone on his cheeks. The knowledge of my death was on him now, and he could not bear it—yet he could not look away. He wanted something from me, some gesture of departure, some soft thing to fold around his hurt when I was gone.

Under the cloak, I curled my hands around the god's hard forearms. I looked at my husband and smiled, and then I looked away. If there was relief in his eyes, I did not want to see it.

Hermes launched toward the ceiling. The stone bore the same painting as the ceiling of my bedchamber, five-armed white stars on a blue field, and they seemed to distort and lengthen as we hurtled toward the roof. I was dizzy again, but sudden panic cut through the blur. I would die. I was going to die. I struggled in the god's arms and then cried out, for it felt as if his hands would sink through my flesh to fasten around my bones.

We went through the roof. I had time to draw one more breath, and the air above the palace whistled cold through my nostrils. Then a sudden rush, a sickening lift of my stomach, and we plunged toward the earth, plunged through the earth, and under it.

HERMES' HANDS DID not hurt my bones any longer. I had no bones to hurt.

Entering the underworld was like coming into a dark room from the sunlit outdoors—not just any room but a quiet storeroom so old that its contents have all been forgotten, where dust drifts in the slanted light from the opened door and settles on the lips of abandoned vessels once shaped by human hands. Like the last stretched moment before one falls heavily asleep. Like being swallowed. And yet like none of those things at all.

We flew, the god and I, wrapped in his fluttering cloak. The space around us was uniform as a cloud, but I saw shapes and patterns below us, patches of darkness, ribbons of gloom, glints of metal or stone. Lines of strange-colored light. I felt as if I were trying to make out the floor of the sea by looking through deep water.

My feet dangled free, skimming over the drab landscape below. I knew I should be frightened, but I wasn't, not of the great height at which we flew, nor of the god who held me. A great, gray calm had settled on me.

"Where will you take me?" I asked the god Hermes. There was

no wind in this false sky, no little god to whip the sounds from my mouth.

"To the shore," he said in my ear. "To cross with the others. Have you a dagger or a bit of bronze to give the boatman?"

"I have nothing." And I didn't, not even a studded hairpin. My hair had come loose and hung down around my face like a maiden's, swaying as we went. I imagined the pins scattered on the palace floor like a constellation, my husband picking them up, cradling them in his palm, staring up at the ceiling. I felt no sorrow when I thought this, no yearning, no anger. I thought of Admetus alone, and then the thought fell from my mind, just as I would plummet to the ground if Hermes dropped me.

But Hermes shifted his grip, and I didn't clutch at him—he could've released me and I would have closed my eyes and fallen. I couldn't feel my body as I had when above ground, the effortless, constant knowledge of all its small irritations and twitches and pleasures. Fallen asleep, we say, when our limbs feel prickly and dead, but this was a different kind of slumber—my body had gone quiet all at once. I should've been frightened, but the blankness felt like relief.

"You must pay the toll, or he will not let you cross," Hermes said as we drifted lower, the dark shore rising up to meet us. Along the edge of the river—for that was the first gray ribbon, the Acheron, running softly through the floor of the underworld—crowded a mass of shades. From above they blurred together, but as we approached I could see their individual bodies. They looked like shadows tangled on the ground. Did I look like that beneath the god's cloak?

"Here you'll stay if you cannot pay Charon," Hermes said.

"Then I will wait with the others who cannot pay."

Hermes was silent, suddenly distracted, as if listening to a far-off call. We hovered over the shore. I strained to hear, twisting my head against his shoulder until I could just barely catch the sound, a low, deep murmur that was not coming from the crowd of shades milling beneath my feet.

"I will take you to Hades and Persephone," Hermes said, and we ascended again. "They wish to see you."

"But I must cross the river to enter," I said. "Am I not dead then?"

"Lady," the god said, "you are."

The stranded shades looked up as we skimmed over their heads, some of them standing with their mouths open like baby birds or amazed children. Some of them were children. Their faces were worn away by death, their features soft as rubbed stone. They looked like a group of clay figures, each one similar to the next.

The boatman was coming toward the dark shore, his empty boat skimming the surface of the water. His back hunched as he shoved his pole down into the silty riverbed, his white head bent downward, and he didn't look up as we flew above. He looked like an old grandfather, like an old king. Faintly I remembered Admetus's parents at the feast table, how they had clutched each other and stared at their son with watery eyes. The shades on the dark shore reached out for the ferryman's boat, reaching out like Admetus had then, their hands closing on nothing.

On the opposite bank, a broad path led toward the rest of the underworld. A few shades lingered and stared across the water as if they might beg Charon to return and ferry them back to life. Beyond them paced the black hound Cerberus, a creature of nightmares and of stories told in the frightened haze of half sleep, dragging his long chain back and forth in front of the entrance to a dim little cave. He was smaller than I had expected and skinny around the ribs. His middle head sighted us first, then all three heads lifted to snarl at the god's winged heels. His six black eyes shone wet.

Hermes shifted me in his arms and snapped his fingers at the dog, firing a bright spark that made the beast's two outer heads snuffle subserviently in the dirt. The middle head let out a protesting howl.

"Quiet," Hermes said, and Cerberus subsided, circling on his chain, his middle head lowering with a choral growl. I looked back as we flew over the beast—his tail had begun to swing back and forth, back and forth, like that of any hound recognizing a frequent visitor.

We'd passed the guardian; we were in the underworld proper, Hades' domain. Here were the wide, pale fields, filled with asphodel. The flower of the dead stood out from the ground in clumps, stiff and prickly, sticking up between the forms of the shades that wandered over the fields. I'd seen the flower by graves; I'd planted it by my sister's grave myself, pressing dirt around its roots. I remembered the little starlike tufts of petal, the burst bulbs, the way the slave boys had heated them in the fire and knocked them against stones to make them explode. Hippothoe had learned the trick of it—

She was here, somewhere, among the flowers of the field, among the dead who wandered in their pale robes. They dotted the landscape as far as I could see. They seemed to look straight ahead as they walked, but I watched them knock into one another, stumble slightly, and move on without a word. From this height their faces were as interchangeable as masks, and I felt the first cold touch of something like despair stroking at my gullet. There were so many dead, so many. Where was Hippothoe? How would I find her?

It seemed that we sped over leagues of field, asphodel and shades thronging below us. Ahead the ground flattened and the left edge of the field seemed to fall off into darkness—not a gray darkness like the rest of the underworld, but a hungry black depth like the yawn of a giant mouth. To the right stretched a forest, lit from within with a white-gold glow like sunrise on a wintry day. It was a light like Apollo's. I closed my eyes against it, but my eyelids seemed faintly transparent, as if a thin veil of skin couldn't keep the underworld out.

I saw the palace through my lifting eyelashes. I don't know why I hadn't seen it immediately, for it sat equidistant between the cold light and the dark pit, behind a towering gate of gray shimmering stone. It was Hades' palace; I knew it at once. It bore no carven lions or marks of kingship but was built of stone blocks with surfaces smooth as ocean-rounded pebbles. I wondered if the earth had worked these stones in her mouth for Hades, softened and then spit them out for his use. The walls of the palace were enfolding as a grave, but I almost liked the look of them. Here Hermes would deliver me; here I would be greeted by my new lord. This was a process I knew, the act of being transported by a man from one palace to another, given as a possession between kings.

Hermes twisted, swerving sideways, and the adamantine gate rose up before us. It stood free at the end of the plain, an arch of stone with no walls winging out from its sides—the king and queen of the underworld would never be besieged in this palace. We lit on the ground. I hardly felt my feet touch the dirt. Hermes moved away, his cloak slipping from my shoulders, and I looked down at my quiet body. My clothing had disappeared when I left the world, and instead of bright finery, I wore a colorless shift made of some thin, plain fabric beneath which I could see the curves of my breasts and hips. This was no garment for an Achaean woman—it was not a matron's bodice, cut for display, but it was not a maiden's careful wrapping either. I put my hands to my breasts in shock, thinking to cover them, but my palms were dead and dull, and I could barely feel the bumps of my nipples under the cloth. I look like a slave girl, I thought, and then: I look like a shade.

My hands fell to my sides. I looked to Hermes, who stood, watching me. His sleek face was troubled, his fine brow twisted in puzzlement.

"There is no shame here," he said. "It is strange that you should feel it."

At first I didn't understand his words. No shame? I was a queen and a wife and I stood dressed like a slave girl in the courtyard of a god's palace. I stared, incredulous, but Hermes looked on me without embarrassment. No shame. He turned finally and pointed to the nearest pillar of the great gate, which arched above our heads. Its surface was dully reflective, like stirred water, and in it I was a tall, pale smudge distorted by the bumps and twists in the metallic rock. Even the paint on my face had vanished. The metal showed me a white oval, my cheekbones stark, my lips pink-gray.

I looked like Hippothoe had when last I saw her. I was dead.

"So you see," Hermes said at the same moment that I turned to him and asked, "What must I do?"

The god swept his cloak back around his body, preparing to leave. Again I felt the hum of his presence, heard the sound of him like a stirring of feathers in an empty room.

"Lord Hermes—where are you going?" There was nothing for me to fear here; there was nothing here, nothing but the dead and the gods who ruled them. But still I did not want Hermes to leave. "What must I do?"

"I go back to the world," he said.

If he'd been my husband, I might have folded my hand around his arm, held onto him until he relented, but I couldn't touch a god like that. "Will you not stay?" I asked him, looking away from his dark, silent eyes. "Only to escort me to the palace."

"I do not venture inside that palace." His voice was soft as rock-tumbled linen, not fluting sweet like Apollo's. I wanted to ask him again to stay, but I could not. I didn't know what subterranean enmity or alliance kept him out of the royal house. The only story of the underworld I knew well was the goddess Persephone's—the bards were always singing it and the kitchen women talking of it, and Phylomache, who talked of the gods just as she talked of any gossip-worthy mortal event, had sighed over it in my hearing.

"The king and queen await you," Hermes said, and then he did reach out to me the way I'd once dreamed a god might, laying his thumbs along my cheekbones and turning my face up as he bent to kiss it. His lips were like a spark on my forehead, and for a moment I could feel my body as that spark jolted through my blood. Then it was gone, the light pressure of his hands gone also, and I was left staring up at him in a daze as if I were one of the shades by the river. He crouched and sprang, the cloak billowing around him, and flew into the gray dome of the underworld.

I put my hands up to my cheeks, brushed my temples. I could feel some ghost of my own touch, some memory of skin, but no real sensation. I turned back to my blurred reflection in the pillar's surface: pale, thin face; hair the color of dirt; eyes like discs of battered copper. I touched the gate, trying to recall when I had seen that stone before, when I had learned its name. My brother Pelopia had brought a piece of it home once, a gift from some sea nymph he had met on the shore. I remembered the way he'd cupped the smooth, glossy pebble in the palm of his hand, how his touch had made it steam. He'd chipped at the courtyard wall with the round pebble and knocked bits of stone free. "It's adamant," he'd said. "She gave it to me." He'd folded his fingers around the pebble as if it were the nymph's hand he held in his own. I don't believe he saw her again.

I stepped through the gate and stood before the broad doors of the palace of Hades. It was no taller than my father's palace or my husband's, the roof standing at the height of four men. It was not a grand and carven building like the eastern palaces spoken of by visiting seamen. But the walls were smoky crystal, and when I moved toward the window set into the wall beside the closed doors, it wavered and vanished, the wall around it smacking shut.

At first I thought the courtyard was empty, but I saw a clump of shades standing near the palace wall. They turned when I approached them, though my feet were silent on the ground, and whispered to each other in grass-dry voices. They didn't speak to me. I took another step toward them, and the group swayed drunkenly toward me. I put my hands out and they split around me like a wave, most of them stumbling through the adamantine gate. One remained, just out of my reach.

I couldn't tell exactly how old she'd been when she died—older than I had ever gotten. I wanted to touch her the way one might want to touch a corpse, to feel the change in the density of the flesh, the cold, altered solidity of death. But she wasn't solid. I couldn't see curves or bone beneath her shift, only a hazy human shape like something a child might scratch in the dirt with a stick. I lifted my hand to trace the line of her jaw and felt a tickle like goose down beneath my fingertips. Eddies of shade spun off of her, tendrils of self dissipating into nothing, and I jerked my hand back, resisting the urge to wipe my fingers on my shift. She did not recoil. She tilted her head and regarded me, and the look in her eyes reminded me of some of my father's slower hunting birds, a glossy, alien stupidity.

I could not possibly look like that.

I backed away from her and stumbled up the steps to the heavy palace doors and touched the great bronze knot set in the center of the right-hand door. It felt warm, and wrong somehow, and my stomach sank the way it had when I'd had to push on Phylomache's belly to force out the afterbirth. Dizzy, I put my other palm against the door; it was fashioned of some dark wood rather than crystal, a rich brown-red like dried blood, and I could almost feel the grain.

The door stuck at first and then pulled open easily. The hinges, like everything else in the underworld, made little noise. Even the entrance hall didn't ring with silence the way it would have in a mortal's palace. Any sound was smothered, as if the room were hung with tapestries, but there were no weavings, only a faint light bouncing from the crystalline walls. From within the walls seemed thinner, and through them I saw shades moving like clouds outside the palace. The hall seemed plain and low until I glanced up at the ceiling and saw a field of stars rotating slowly over my head, endless darkness and ribbons of light. So this was what we mimicked with our lapis and lead, this tamed celestial beauty? I stretched my hand out, but the ceiling was too high to reach—all I managed to do was block out the stars.

There was a slight grinding noise, then a clack like the sound of closing teeth, and a window opened in a solid stretch of wall to my left. I snatched my hand down and fell back a step, startled. But the window remained. Through it I saw the shade-crowded plain, and beyond it a structure like a king's dais built hundreds of times too large. I knew it must be the throne of the judges, where old kings dispensed with the recently dead—where Admetus would have gone to be judged for his cowardice, had I not spoken in his place.

When I turned away from the window I felt faint, too light, as if I could float like the other shades did. But I looked down and saw that my feet were still on the ground, bare on the palace floor. I still had the same high arches and long, skinny toes, even if they did appear pale and insubstantial.

My heart jerked in my chest. Just once, first, like the yank of a rope, or like hearing from a distance the sound of a voice I loved. I listened as I had listened before in Hermes' arms, but I heard nothing, just the swallowing silence of the place, the insulation of earth.

The second heave pulled me bodily forward. I stumbled on the smooth stone floor and threw my arms out for balance. It felt as though a ghostly finger were hooked beneath my ribs, drawing me toward the center of the palace.

The king and queen wanted to see me, Hermes had said. I believed him now.

The long pillar-lined hall I stepped into seemed to terminate in a golden mist. Uncertain, I watched it hover at the hall's end. It seemed harmless enough, but it might be a god in disguise, a trap, some subtler guardian than the three-headed beast. I crept toward it. As I approached the end of the hall, I saw that what I had thought was like a golden cloud was actually a set of woven golden hangings, each thin strand bright with jewel chips. I touched one of the curtains and it rolled and sparkled like a cold wave. Through it I saw the faintest impression of the room within, a great dark space with two bright figures at its center.

The ache in my chest sharpened. I parted the golden curtains and entered the megaron.

They sat on thrones of adamant and ebony—thrones of equal size, the curled armrests inches apart—and their hands, hanging between the thrones, were loosely entwined. Hades looked as grave as I had imagined him—bearded, his eyes sad and liquid as a deer's. He wore a tunic of some thick gray material that appeared as sleek as fur, and beneath it his bare legs were muscular and pale against the base of his ebony throne. His hair fell about his shoulders in dark ringlets as neat as a woman's, and he wore a silver crown that seemed to twist into the strands of his hair.

I looked to him first because he was king—because men spoke first and women waited in silence. I belonged to him and I owed him my obeisance. I knew the ways of royal women. His queen might have her limited power in this world, but I had none, and she would pay me no mind. I dipped my head to the lord Hades, my hands by my sides, wishing for a skirt to spread around my suppliant knees.

I waited for Hades to speak. He did not, but when I raised my head he was smiling a little as his thumb stroked his wife's fingers. He seemed to be waiting. I looked to the queen, my eyes slipping up her slender white arm to the fine arch of her shoulder and the pale column of her neck.

The sight of her face undid me. My fists clenched around handfuls of my shift and I felt the cloth fold between my fingers, felt the prickling of my flesh beneath—the waking of my lifeless body.

THE GODDESS PERSEPHONE'S eyes were gray and reflective as adamant, set wide in her girlish face. Her cheek was leached of color, but its curve was apple sweet. Her hair was golden and smooth as flax, her thin lips the stunning red of pomegranates. Her crown was neither gold nor silver but a narrow sharp-edged circlet of adamant, and she wore a dress almost like my shift, fine gray cloth that clung to her slim body. Like me, she was a queen dressed as a slave or a shade. But she was not like me. She had a remote and dream-like beauty, a feverish loveliness that called Hippothoe's face to mind. It was the kind of beauty death lends to a beloved face, a beauty that spoke of last looks and last kisses, of tears falling unheeded onto cooling skin.

She said my name, and her voice was as clear as the ring of a blade against armor. I stared at her, my mouth open.

"The wife of Admetus," the goddess continued, "who so loved him that she died to preserve his life. Is that who you are?"

Suddenly, with her gaze upon me, I didn't know. "I believe so, lady," I said with an unsteady formality.

"Alcestis," she said again, and smiled. Her smile was crescent shaped and cold as the moon, and she pronounced my name as sibilantly as a snake might. "And you have come here to take his death as your own."

I nodded.

"You do not seem convinced. And for my part I would have you certain, Alcestis." Her voice grew dry as she spoke and her fingers flexed around her husband's hand. The rope of gold encircling her neck twisted and slipped against her skin.

"What other reason might I have to die?" I asked. I had not had a quiet voice in the world above, but here all my words sounded like whispers. The entire room was quieter than anything alive. No servants moved about, no animals lowed outside the palace. Always, in the world above, I had felt myself surrounded by life. Here there was none.

"What other reason," she said, amused, and tilted her head to give the king a sideways look. "She loves her king so much, husband, that she would live as well as die for him."

Hades looked back at her. His eyes were fire-bright, and his fingers moved out of her grip, up and over her wrist in a slow caress.

"Be silent," Persephone said to him, but she did not tug her hand away. Hades lowered his head and I saw the part of his dark hair, like a split in armor. This was what my father had always feared, that even a slip of a girl like me might see a king's weakness. When the queen turned back to me, her face was soft. She looked happy. She leaned toward me and asked, "Why did your husband fear death so? All must die."

"Apollo promised, lady." I looked down. "To spare him from the Fates."

"Ah," Persephone said. "Apollo promised. Apollo makes many promises, but rarely does he make them to kings. Though

I have yet to see your husband." She said it musingly, an antici-
patory flavor to her words, as if she were looking forward to
questioning Admetus herself. I thought of my husband standing in my place, the queen's stone-gray eyes pinning him here,
and I felt a little swell of satisfaction. She would force him to
speak about Apollo; she would not be ignored.

The queen smiled, a curl of her lips that felt like a curl of
her arms reaching out to touch or examine me. Did she know
my thoughts? I tried to shrink back, but she caught me easily,
absentmindedly, with another yank in my chest. Her eyes drifted
away from me toward her husband, the dark and silent king.

"Did you truly choose to die for Admetus for the reason of
love?" she asked, a hint of wistfulness in her tone.

I looked to Hades again, flustered, but he had not raised his
head.

"Look at me, Alcestis," the queen said sharply, turning back.
"It is I who ask, not he."

"It was my duty to go in his place. He is my lord—he is
worth more than I."

"Surely not," she said, amused again. "A death is a death,
Alcestis. Some are better earned than others, but all shades hold
the same value. To believe otherwise is mere self-love."

Admetus didn't love himself nearly so well as he loved
Apollo, but Persephone wore her calm like a loosely pinned
cloak. I couldn't argue with her. I nodded and looked down at
my feet. I would've knelt before the lord Hades in supplica-
tion if I had thought he could halt this game of questions, but
I knew the goddess would stop me before my knees touched
the stone. I might have spoken to Phylomache about things
such as this, but never to anyone else, never in front of a man.
Persephone was not an Achaean woman—not a woman at all.

But she knew our ways, and she must have known her questions would upset me. She did not seem to care.

"You must have imagined," she said, "that if one of you was ever threatened with death, your husband would have chosen to sacrifice himself for you, as befits a lord of the Achaeans."

I raised my head. Her eyes widened, her fine eyebrows flicking up. My voice came out strangled. "What do you want of me? I cannot explain my husband's behavior. It is not for me to judge."

"We want nothing of you." Hades had spoken, not his wife, and I flinched at the sound of his voice, for he sounded at once like my father and my husband. When he looked at me, his face was serious, almost sad. He did not seem as easily amused as Persephone. "No wanting, and no judging. Not for you."

"Then what must I do?" I asked desperately, as I had asked Hermes. Everything was wrong: the improper questions and missed cues, the way Hades bent his head to Persephone, the feline look she wore now, as if preparing to pounce. I couldn't guess my place in their kingdom and I wanted them to instruct me. I had always been told what to do.

"There are no duties here. Not for those in the asphodel fields. In Tartarus," Persephone said, smiling again, "and in the fields of Elysium, yes. But not for those who simply die. And not for you, Alcestis, for you are a wonder. You still know yourself." Her gaze had softened, and her eyes glistened like the edges of melting ice.

I was tempted to tell her that I was the only person I had ever known well, besides Hippothoe, and that it was perhaps no surprise that I would not let myself go easily. But she was right. I'd seen the blank eyes of the other shades, the depths of emptiness in their once-lively faces. I was not yet so reduced.

Hades released his wife's hand. She frowned as he leaned toward me, his hair falling around his dusky throat. "Yet there is something you want of us."

I shook my head.

"Come, Alcestis," he said, and his low voice was as warm as Persephone's was cold. "Do not dissemble. You are so newly dead, I cannot help but know your mind."

The idea made me feel dully ill, but I would not show it. I lifted my chin in the manner that had earned me many a slap from Pelias. "If you could tell me, my lord—where is my sister?"

"Which sister?"

"The only one who—do you mean that Pisidice has died?"

Hades thought for a moment. "No," he said finally. "Not that sister. The wild-haired girl with evil in her chest. Hippothoe."

There was no evil in her, I thought fiercely, staring at the ground so that I wouldn't insult the god with my anger. Only sickness, and weakness, and youth.

"I do not think she likes that, husband." Persephone smiled down upon me graciously; it was the smile I'd been trained to give to slaves and village children. "Perhaps a little gentleness for one so recently dead, if you have learned that in our years together."

Thoughts flitted between them like arrows, volleys of meaning tossed back and forth. Hades looked away first and Persephone shifted on her throne, triumphant.

"Forgive me, Lady Alcestis," Hades said, almost humbly. "I cannot tell you where your sister wanders. She has been dead these seven years. She does not appear brightly in my mind."

I didn't understand. "You do not know her?"

"I am sorry," said the god.

"But—my mother? Are there any here whom I might find? Any from Iolcus?"

Persephone was watching me, her lips slightly open in fascination. "There must be one, husband, of all the Iolcan royal dead," she said slowly.

Were there so many then? Our line was not ancient; my father's father had built the palace, his men laboring to cart in the blocks and raise the walls against invaders. Before him there had been nothing, only a good port wasted in the hands of villagers who offered no resistance to Cretheus's men.

"Your father's mother," Hades said. "The lady Tyro. She is not long dead, and I remember her well."

The lady Tyro dead and I had not heard of it? After all the rituals, all the times Pelias had invoked her name in appeal to his father, he had not sent word of her death to his brother, or to her grandchildren.

Or perhaps Admetus had not thought it necessary to tell me.

"Where does she—" I paused, unsure what to say. "Where is she?"

Hades' eyelids slipped low for a moment, giving his lean face a sleepy cast, and after a moment I realized with a shudder that he was tracking her in his mind. "She wanders past the asphodel fields, by the vale of mourning," he said, "though she does not mourn. You shall go and find her, and she shall know you. All your ancestors shall."

"How shall I know her?" I asked, not certain I wanted to know what sort of woman would have loved Poseidon and produced my father.

"By her history," Persephone said, in a voice gone sweet with delight. Her eyes were not sleepy; they were round and bright, fixed on me. "For she dared great things for love, as you have done."

"I have done no great things," I mumbled.

"No? Then perhaps you shall yet. Go now, and see your way to your grandmother." She flicked a dismissive hand at me, and suddenly my eyes seemed clearer and the lines of her slim body sharper. She watched me, still smiling. Her smile felt like an invitation and a vivisection, as if she wanted first to take me in her arms and then to split open my chest with her narrow white hands, to read me like an omen, to pull meaning from every visceral wrinkle.

I dipped my head to her and then to the dark lord Hades, who still sat brooding and silent at her side. She turned her face away as I bowed and left me to go; I felt her hold on me loosen, like fingers slipping free of my heart.

I wanted to look back at her, but I fled instead. The edges of the golden curtain scraped against my bare head as I left the megaron, and I ran down the long hall and beneath the entry's whirling stars, my feet still terribly silent on the stone floor. Then out, shoving at the heavy door while its hinges protested with a shriek like a child's. Once free I bolted for the adamantine gate, pushing past the blurry bodies of the shades milling in the courtyard.

One of them caught my arm as I passed, dead hand sliding reptile cool over my bare arm. I threw it off, twisting around a shudder, and looked up into its blank face. The shade was a man, or had been, thick waisted and thin haired, no mark of death on him other than the gray softening of the underworld. He groped for my hand and I yanked it away. Some hint of hurt surfaced in his murky eyes and I stared at him, fascinated and confused.

"Lady, do you know my boy?" he said heavily, words slurred together. He lifted his hand again and I flinched. "Do you know my Timios? Only as tall as this, as my hand here."

We both looked at his hand, fluttering between us like a trapped bird.

"How is it that you speak?" I asked, as gently as I would have spoken to one of Phylomache's daughters. "Have you just now come from the world above?"

"Just come?" he echoed, and looked over the courtyard as if he had never seen it before. His eyes narrowed, and then the stunned look seeped back into them. "I don't know. But do you know my boy? You must tell me. I've looked everywhere. I cannot find him. I call for him and he doesn't answer." His eyes grew darker as he talked, hollows beneath his brows.

"I don't know him," I said. I reached for his hand, but he drew it back, folding his arm against his chest as if it enclosed his son. "Perhaps the lord Hades—"

The man backed away. "Speak not of him," he whispered. "He takes. He only takes."

I thought of Hades, with his hand soft on his wife's wrist and his eyes contrite and all the newly dead still shining in his mind. What could he take from me?

I said, "I will look for the boy Timios. I'll tell him that you search."

Again the pitiful spark in his eyes. He seized my hand, his touch almost solid, and kissed it like a slave might, his lips a moth brush against my knuckles. "I thank you, lady, I thank you. May the gods bless you. May they give you many children, and a fine house, and . . ." But there his voice failed, as if he could not recall the blessings life had once held. "I thank you," he said again, in a small, broken voice. I fled.

Past the gate I stopped running. There was no struggle or intensity in it now; it was as easy as dying. My chest was still and my shift unstained with sweat. I wanted a body, a body that would know how to be properly afraid. I wanted heaving breath or a living heart to drum against my ribs. This was freedom, but it was the freedom of an unmoored ship floating lost on a mirrored sea.

I took the path that led from the gate to the asphodel fields; I didn't know what else to do. I was to go past the asphodel fields, Hades had said, by the vale of mourning—as if one part of the world's underbelly were more melancholy than another. And how would I know this vale? Perhaps it would be marked by a stone stele with a carven tear. Or perhaps a funeral slab engraved with the names of the dead, all the dead, the silenced boys and vanished girls, the lost fathers and the weeping mothers. Even if the gods did honor us in that way, I'd never be able to read the names—not even my own.

I stepped off the path into the field, brushing stalks of asphodel with my fingertips. Shades moved in front of me with the slow purposelessness of grazing sheep. Following some imagined trail, maybe, a lover's feet on the ground. I knew slave girls who swore they could recognize the outline of a friend's foot in the dirt, the silly dots of toes, the sinuous curve of the lifting arch. The ground of the underworld bore no footprints. When I looked up, some of the shades had turned to look back at me. I was beginning to see little differences among them, hints of intelligence in the eyes of some.

The ground was hilly now, and there were ghosts in the lines of the hills, shades who sat on the dirt quiet as shrines. They didn't move when I approached. Some of them were weeping, their shoulders trembling and their heads bowed. Women walked with babies in their arms, but the babes were too calm, silent and inhuman as cloth dolls, and the mothers crooned idiot songs that had long since lost any semblance of language. I'd seen their hollow-eyed look in the faces of starving villagers come to supplicate at my father's kingly feet, in slave boys with bare-ribbed bodies who had taken ill of a white fever and died laughing and thrashing in the funerary circle, where they'd been abandoned so they would not sicken the entire palace. I had seen this look in Hippothoe's slackened face, and I'd known that the look was death, but always it was a passing look, succeeded by peace and silence. Here all faces wore the look of death and wore it forever.

I could hear the hound Cerberus barking, his fearsome voice reduced by distance. Where had I wandered? From above, the asphodel fields hadn't looked so large, but all things seem easy and near when one is being transported by a god. I stood as tall as I could and tried to look over the hills. I couldn't see far, but I noticed a faint bluish light rising beyond a distant hill, a light that looked like no god I knew.

I turned toward the light and walked for what seemed like hours, though my body did not tire. Eventually the field grew rocky and bare, the asphodel rising up weakly between the stones. I came to the crest of a hill and beyond the hill I saw the vale of mourning.

It needed no marker. Along the rocky valley bottom lay the Phlegethon, the river of fire, and shades stood by the river's bank, wavery in the heat, the flames shining blue-white through their bodies, like water churned into froth. Pelopia had told me once that a smelter's flame burned blue when he cast bronze, but I hadn't believed him. From the hill, the flames of the Phlegethon looked cool and pure, like a mist so enveloping it seems to erase the world.

I climbed over the ridge of the hill and made my way down into the sloping valley. A girl's shade looked up at me as I passed the rock where she sat. She was silent and strange, but there was a calm in her eyes, a reflected gleam from the river that gave her face a look of contentment. I felt myself smile, but she did not smile in return.

The Phlegethon cast a pale glow into the gray sky, the light I had seen from the hill. I stared up at it, dazzled. A loose group of shades stood near the flames. They would catch fire, I thought, standing so close to the bank—they leaned toward the heat as if they wished to—but the matter of a shade's body was not quick to ignite. Memory does not go up in flames.

"Girl," someone called in a croaky, rough-edged voice. "Pelias's daughter. Girl. Come here."

The voice had come from behind me. I turned, stepping around two shades who stood like twin trees, their feet nearly touching but their torsos swaying apart. A woman lay on a flat patch of ground near the river's edge, stretched out like a sleeping servant, her arms folded peacefully across her belly. She'd lifted her head slightly. When she saw me looking at her, she lay back down, as if the effort of leaning up from the ground had cost her dearly. Slowly, reluctantly, I went to her.

In the glow of the fiery blue river, Tyro looked like a woman seen by moonlight rather than a shade. She had broad cheekbones and wide-set eyes, and my father lurked in the fine line of her nose, the strong chin. I could see where wrinkles had once seamed her face—they were still visible as tiny feathered lines of light, the way fine cracks glow in an old ivory jar when one places a candle inside it. I understood what Hades had meant when he spoke of newly dead shades appearing brightly in his mind; my grandmother was faded, but she had yet to lose her light.

She squinted at me from the ground. I must have looked strange with the glow of the river behind me and my odd half-solid body dense inside my shift. "Daughter of my son," Tyro said. "Vessel of seawater. Sit."

I settled beside her, pulling my bent legs up to my chest under my shift and wrapping my arms around my knees. I could feel the faintest brush of bare flesh against bare flesh, the softness of my breasts against my thighs. "Mother of my father, honorable Tyro," I said. "I don't like this place."

"No, nor should you."

"I've been looking for you. I saw—there are awful things here."

"Look at the river," she said. "Do you not think it beautiful?"

I looked at the river. It was indeed beautiful. "Yes," I said.

"Do not speak to me of awful things," she said. "I birthed your father, you know. He bit me when I nursed him. As if I were a sow." She rolled her head sideways, smiled at me. "But now you have no need to worry. He lives."

"He does."

"Childbirth or illness," she said suddenly. She meant it as a question, I saw, and I shook my head, unsure how to explain. "Strange. You look too fresh for murder. I see no marks of blood upon you."

"No blood," I said. "The god Apollo—he promised my husband that he'd intercede with the Fates when death came for him. When it was his time. He was—we were holding a feast for Artemis when the messenger arrived. I took his place." It was easier to say this time, without Persephone's confusing presence, but still I stumbled when I recalled Admetus's cowardice.

My grandmother looked away. "Brave girl," she said, though

she didn't sound entirely approving. And then: "You have the reek of god upon you."

"The god Hermes brought me here."

"Not that god," she said. "When did you come? Only just now?"

I nodded, glancing at another shade who stared at us and then moved on. Few of them seemed to notice us on the ground, though none of them had trod upon us yet. I wondered if their misty feet would sink through my body or if their toes would bump against my hips, slip on my thighs. "Hermes took me to the palace. I was sent for."

A long silence.

"Lie down, child," she said finally, jerking her head toward the ground by her arm. I unfolded my legs and stretched them out on the powdery dirt, my ankles emerging pearly gray from beneath my shift. I lay down and looked up at the pale bluish sky-ceiling. There were no stars above us here.

Her hair was spread out on the ground between us like a dull silvery net, loose like a maiden's. Perhaps she had died in the morning, before a slave could braid her hair. Or maybe she too had left her hairpins behind on the floor of some echoing room in her villa when Hermes came to spirit her away.

"Where is my sister?" I whispered, half afraid of her answer. "Where is my mother? Do you know them? Have you seen them? Do you know where they wait?"

"Of course I know them. Seen them, that I have not. No—your mother, Anaxibia, I saw once, and she spat at me. Tried to, at least." Tyro was chuckling. It sounded like the rasp of wheat chaff in the wind. "Never forgave me for having more life than she did. Not the forgiving kind."

"How is it you know me?" I rolled onto my side so that I

could study her face. She smiled again, and I thought her skin might crack like the shell of a cooked egg rolled between a servant girl's palms. Her lips spread over gray teeth.

"Your blood," she said. "And the gods' favor. It marks you."

"I've earned no favor," I said, stricken. Admetus had earned favor, and favor was the scent of laurel in the sunlight, bitter when crushed. I wanted no favor from a god.

"Dying in a man's place? You should be in Elysium, child, drinking wine from a two-handled cup. You should have a slave boy to kiss your hand when you lay it along your thigh, as a dog kisses the hand of its master. You have earned favor." She looked at me through narrowed eyes, little slits of murky light. "Had you not, yet you might still have drawn her eye. You have the look of Poseidon about you."

I twisted my head to look at the river, where the flames rushed past quick as water. Did she come here to stare into the blue light and remember her Olympian lover? Had she once smelled of salt water and wakened in the morning to find sand in the creases of her fingers? I felt a flash of sympathy for Cretheus, the one whom she had left in a cold bed to stare at the constellations on the ceiling.

"Nothing to say to that, Alcestis?" My father's mother made a rattle like one of Hippothoe's coughs; it might have been a laugh. She shifted and stood—a slow, creaking process even in death, as if her bones had not forgotten their aches—and crossed her arms over her breasts the way the head maid in Iolcus always had before she'd scolded me. "Call me Tyro," she said. "None of the others can remember my name, and I like to hear it now and again. Reminds me of days when I lived and wore it."

I scrambled up to stand next to her. She reached out with

both hands and her fingers felt like cool mist against my cheeks. "Watch for your mother, but do not hope for much. She is overfull of blame even now, and spills it at the slightest touch. You have little enough of life left in you. Spend it on something else."

"And what of Hippothoe? My sister. What of my sister?"

"What of her? Nothing, I expect. And I know nothing more. Pelias yet lives, and Iolcus stands. Nothing else concerns me."

I touched her thin gray shoulder and shivered at the downy feel of her body. "You could accompany me, Tyro. To help me look for them."

"What good would that do?" she asked, shaking off my hand.

"Come," I said again, feeling suddenly desperate. "Please. I don't want to go alone through the asphodel fields. The others frighten me."

"Frighten you?" She turned away, looking toward the river. Blue light cast sideways shadows across her face. Her voice had gone distant and when she looked back at me, her eyes were like cloudy marbles. "What have you to fear, granddaughter of the sea?" she asked me, and I could not answer.

10 I LEFT MY grandmother in the deep vale and walked along the rocky bank of the Phlegethon. I felt dizzy, but I didn't spread my arms for balance. What did it matter if I fell? My body would not break.

I climbed out of the valley, where the river fell in a strange bright stream from the plain above, and found a smooth boulder near the top of the cliff. I pulled myself up onto it and sat, folding my legs before me and peering down into the vale. From this height I couldn't recognize my grandmother among the gray forms on the bank. I could pretend, at least for a moment, that no one here knew me. I still felt naked, though I wasn't cold. The atmosphere was windless, the air perfectly neutral in temperature. It was not late fall here; this place was perpetual and without seasons.

I rested my temple on my knee and closed my thin eyelids. I wished for the warmth of my husband's hands on my shoulders. There had been a morning once, not long after we were wed, when he had awakened me with a series of dry kisses along my shoulders and trailed his hands along the furrow of my spine. I had been smiling before I opened my eyes, and it was only when I rolled over to kiss his mouth that I had seen the look of uneasy determination on his face. I had kissed his cheek and stroked the silky skin between his shoulder blades until he lay warm and quiet against me, and the slave girls had given me envious looks when they attended me late in the morning.

It was one of the better memories I had of Admetus.

If what I had seen of the underworld was true, that memory would vanish. I could clasp my recollections to me as tightly as I was able and still they would slip from my mind as the feeling of touch was slipping from my fingers. I wouldn't remember the savor of his skin or the rough tangles of Hippothoe's hair, how it had snagged on my fingernails and made my face itch as I slept. Already I found it difficult to keep him, or Hippothoe, in mind without effort. If I tried to conjure them up, I saw Persephone's face.

I slid off of the boulder and picked my way down the rocky hill into the asphodel fields, unsure where to go. It was hard not to feel that my freedom to roam the underworld must be some kind of test—that if I toured obediently through its dark regions, I would be rewarded with Hippothoe.

Eventually I entered a dark cypress wood. The forest felt empty, no leaves on the ground, no broken twigs. No calling birds. I plucked at a branch, bending a feathery leaf between my fingers, and it sprang back to its original shape with no mark on it. I'd been in a forest only once, not long after Hippothoe died, when I had bothered Pisidice to let me come along with her when she went out to supervise the washing. I'd gotten myself covered in pine sap, and the slave girls had had to wash me too, while Pisidice stood over me and shouted. Now I touched one of the cypress trunks and my soft fingers came away clean and dry.

I slipped around the low-hanging branches, pushing them away from my face. Then the woods came to an abrupt end, a line of trees so sudden and straight that they must have been placed by the gods, and I walked into a clearing full of chilly light.

Around the heroes' quarter stood a glowing barrier like a broad-lit circle cast by a torch to keep the dark at bay. But the light of Elysium burned too brightly, flaring in my eyes like perpetual lightning and whitening the figures within. The light was cold, like eternal dawn that never blossoms into day, but it drew the dead just as the flaming river had. Shades lined its edges, their hands smudges on the wall of light. I peered over the shoulder of the tall shade in front of me.

A great table sat in the courtyard of a great palace, far grander than the smoky crystal building that housed the king and queen. Behind the palace spread golden-green fields of wheat, grass dotted with grazing horses and cattle, pens holding sheep and goats. There were stands of white beech trees and dense pine, and a neat, pleasant stream ran along the side of the courtyard. I could see a sunlit sky just streaked with cloud and long late-afternoon shadows stretching from the men's feet. The scene looked like a mural, pretty and static.

This was Elysium: a continuous feast, a table piled high with meat and every man served the hero's portion. Nothing but heroes' portions in these fields, no man made to feel less than godly. At the table sat men clothed in the skins of wild beasts, with spectral swords still buckled to their sides and greaves strapped to their shins. Their armor clinked and sang when they moved, and they moved like gods, easy in their bodies, not one of them aged or wounded or sobbing into his hands. They looked like living men. From time to time, one of them hooked a serving girl or boy into his lap and pressed his face into the slave's hair. The boys smiled and twisted in the men's laps, and the girls giggled and covered their mouths as if to hide delighted grins. Every girl, every boy, every hero—all perfectly joyous.

I pressed closer among the throng of observers. I didn't recognize the men at the table, though I knew their lazy, proud expressions and the cut of their royal muscles. My brother Acastus had looked like this before he left for Mycenae, skin tanned golden by the sun and always bearing a faint slick of oil, as if he had just come from wrestling a friend. But beneath the joy I saw strain in their immortal faces, in the tautness of youthful flesh in a world full of dissipating mist. They did not belong in the underworld, and though the brilliant world within the bubble looked nothing like the gray landscape outside it, they were not fooled. One hero's hand pressed hard at his temple as if to stave off a headache; another man sat with a slave girl on his lap and touched her, and yet looked away from her with frightened eyes that didn't match his obscene grin. When she stood, she moved with the rolling ease of a shade.

The heroes looked out toward us often, little glances cast furtively between jokes. They couldn't see us, but perhaps they could feel us watching them the way the slaves watched royal feasts from the kitchen hall, hungry and wistful and resigned.

I pushed around the shade in front of me and put my hands on the curtain of light. It crackled beneath my touch, tiny bolts of light dancing away from my fingertips. Slowly, the men at the grand table looked up, looked at one another, looked toward me.

I backed away, knocking into shades who had come up behind me to watch the heroes and muttering a choked apology. The other shades took no notice as I stumbled back into the forest. The palace must be to my left, I thought, and I tried to run in that direction, but the woods darkened around me and, without a sun to guide me, I couldn't tell which way to go. I faltered and spun as I ran, batting at the thin branches that whipped across my face and watching for a path, and finally I caught my foot on a cypress root and tumbled to the clean ground.

I sat for a moment with my hands braced on the dirt and my eyes closed. My foot tingled slightly; I'd knocked it into something when I rolled on the ground. I touched my ankle, grateful for the sensation, and when I opened my eyes I saw a small wooden arch twined all about with gray-brown vines and white flowers and a path of flat stones proceeding from it. It had not been there before I fell.

I got up ungracefully and went to the arch. When I touched the gnarled wood, I felt something strange—a more delicate sensation than the imperious summons I'd received in the palace of Hades, but similar, as if a soft hand were stroking the surface of my heart. I knew whose touch I felt, and I didn't think to resist. I went through the arch.

On the other side was a garden in which all the trees were dead and all the flowers wilted. Immediately behind the arch stood olive trees heavy with black fruit, hard beneath my fingers. I tried to tug an olive from its branch, but it wouldn't come away in my hand. The berries farther along the path clung just as fiercely to their stems. The flowers smelled of cold: the spike of air in your nostrils when winter seizes the world.

The queen of the underworld sat beneath a pomegranate tree, its branches forming a bower over her head. This tree, like the others, was stiff and dead, and beneath its arched covering the goddess shone jewel-bright.

I took a step and Persephone lifted her golden head. She held a pomegranate poised halfway to her mouth, and its juice dripped down her white hand, over the fine bump of her wrist and along her forearm. The fruits on the tree were pinkish gray, their waxy skins shriveled and bumpy, but the fruit in her hand had a soft, glossy skin and plump red kernels in its honeycomb of pith. I wasn't hungry, but I could not pull my eyes away from the pomegranate in her pretty hand, the juice like blood in runnels on her skin.

She raised her arm, licked at the line of juice, and smiled at me with stained lips.

"Alcestis," she said. "Do come sit."

"You can't eat that," I said, startled into rudeness.

She lifted one eyebrow in genteel confusion.

I dropped to my knees before her, gesturing toward the pomegranate. "The fruit, my lady. I've heard the story. I know what it must mean if you eat."

"Oh," she said with a laugh slow as water over stones, "this holds no danger for me now. The deal has been struck, you see, and all have agreed to its terms. So I may consume whatever I wish, and no one may forbid me."

The golden chain had vanished and now she wore a bronze circlet about her throat, its fit snug enough that a mortal might have had trouble breathing. It didn't seem to cause her discomfort, though, and the rub of the metal raised no color on her skin. She lifted her free hand to touch it as I stared, leaving a smudge of juice on her neck, and smiled at me again when I ducked my head in embarrassment.

"Charming." She licked her fingers. "Yet not obedient. I asked you to sit, not to kneel like a supplicant, Alcestis of Pherae. There is plenty of grass to share." The grass freshened and greened when she patted it. I thought of my grandmother lying on the rough ground by the Phlegethon, of how the light in her eyes had dimmed when she rose. Persephone's gray eyes were brilliant with amusement. She held the pomegranate out to me as I crawled up to sit beside her.

"Will you eat?" she asked. Her sly smile lightened her face, made it young and mischievous, less stone carven. I had no stomach for the fruit, but my fingers itched to take it, to dig into the red kernels until their juice burst on my hands. Such color in this place—I hadn't thought it possible. Still, I shook my head. I knew her story.

"What is this place?" I asked her. "I fell in the woods and when I looked up there was a gate. But there are no walls, not like the heroes'—" She was giving me a curious look, not entirely friendly. I swallowed the rest of my thought. "Not like a mortal palace."

"No, there is no need for such barbarities here. I wished you to see it, so you did." She picked several kernels from the fruit and crunched them between her teeth, spitting the seeds delicately into her cupped palm and then dropping them in a neat pile beside her.

"You say you have heard my tale," she said. "And who told it to you?"

"The village bard in Iolcus knows stories of the gods. He came to the palace for feasts when my father wanted to hear tales. But he tells mostly of Poseidon and the Olympians." She was still watching me expectantly, the pomegranate forgotten in her hand. "I do not know much," I said. "My husband did not even talk often of Apollo. And no man likes to speak of goddesses overmuch."

"That I know well. They call on us readily enough when they need us, but they never give us honor. Their fear is unbecoming."

I was not sure that I thought the men's fear so unreasonable now, sitting on the grass beside this goddess in a dead garden, watching her suck the juice from the fruit that had doomed her. But I nodded. I didn't want to anger her. I could imagine that beautiful face contorted in rage, with a vase figure's twisted lips and black eyes, her hair flying out around her.

"I will tell you my tale," she said, almost gaily. "The mortal singers get so many things wrong in the telling, trying to fit our deeds to their ghastly music. It sounds like dying goats. I wish they would choose some other way to honor us, but one cannot argue with devotion. We are not ungrateful."

I'd thought the bard's tunes fine, but I murmured agreement.

"I lived with my mother then. She was always overcareful with me, and I did not like it. I thought I knew what was safe. I was a maiden, and she had given me girls to attend me when I went down from the mountain of Olympus. They were pretty girls, but not as pretty as I. In the field below the mountain there were flowers. We often went to pick them, my girls and I. The lord of the gods had a liking for me and I thought he would always protect me if I needed it. I went out to pick flowers that day, and I did not worry. I did not know that Hades was watching me. I had met him when he came to Olympus, but his visits were rare and his manner unpleasant, and I had never considered him as anything but an uncle.

"He took me for his wife. He took me," she repeated, and glanced over at me as if to be sure that I was listening. I nodded. I understood well enough. She looked down again, her golden eyelashes fluttering against her flushed cheeks. Her smile grew wider, but her fingers dug into the pomegranate's flesh. "And we were wed, and I was queen, and there are rewards due a queen. You know this."

I nodded again, watching her hands.

"I ate the fruit. No one had warned me. I did not think. It looked so beautiful and sweet, and the garden was empty. I did not even think anyone had seen me eat. It did not taste quite right," she added suddenly. "Nothing here does. But I have learned to like the taste. It tastes like dust, and memories, and there is salt in it, like mortal tears. I cannot explain it to one who will not eat. But it lingers in the mouth.

"I thought I could still go back. My mother was miserable, you see, and so the mortals grew miserable, and misery pours no libations. But when Hermes came to order me back, my husband had the seeds in his hand. He had been carrying them ever since I ate."

She looked at me, her eyes glossy and flat like a sea becalmed. I wanted to ask her why she was telling me this—it was the story I knew—but I recognized the acid edge to her voice. Phylomache had done this when my father had insulted her in some fashion: told the story over and over, like opening a wound to bleed it clean. But some wounds never bleed clean, and Persephone, her mouth and fingertips reddened with juice, did not look eager to forgive.

She seemed to be waiting for me to speak.

"It is fall now," I said, "in the world above. The winds had changed on the shore, the slaves told me. Before I died."

Persephone smiled. The leaves above her head glistened waxy green for a moment and then faded. "Yes, now my mother grieves and cools the world, and when I return all will begin to blossom as if I had never left." She looked down at the fruit in her hands and let out a frustrated sigh. "Every year it is the same, in the light with her and then in the dark with him. Sometimes I think I shall just stay here, in the underworld.

I will refuse when Hermes comes for me, and if Zeus dislikes it so much he can come to fetch me himself. I should like to see Cerberus bark at him when he comes, old god with his old lightning bolts, as if he could hurt us here." By the end of this speech, she was muttering like an old woman. I stared at her, thinking of winter eternal, frozen crops and storm-lashed seas and ground so hard no pick could dent it.

"You cannot stay," I said, but she cut me off with an airy wave. She had so many smiles, like differently weighted blades.

"I would not, I know it. If I chose a place to stay, I would live with my mother in the sunlight and pick flowers in the field with my girls and let them weave my hair with vines. We would bathe in the river and hang our clothes from tree branches, and no one would dare interrupt our peace."

I could see the field as she spoke of it. And then I began to see things that I could never have imagined on my own: a black chariot rattling over the edge of a gaping chasm in the earth, a rainbow broad and flat as a road, a ring of golden thrones around a roaring column of fire, and a woman petting the flames with the tenderness reserved for a child. I saw Hades reach out for Persephone's hand, saw her frozen for a moment as she considered, and then saw her arm rise away from her side and float toward him as if she could not control it.

Something touched my shoulder, and I started, blinking and shivering. Persephone had dropped the pomegranate and it lay forgotten near her foot. She touched my arm again—not to rouse me this time, but with a look that would've rested easily on the face of Phylomache's two-year-old daughter, a look that said: *I will do this, and you will not stop me.* Her fingers were sticky and her touch made light burst beneath my skin. I could feel my skin again, could feel the burning line she left as she trailed one finger from my shoulder to my elbow. I watched her fingertip move and my cheeks tingled hot and cold, like fever in summer.

"Alcestis," she said, considering, "you listen well. It is a good trait in a mortal, knowing when to be silent."

I laughed, then shut my mouth abruptly. "It is only because I do not know what to say, goddess."

"Oh, do not call me that. You shall call me Persephone. If you must title me, call me your queen, and I will be satisfied." She pulled her hand away and peered at it as if searching for some remnant of my shade flesh on her white fingertip. I stole a glance at my arm; it looked almost solid, almost pearl colored, not gray. The place where she had touched me glowed faintly pink.

"Did you find your father's mother?" The challenge in her eyes had vanished. She looked younger than I, like a barely bleeding girl wed and broken too early, and concerned for me. I put my hand on the dry grass between us, steadying myself, then drew it back quickly; I couldn't stand to have her touch me again, not so soon. I couldn't think when she touched me.

"I did," I said. "She was where the lord Hades told me to look."

A small gesture: of course, said her graceful hands. She had that kind of confidence in her husband's power. "And did she know you?"

"Yes," I said slowly. I didn't know how to describe my god-beloved grandmother. She was dead, that was all. A little glow left to her still, but she would set like the moon in morning, the horizon gulping up her shine. And what of my sister, whom even Tyro had not seen? How had I sat so long beside the queen of the underworld and forgotten to ask of her?

Persephone didn't seem to have noticed my hesitation. "And you knew her. Good. She will help you if you have need. The first days—the first days are not easy. I remember." She bent forward and retrieved the errant pomegranate, picking idly at the membrane between the seeds and peeling pieces of it away.

"But I have not found my sister. My Hippothoe, who died when I was young."

Persephone's fingers stilled and then began plucking at the fruit again. "You will find her. You must be patient." Her voice was light and almost cloying. I thought of touching her white hand, the tiny angled hollow at the base of her thumb.

"Lady—Persephone," I said, pleading.

Her gray eyes flicked up. "Lady Alcestis," she said. I listened for mockery; it was a habit born of years of conversing with Pisidice. She would have spoken derisively, but Persephone did not. She looked at me gravely, waiting.

"She is all I have."

"Your father's mother," she said mildly. "The lady Tyro. You told me—"

"Tyro is a shade," I said. "I want my sister."

"The feeling will pass, Alcestis." Her eyes were bright again, the sheen in them like the gloss of fever or tears. "All feelings do."

"I know that," I said. "I see the others here; they have no feelings. They have nothing. But I have not forgotten my life yet. I do not feel—I don't feel like I am dead. I don't think I died the right way." My voice grew fierce. I was certain she would laugh at me.

"The right way," Persephone said faintly, as if startled. "Oh, Alcestis. There are so many ways to die, and most are terrible or boring or terrible and boring. You have been lucky. It did not hurt much, and you arrived here as you were when you left the world. It is like a song, your death."

I was silent. She touched my arm again, a quick tap, a flint strike.

"Tell it to me again. Your death and how it came about."

"I told you of it when I arrived here," I said. I should have called her queen, but I couldn't say it.

"Tell it," she repeated. "I want to remember it."

Then I understood. "Even when I forget?"

"Even so."

"I married Admetus to escape my father," I said. "He loved Apollo, and Apollo loved him and swore to save him from death. But he didn't tell Admetus how he would be saved. I saved him, and I came here."

"To me."

"To death," I said. Persephone looked down at the pome-granate in her hands, and for a moment I saw it as she did—the flesh, once so tempting, now robbed of its danger and pleasure, tasting of dust.

"And then?"

"And then I don't know what happens," I said snappishly, forgetting myself, forgetting the goddess. Her cheeks grew pink, and now she laughed, a sound that stirred the branches above her shining hair.

"Well, I am no seer to tell the future. But I can," she said with a confiding air, "often recall the past. And I see that you can as well, for I could tell you knew your grandmother's story when I spoke of it in the palace."

"My father did not let us forget it."

"No," Persephone said. "Indeed. So you are the child of a child of a god, the lord Poseidon. And you lived sixteen years in the world without knowing yourself different in any way?" She put the pomegranate down again and leaned toward me. "You woke in the morning, every morning, and you did not feel yourself filled with the force of the universe and your godly ancestors?"

I hadn't felt myself filled with anything but exhaustion most mornings. Occasionally my head had ached with wine or the residue of tears. On rare mornings, I'd risen with a sense of vague and unfocused joy, as if the sun had leapt up in my chest instead of in the sky, but those days had come infrequently after my father's marriage and even less frequently after my own. I shook my head.

The goddess frowned and the leaves over her head drooped. "You were only—Alcestis?"

"Yes."

She reached out suddenly and put one sticky, sparking hand on my knee. "How lovely," she said with the force of a spear thudding into earth. Then, wondering: "How strange."

"YOU MUST COME to the palace," the goddess said, and laughed when I did not respond. "Come! You are reluctant as a maiden. What have you to fear, Alcestis? I shall not lift you above my shoulders and cast you down into the pit. That is my lord's sport, and he plays only with men. Come, come. We shall feast tonight." She stood at once and shook a few pomegranate seeds from her skirts, letting them tumble into the dying grass.

"How long have I been here?" I looked around the garden. "How do you know it is night?"

"It is what time I choose, and I choose night." Persephone bent and picked up the half-eaten pomegranate, her hair pouring around her face like honey. She looked at me as she straightened, and tossed the pomegranate into the air and caught it, tossed it and caught it, then held out her other hand. "Well?"

I reached out hesitantly, and she seized me, pulling me up from the ground without effort.

"You pay me little attention, Alcestis," she said, and tugged on my hand, sending a pulse of feeling along my arm and into my chest. I opened my mouth to apologize, but she shook her head magnanimously and smiled as broadly as a man. "I forget that you are dead. I am sorry. You must still dwell on thoughts of your husband."

I hadn't thought of my husband since before I found the Elysian Fields. "No," I said, looking down at our joined hands. "He fades from my mind. But there is not much to forget."

"I do not think I believe you, that your husband could be so easily dismissed. A king of the Achaeans." She tossed the pomegranate once more. "Yet you were fallow when you died, and it is a woman's right to hold her mind back, though she cannot reserve her body as her own. Even if there is not much to forget, I shall help you do it."

My father had said that while it was unfortunate to ask for a goddess's help, it was worse to receive it unasked, for Olympian women always had dark motives lurking in their hearts. Persephone wore her darkness as Hermes wore his cloak, wrapped ragged around her body, but her eyes were soft now, compassionate. She knew I had not yet conceived. I moved my fingers slightly and her grip tightened.

"Come," she said again. "We will go to the palace. There is little else for one like you to do in this place."

I let her pull me along. She led me out of the garden into the wood, and there were shades around us again, as pallid and thin as the cypress trunks. They looked toward us as we passed, dimly curious.

We left the woods and the palace rose like smoke ahead of us. Persephone still gripped my hand, the pad of her thumb pressed against the center of my palm. I would have thought a goddess would stride quickly, long legs stretching over her domain as she walked, each step new evidence of her conquering power, but Persephone kept a slow pace. Her hips rolled as she walked and the rippling hem of her shift skimmed the brown grass.

We came to the adamantine gate. It hummed discordantly as Persephone passed beneath it, like the sound of an ill-tuned lyre, strings warped by heat or damp. I looked at Persephone as the note sounded. Her chin was held high as she walked, the slant of her cheekbone cliff sharp. She didn't seem to hear it.

The courtyard was empty of shades. Hades stood by the palace doors wearing a bleak expression and a silver torque to match Persephone's bronze. He did not look especially threatening, standing there with his big hands at his sides and dark strands of hair falling over his eyes. He looked like a sad youth. Yet still I shrank back, straining against Persephone's grip. She stopped and turned until her eyes met mine.

"Welcome," she said, looking into my face. She spoke in a deep voice; it wasn't her own. "Good day, my lady. I am glad to see you have returned. Good day, Lady Alcestis."

Movement: Hades inclining his head, agreeing, mouthing the same words she spoke. I looked toward him, but Persephone squeezed my hand hard enough that I felt a flash of something, white cold and close to pain.

"Good day," I whispered.

"Will you not come in?"

I couldn't speak to Hades while looking at his wife, couldn't keep my head raised as I addressed a god. I looked down at the silver straps of the goddess's sandals. She swung our entangled hands forward and nodded toward the palace. "Enter," she said. Hades' lips moved to echo her command.

She released my hand and walked toward her husband with her head bowed. The palace doors opened for her, and he watched her go inside, still moving at a slow and swaying pace. She did not hurry for his pleasure.

He spoke to me without looking away from her. His voice was rough as if from sickness. "Enter," he said, and then went through the doors.

I did. The dark hall swallowed me, and I followed their glowing forms until we reached the megaron, where I had seen them first. Inside there were no thrones now but plates of food on a long wooden table and a stone bench behind it, where Persephone and Hades sat. Persephone gestured: another block of stone sprang free of the wall and screeched across the floor to the table. The gap in the wall sealed itself with a wet sound like a mouth closing.

The king and queen sat, waiting. I stared at the table, the familiar-looking spread of food. Like an Achaean feast, but without the roar of men's talk and the splatter of spilled wine. Elysium had felt more familiar to me than this. I looked to Persephone, unsure what I should do.

"Sit," she said, and when I did, the stone felt soft as wool.

No slave girls circulated with platters: the gods served themselves and offered me nothing. I ascribed this to politeness at first—they wouldn't wish to give me food that I could not eat—but I began to wonder if they even remembered my presence. They didn't look at me nor did they look often at each other, but it seemed they did not need to. They moved in unison, or near it, just a slight discordance to their movements, like the sour note of the adamantine gate. Hades lifted a piece of meat to his lips, and Persephone paused for the length of a breath before mirroring his motion. It was the very slightest kind of deference.

I waited while they performed this ritual. I thought Hades

might chastise her, but he said nothing, and he smiled, a little, when she held a sliver of fig before her mouth for long moments before biting into it. This game was not new to them nor was it brief. I sat in silence, no longer expecting to be offered the hospitality a mortal host was bound to give. They would not give me anything and they wanted to be sure I knew it.

Persephone put down her bronze goblet and looked to her husband. As she turned, her gaze swept across my face, her eyes glowing with interest. It didn't matter if she looked at me, of course; I was a woman and dead, so I was doubly at her mercy. It was her right to look. But she didn't direct her glances with care as a mortal woman would. The women I knew lowered their lashes to veil their eyes and looked at men sideways. Persephone treated the world as if it were there for her to see.

She and Hades stared at one another with eyes sharp as teeth. Then the goddess shifted her gray eyes to me and began to speak. Her voice wasn't honeyed as it had been in the garden, but flat and bespelling, like the murmur of an oracle. Hades, intent, did not interrupt her once. These are not the things one tells when one recounts a speech: her fingers plucking at her skirt, the slip of a lock of hair across her cheek, the weight of the god her husband's eyes on her throat as she swallowed. Any bard would leave them out. But I noticed them.

This is what she said:

"I told you, Alcestis, the story of my abduction from the world above. But I did not tell you all, and the bards do not either. It is not a fault of theirs; they do not know. Only those who were there know what occurred, and now you shall know also.

"It was a warm day. Now I would say it was summer, but there was no summer then—my lord made summer, as he made winter—there were only warm days and cool ones, better growing weather and worse. This was good growing weather. It had been good for a long time, and I had been growing. I would go into the fields with my maidens, away from my mother's eye, and lie beneath my uncle's light. I would stay out until the horses had crossed the horizon and carried the sun away, and when Selene came from the east to sing her cold songs, I would sit in the gray grass and listen, unheeding all else.

"That day I had flowers in my hair. My maidens had just braided it, all the stems woven in and the blossoms above my ears and down my back. I was happy in the sun, with my flowers. I did not see him when he burst from the earth. I heard my maidens shriek, a sound I had never heard a woman make, and I opened my eyes to see my uncle above me, dark as a thunderhead.

"I did not try to run away or plead the aid of a relation. I could not rely upon any god to help me—they were as likely to transform me as save me, and I was not made for a vegetable life or the crawling existence of an insect in the dirt. The flowers I spoke of—when he stole me, they fell all over the field and into the pit, and when we landed, the flowers were spread over the ground below us. They had wilted when they touched the soil. The merest touch and they faded. Then I knew where we were and what he had done.

"He pulled me from the chariot. I allowed myself to be pulled, for it was the only action I could imagine. Alcestis, you will know what I mean. He took me to the palace and the shades thronged around us. They nudged like sheep. I was not right to their eyes. I was unchanged. I could not dampen myself, as you cannot.

"I stayed with him, for I could not escape. I thought I could preserve myself from ruin, and so I did not let him touch me.

I did not let him claim me. I had that power. I was pure when my mother came to bring me home.

"Above the ground, I had eaten what I liked, for it was all of my mother's making. I ate the pomegranate seeds, and though their taste was strange, I did not think I had done wrong. I thought no one had seen me. That is the part of the story you know, Alcestis.

"I have a temple above the ground. Many temples, but there is one I love best. Men come to the temple and pray to me, for they think I will aid them. They think the temple was built for that purpose. They pay no attention to the maidens who serve, for they are maidens consecrated to a goddess, and cannot be captured or slaughtered or beaten until they cry. They are the maidens who were with me that day when he came into the field. They serve me as they did when I lived with my mother; they are always overjoyed to see me when I return from below the earth.

"They wear white shifts and flowers in their hair, like brides, but they are my brides, brides only to me. No man shall have them, and no god either. The touch of a man would repulse them, for they have known my touch and my kiss. The flowers in their hair shall never fade, but if a man were to smell them, to press his nose against those flowers in their hair, to him they would smell like ash in a cold hearth.

"In the summer I live with my maidens. I surround myself with them, and they are very beautiful and very fresh, as I once was. They are as tempting as fruit. Yet since I am wed I do not kiss them or touch them, even when I am above the ground. I let them serve me, and the serving pleases them and gives them purpose, all the purpose they need and more purpose than they would gain as wives of men.

"You, Alcestis," she said, her voice lightening, "you would have made a good maiden." Her eyes were on me; she had been watching me as she spoke, delivering her speech slowly and with relish, as if each word tasted honey-sweet. She expected me to smile and thank her, to sit in stupefaction as I had in the garden. And I did want to thank her—I did want to smile. But I would not.

"I was a good maiden," I said, "till a man took me. But I have told you that story."

She blinked. "Defiant," said the goddess. "The tiniest flame, the smallest pile of kindling smoldering in the dark."

She reached out to her husband and Hades folded her hand in his own. They stared at me across the spread table, over the fruit and the meat, and the bread and the cakes.

"Shall I tell you another story?" I asked.

Her eyes brightened, as I had known they would. She pulled her hand free of her husband's and leaned toward me, her hair brushing the table.

"It is the tale of a young girl," I said, "a granddaughter of the sea god, who came to the underworld before her time. She died in the night unexpectedly, and the house was quiet with mourning for her. They buried her in the grave circle, performed the correct rituals. But there was one who looked for her always, who was made miserable by the girl's death and believed it a mistake of the gods."

Persephone had laid her hand upon the table, beside a red-juiced platter of meat. Her fingers crept forward as I spoke, scaling the grain of the wood. My hands sat in my lap; I could have touched the rise of her knuckles, where bone shone like marble through her divine skin.

"You have a stronger trust in your husband than you would admit," she said.

"That one was not my husband. It was me. I watched over my sister when she died, and spoke to her grave after she was buried."

She sat back and took her white hand away. I bent toward her, clenching my hands in my lap, hot with a sudden hatred. "Why this retreat? You ask me to tell my story, but the story of my sister holds no interest for you?"

"Your sister does not sit before me," the goddess said. "And that is enough and should satisfy you. But I will answer you further. She died of a fever?"

"A cough."

"And she was young, a virgin, unmarried?"

"She was ten years of age."

Persephone waited.

"She was skinny as a larch, and noisy, and not pretty," I said. "She didn't have to fear marriage yet."

She leaned toward me again, her voice entreating. "You see, Alcestis—you must see—how little fascination her story holds. It is like many others. Children die, and are mourned, and come among the other shades. We think on them when they arrive, and yet they fade quickly. I do not even remember her name. But you, Alcestis, you I have no trouble recalling. You stay in my mind."

I bolted up, half stumbling over the block of stone I'd been sitting on. Persephone watched me the way a man might watch a fractious yearling horse: indulgently, but with an edge of concern, a worry that I might require effort to tame. I believe she'd thought her words would make me soften in adoration. "Her name was Hippothoe," I said. "And I don't care if her story is so dull it sends you to sleep. She is my sister and I will find her whether you help me or not."

"This grows tiresome," Persephone said. "My lord has told you that your sister is not fresh in his mind. He does not lie about the dead, Alcestis. You cannot ask more of him. If I can help you, I shall, but I know no more than you. The realm of the dead is full of lost siblings. Did you think your sister would be waiting for you at the river's edge?"

"I thought I would be able to find her." A swell of feeling came over me, of the sort that might have preceded tears. I put my hand to my cheek, expecting it to be wet, but my fingers pushed into dry softness and I shuddered. "I must find her."

"Why this urgency?" Persephone asked. She looked tense; I hadn't seen that expression before, a crinkling around the corners of her eyes that made her look mortal and worried—as if she harbored fears that could oppress her adamantine heart.

"Do you truly not understand?" I asked, disbelieving.

She shook her head slowly. The piece of golden hair fell along her cheek again, brushing at the edge of her mouth.

"Did your goddess mother wait to search for you when you disappeared?"

"She did," Hades said, and Persephone and I turned in surprise. "She asked the help of Zeus first, and that is how I won."

He sat languidly on the stone bench, the line of his mouth set. How strange it was—a god sitting before me, lord of all I was, and I had not looked at him since Persephone had begun her speech. I hadn't hidden my eyes out of fright or respect; I'd just ignored him, as Persephone did, more easily than I had ever ignored Admetus. He exerted no force on me and demanded no attention, and fearsome as Persephone was, his blank patience unnerved me more.

I began to speak, but he waved me quiet.

"It is the truth, and my wife would be wise to admit it."

Persephone too was momentarily silenced.

"Speak, wife," he said. "I do not forbid it."

She gave him a look that seemed to say, as if you could forbid it. When she spoke, she directed her words to me: "My mother knew her place. And you, Alcestis of Pherae, you ought to know yours."

I saw myself perched on her lap like a petted child, my mouth moving and my eyes alight with joy. She'd have me tell my story until she was satisfied, and she would never be satisfied. She'd train me to speak on her command, laugh on her command, breathe on her command. The brush of her hand against my wrist would restrain me and the brilliance of her smile reward me. I would be her maiden.

I took a step back blindly, and the vision disappeared. Persephone was frowning, a slight wrinkle between her neat brows, and her eyes were storm dark. She shifted, cloth whispering, and Hades seized the back of her neck as if she were a kitten, his hand buried in her golden hair. Her mouth came open slightly, but she made no sound, and he said nothing either.

"I thank you," I said in a faint voice, "for your hospitality, my lord, my lady. But I must go."

I fled the megaron. The hallway seemed ever dimmer, as if clouds had gathered outside the translucent walls of the palace, but I ran through it and burst into the entry hall and out through the doors to the courtyard. The familiar tug in my chest tightened to a wrench as Persephone called me back to her. But I would not go.

The adamantine gate shrieked when I passed beneath it. Down the road I ran, up the crest of a hill I hadn't seen before. The landscape had changed. At the edge of the hill I stood and looked out across the asphodel fields, at the crop of shades swaying mindlessly through the flowers. The Acheron flowed black in the distance. I thought of Hermes there, across the river, slipping in and out of the underworld with shades wrapped in his cloak. If I crept to the riverbank, past the sad hound in his cave, would the ferryman take me across? I could show him the pink prints of Persephone's fingers as my fare. Then I would wait for Hermes among the shades and beg him when he landed with some newly dead girl, beg him to take me back. I'd hide in a cave for the rest of my years if I must, never see my husband again, nor his parents, nor my brothers, never see Pherae or Iolcus. I'd be silent all my life.

I raised my eyes to the blurry ceiling of the underworld, but Hermes did not come.

If I could find some face that had not crumbled into senselessness. If I could find my father's mother, once more. If I could find Hippothoe—

I cried out my sister's name.

No one answered. I called again, my voice coming harsh from my throat, loud as a shout in battle. This was my battle, and I did not care if the gods in the palace heard me, if they paused to marvel at the depth of my sadness. I would call, and she would come. It was simple. How had I not thought to try this before?

"Hippothoe," I called, "Hippothoe, it is your sister—come!"

Then I heard another name called in the distance, an Achaean name, a man's name. There was another stretching silence, and just as it grew hollow, a man cried out for a woman. Then came another shout, the sound of the names achingly similar— another, this time a man's name, and then three names in succession, each ending in a swallowed sob as a mother bellowed for her lost children. *Where have you gone?* she moaned. *Where have you all gone?*

Before her pleas ended, another howl had begun. Names rose across the underworld like wisps of flame, burning and smothering in an instant, never answered by a shout of recognition or a screech of joy.

In the field of asphodel, I lay down and listened to the dead voices calling.

THE ASPHODEL BENT over me like the arch of a vault. I lay with my hands flat over my eyes, slivers of gray light sliding between my knuckles. Some of the names sounded familiar, but surely it was only the system of naming among the Achaeans—surely I didn't know as many of the mourned dead as I thought—surely I couldn't know so many.

The calling of names slowed, then ceased, one last wail dying in the still atmosphere: *Larisa*, cried some woman, some sister or mother or lover. I had known a Larisa in Iolcus, a village girl who'd drawn Acastus's eye, with a head of soft black curls and eyebrows like straight painted lines of kohl. For months I had seen her around the palace, waiting in the courtyard or by the gate, never speaking to anyone but my brother. She'd borne him a child. I remembered the head maid talking of it to one of the slave girls; the babe had been sickly, and they'd said she'd never find a husband among the village men. The slave girl had whispered: perhaps she'll try the god of the sea.

I tried to imagine what it would be like when I found

Hippothoe: how delighted she would be, how loud her laugh would sound in this quiet darkness. She would look as I remembered her, all bones and curls and joy, and she would throw her arms about me at once, and I would not slip through her embrace like mist, nor would she slip through mine.

I knew I should rise at once and go to find her. I should walk across the underworld, determined and untiring, until she appeared in my path. In my wanderings I would seem no different from the other shades stumbling aimless through the fields.

I couldn't make myself stand. I was afraid of the shades; I was afraid of finding Hippothoe, even as I wanted nothing more than to find her. If I loved her, I thought, if I truly loved her, I would've found her already. The next thought blossomed in my mind like a poison-petaled flower: if she loved me, she would have found me.

I scrambled up from the dusty ground. But when I stepped out of the asphodel field onto the road, I took only a few strides before stopping, unsure which way to go.

I turned back toward the palace, the fortress, their stronghold. I felt Persephone's thrall, and I hated myself for sitting lumpen and stupid in her power. But still I wanted her near me, wanted her to help me and hold me.

"For what do you wait, my lady?" The voice was pitched like a youth's, but coarse with age. An old man's shade leaned on a staff, one arm hooked around it as if he still needed it to bear some of his weight. He was gaunt as a sail stretched by wind, and his shift hung slack from his sloping shoulders, but his beaky nose and narrow face remained unblurred. He had spoken as if he knew me, but I did not know him.

He stood waiting for my answer, his mouth half open in an

expectant smile; he had died without losing his teeth. He was looking over my right shoulder, not at my face nor even at my hands, as a shy man might have done. I took a step away from him and he tilted his head as if listening. His eyelids fluttered and his mouth opened and closed with a slick little sound, but still he gazed toward me with his hatchling's smile, his hopeful and unfamiliar face.

He was blind.

"Who are you?" I asked him, before remembering that he might not know his own name. "What were you called, when you lived?"

The old man's eyes found my face. "Tiresias," he said, and his eyelashes flittered again when I flinched in surprise. I'd heard his name when I was alive, but I'd known it as a word in a song, something to be painted beneath a figure on a vase: Tiresias the seer, an idea unconnected to the man. He continued, "Also the seer, also the blind man, also the woman. As you are called Alcestis, also the sacrifice, also the wife. And what do they call you, those who live within?" His eyes slid away toward the palace. "You would like to go back, I think."

He was right. I wanted to return to the palace, wanted to hear the goddess call for me, to feel that pull inside my rib cage. I'd been wishing for it even harder than I had been wishing for my sister's presence. I looked down at the ground, ashamed.

"Come, come," he said in his hybrid voice. "This is not my purpose." He was a rare shade, to have a purpose, to remember it.

"Say what is your purpose then," I said. "Or tell me mine. I think I have lost it."

The old seer came closer and reached out with his free hand as if he intended to touch my arm. I drew back. Even in the low light of the underworld, I could see the milky film in his eyes.

His gray hair hung lank. For a moment I thought he resembled Admetus's father, and then I chided myself—they were both old and frail, that was all. They looked no more alike than Phylomache and I had, both being young women. But they did share a look of frustration and weariness.

"You do not understand," Tiresias said. "I cannot speak to you so clearly, though I would tell you truth. I will say what I can and it will not be enough, but it may serve."

I was growing frustrated too. "I do not see what you mean."

"No," he said, grimly amused. Then he said: "This morning at dawn I dropped a sword in the river."

"What?"

"This morning at dawn I dropped a sword in the river." He spoke forcefully, but his words still made no sense to me. He had not been a warrior or a king.

"Grandsire, I don't know what you're saying. I don't look for swords—I am looking for my sister. Can you tell me where to find her?"

This time he shook his head, mouth tightly clenched. There was a long pause. I looked back toward the palace. Would she never call me in?

"The wind shall come and knock the eggs from the nest."

I waited.

"They will split on the ground," he said anxiously. "The eggs will split. Do you see?"

I realized why I had thought he looked like Admetus's father: they shared the exhaustion of struggling to force a distorted mouth to form language or to coax a prophecy from a cursed tongue. This was the oracle's anguish. "I see," I said. "Tell me what you can, Grandsire."

He lifted his head, and though his pale eyes were difficult to read, I thought he looked grateful. "The first arrow may not be so bad, but the second one pierces deeply," he said.

There were no weapons here, save Hades' spear and the ghostly blades of the heroes in Elysium. I nodded, realized he could not see me nod, and said, "Yes. Is that all? Can you tell me more?"

"That is not all," he said, shifting his grip on the staff and thumping it on the ground in frustration. "That is not all."

His anger worried me. What more had he to tell me? What might I possibly need to know here, other than how to find Hippothoe? "Grandsire," I said, "my sister—"

"No," he barked. "Guard the fruit," he said. "You must be wary."

"Of the fruit? In the garden?"

"Yes," he hissed, obviously relieved to be able to answer. "The snake coils within the flesh, waiting to strike."

"That I know," I said, relieved in turn. Was that all he sought to warn me against? "The queen herself has shown me the fruit, and eaten it before me, and tried to tempt me with it, but I'll have none."

Tiresias bowed his head silently, his brows drawing together in worry. My relief faded. I had been proud of myself for resisting the pomegranate, but I'd had no stomach for the fruit. That was no great triumph. And here was the seer, struggling, still trying to tell me of some danger that had followed me into the underworld.

"You unnerve me, Grandsire," I whispered, and the old man laughed, a weary sound, and pressed one hand to his stomach as if the laughter pained him.

"Yes, I do," he said. "For that you must pardon me. I cannot help it. To you I must speak all wisdom and no sense."

"I'm sure your words will aid me," I said uncertainly.

"Then you are more certain than I."

"Grandsire, my sister," I said again.

Tiresias lifted his head, his eyes like pits of mist. "I cannot help you," he said.

He turned away, feeling the ground before him with his staff. I felt I should rush to him and lead him, for even in the underworld the ground had dips and rocks and other dangers, but he continued down the road without erring, as easily as if he could see.

I watched him until he'd vanished into the muddle of shades traveling the road, another gray figure among a gray host. I thought over what he'd said: swords and bird's nests and arrows, fruit in the garden. He'd talked of loss and wariness, as if the dead had anything left to be stolen. Knocked to the ground and split open, he'd said. I'd been split open when Hippothoe died, and when the wound had closed and the scar had formed I had become impenetrable. Nothing could get in.

I couldn't dismiss him, couldn't forget what he had said. He was Tiresias, the seer, who had spoken to men who now graced the benches of the Elysian feast or curled despondent in Tartarean cells. He must know more than I.

And yet, for all his warnings, I thought, he had not told me to beware of the palace.

I walked toward it. The gods were inside, I knew; the palace looked different when they inhabited it, the smoky color of the walls lighter and more reflective. Their presence lit the building from its center, where they burned on their twin thrones.

I wouldn't go to Persephone's garden, but surely I might go into the palace to wait in the great hall. They would not grudge me that; any weary traveler could rest in a hall for a while. I could tell Persephone of Tiresias's strange pronouncements. She would be pleased, I thought, to know that he accorded her such a dangerous role in my story. She'd be thrilled to play the part.

I ducked quickly beneath the silent gate, hoping to avoid waking it—I thought of it now as a great metallic beast—and went to the great doors of the palace. I pulled lightly, but they held fast. Again I pulled. The doors would not admit me.

I looked out through the gate to the asphodel fields, biting down on my lip, though it only stung a little. Fury rose in my throat and sank into a chill drain of humiliation. So they would not let me in—so Tiresias had warned me for nothing. So I was to go and take my place among the shades on the road, the nameless wanderers, the mass of dead, and when I began to forget what Tiresias had said and what Hippothoe's laugh sounded like and why I had given up my life for Admetus, perhaps then Persephone would emerge from her crystalline hold and seek me out. Perhaps she would seize me, as Hades had seized her, and sigh over the sad conclusion of her favorite tale.

I turned toward the forest behind the palace; I couldn't stand the idea of walking that road again. I would look for Hippothoe among the trees. She would not like the crowds of dead in the fields; they would make her uncomfortable, the way they gathered and nudged like lambs.

I walked along the side of the palace, skimming the wall with my fingertips, the stone just a faint chill. I went beyond the length of the central hallway and came to the palace's end. From the outside it seemed dismal and small, more like a tomb than a citadel. I turned the corner and looked into the bleak woods, the dull spaces between the dead trunks, the dull shade forms within them. Beside me the palace wall split and a window grated open.

I meant to walk by without looking in, but I heard something as I passed—a crackle in the air like Zeus contemplating a pitch of lightning. I looked and I stopped and I leaned on the ledge of the window, dizzy, my fingers curled over the stone.

They had not bothered to change the feast table back into thrones, though they'd swept the platters onto the floor. Hades lay upon the table, his head dangling over the edge nearest the window and his black hair streaming down, and he was moaning like a speared beast, a long, slow cry pushed out of his chest. Why had I not heard him from the courtyard? How could the walls have kept in that sound? And Persephone—the queen of the underworld sat astride her husband as if he were a beast, her head thrown back and her golden hair spread silky over her bare breasts. Their bodies were the color of milk. Her brilliant eyes were lidded and sharp teeth flickered in her open mouth. She bent, hiding her face, and Hades howled. I gripped the window ledge harder. A tremble started in my stomach and slipped to my thighs, between them.

They were moving. She was moving. I'd done that, to sate my husband; my hips knew those motions. But we were no gods, and I hadn't moved so fast that my body blurred, hadn't hauled my husband up and pushed him down so hard his head cracked against a table. There was a slick of blood on Persephone's ribs, a seeping mark on Hades' neck. Darkness slid over their skin like roiling clouds.

I saw his hand on her hip, the press of his fingers into her flesh. She was lean as a boy but for the curves of her breasts, sleek flanked and narrow and filled with frantic energy. Hades, beneath her, was beneath my notice. I saw him only as the cause of her pleasure and her fury. And she was furious as a tempest, chanting something, words I could not understand that sounded like curse and prayer at once. I would've given all the wisdom of Tiresias's warnings to know the words that fell from her lips. She had her hands in Hades' hair now, her chin tilted up and her long, fine neck glowing white, no adornment there but sweat, and when Hades surged up to kiss her, I wanted to kill him for hiding her from my sight.

Did her lips still taste of the fruit? If he bit at her tongue, would her blood have the sweet savor of pomegranates? I watched the twisting of her limbs and the twisting of her face, her beautiful clear features going taut and sharp. Never did I think: I should not be watching. Never did I think: what I'm seeing is wrong. It was more beautiful than anything I had ever seen mortals do.

The walls of the palace grew brighter, brighter. Persephone's voice had gone high, spiraling. Hades convulsed beneath her and she screamed and stilled, her eyes flying open, gray shot through with flame. She saw me. Perhaps she had seen me before; perhaps she had been waiting for me, as I had been waiting for her. Her lips closed and opened, wet, shiny.

Alcestis, she mouthed, and the room exploded in light.

The window trembled and slammed shut. I pulled my hand away just in time to save my fingers and stumbled back—but I hit something and spun with a gasp. A silent gray crowd was gathered behind me, watching the flickers and bursts of light within the palace. I was only one of them, part of the audience. When she said my name it was a song, a performance meant to draw me in. I could trust nothing from her mouth.

Her mouth would flare me into fire like Semele, crisp me to ash. Even her fingers had burned me. Had Admetus felt this, the conflagration secret in his heart? I had blamed him when I saw the gentle kisses, smelled the lingering sun. I should have recognized the char of desire gone to coal, glowing still after Apollo left. But I'd never known this feeling before.

The forest crouched dark before me. I stumbled toward it blindly, thinking it better to find some place to hide than to stand there just beyond the walls of the palace while they were—

I couldn't think of it, and yet I couldn't stop thinking of it. My mind stuttered and stuck. Any thought or image was converted to one: Persephone with her head flung back and her mouth open. If I had tried to speak, I would've said her name. *Persephone*, I thought; *Alcestis*.

But I didn't try to speak. I didn't want to speak. I touched my fingers to my own mouth and it felt faintly raw. It *felt*. I snatched my fingers away as if my lips would scorch them. What had she done to me?

I walked into the woods. The low branches did not curve over my head as they had the queen's; they slapped at my face and arms, and I was too distracted to catch them. There were other shades among the trees, lumbering or darting between the trunks, and I shrank away from them. I felt as though a great hole had opened at my center, a tremor-shaken pit, Tartarus blooming in my belly. How had I not known the gods for what they were? Artemis and her vipers had not taught me; Apollo's cursed gift had not opened my closed eyes. I'd thought of them like blessed mortals, capricious and fearsome, demanding but distant. I had never thought of gods in the bedchamber, except to resent Admetus's disloyalty. I had known nothing of their love.

I had to stop as I thought of this, bracing myself against a tree trunk for a moment, my cheeks gone hot.

She'd claimed that Hades had wronged her, made much of the damage she'd suffered because of his love. I didn't doubt her stories—I didn't doubt that she believed them. Had she been mortal I would've thought her a liar. But this was her nature, their nature: always wronged and always wanting, every ploy real to them, every seeming untruth genuine. I'd thought of her as a woman, but she was a god.

I had wandered through the forest onto a grassy little plain. My shift was stuck about with pine needles, as if it were real clothing. I brushed at them and sap stuck to my hands. I rubbed my hands together fiercely and my skidding palms heated as if I were alive. I stared at my skin, disbelieving, and touched a sticky finger to my right forearm. I felt the prod of my fingertip, the catch of the sap lifting the tiny hairs on my skin.

I burst into a run, heading back into the trees. Now I had to push myself to keep running, and I wobbled crazily when I ducked around branches and leapt over stones. I no longer felt weightless. I felt tired and frightened and hot, filled with a sick kind of wonder. When I stopped running, my breath heaved noisily in my chest, and I let out a wheezing moan of distress at the sound of it. I had a living woman's voice now, and Persephone was responsible for it, and for the blood beating in my wrists and neck, the renewed swell of misery in my breast.

I couldn't imagine why she had done it. What possible satisfaction could my revival give her? Why restore me to something like life and yet trap me here, mystified by warnings, unable to find my sister, a witness to things I ought never to have seen?

The bank of the Eridanus lay before me, the river into which Phaeton had fallen, the swallower of ambition. The current swirled deep, and I could not think how to cross it. I felt now that water could drown me, that the Phlegethon could burn me, that the beast Cerberus would tear me with his claws if I dared walk near him.

I leaned against a broad-trunked tree, put my hands over my face, and felt something wet slide between my fingers. I took my hands away and looked at them—tasted the salt in the crease between my fingers—and found that I was crying. True tears, real tears, such as I had not cried since Hippothoe's death. I stood half living amongst the half-dead trees and sobbed into my hands. I could not have said honestly for whom I wept.

13

I DID NOT weep for long. I had always been careful to hide my tears while I lived, and even here, where there was no privacy left, I would keep this to myself.

I went to the edge of the river and bent over to wash my face. My reflection was broken by eddies, my eyes like heated metal and my mouth raw red. I looked like a just-painted temple statue, all my features too sharp and bright. This was how life looked to the dead, garish and distressing.

Along the bank of the Eridanus I went, toward the pale brilliance of Elysium. I'd go to where the shades gathered, to see if Hippothoe was among the crowd of watchers at that transparent wall. I would not wander back toward the palace, and if Persephone came for me I would flee into the forest and evade her as long as I could.

The forest rolled out its gloom around me. I thought I'd seen the glowing wall of Elysium to my left, but when I turned to follow its light, I saw only dim trees. Confused, I stopped, walking in a slow circle to see if I could find that glow again—and noticed that one of the trees to my left looked oddly familiar. Hadn't I passed it before? I went to the tree, touched its bark, but seen up close it didn't look so memorable. I had to keep going; I would not find Hippothoe by standing still. I circled the tree again, trailing my fingers around its trunk, and found myself facing the arched wooden gate that marked the entrance to Persephone's dead garden.

I jolted back against the tree, the cypress branches giving off a thick green scent as I crushed them. I tried to flee, but the gate appeared before me whichever way I faced, until I was whirling and stumbling like a drunk. Finally I stopped, panting again, air burning in my throat. The gate wasn't in front of me. I peered over my shoulder and saw it twitch in the corner of my eye, ready to leap before me if I tried to flee. I closed my eyes, opened them. The gate had not moved.

"All *right*," I said, ducked my head, and stepped through into the garden.

The stone path was empty, the trees still, but I thought she must be there, waiting for me. The whole place was full of her. I could feel the hoofbeat pattern of my heart within my chest, fast and uneven. Tiresias had said—what? Something about snakes in the fruit, being on guard, being wary.

I'd passed beyond wariness into a state of nervous, prickling irritation. I went down the path, tapping at the stones before I stepped onto them as if they might give way. Soon I saw that the garden was empty. I should've been reassured, but anger shot arrowlike through my chest. She thought I would wait for her like a dog, but I had finished with waiting. I stalked toward the gate.

I walked into the space between the wooden pillars of the gate with a thunk, as if I had walked into a wall. Stunned, I fell back, my hand to my ringing forehead. My fingers skidded on sweat and I felt a weird burst of vindication. I had forgotten how necessary it was to have my body reflect my sentiments, to know that I was not imagining the threats I faced.

"Let me out," I told the gate, and pushed at the hard air. The gate was silent, and I wished for the animal reactions of the adamantine gate, its strange purrs and murmurs. "Let me out. I want to leave."

I half feared that the wooden gate would spring out to entrap me, twining branches or roots about my limbs. It didn't, but it would not permit me to leave either. I ran among the trees in the garden, feeling for another portal, but the invisible wall within the gate extended outside of it too. Every gap between trunks or space between bushes repelled me. Back to the gate I went and pounded on it with my fists, relishing each impact, the way my bones pressed my flesh against the wood. "Let me go, let me go," I hissed.

"Why, Alcestis?" said Persephone behind me. I hadn't heard her approach; her tread was soundless on the mossy ground. Or perhaps she hadn't wished me to hear.

I didn't turn. I didn't want her to see my tear-stained face, the mortal shine in my eyes. I didn't want her to know that she had won. I spoke flatly. "I'm looking for my sister, and I am quite sure she is not in here."

"You are right, though I do not know why you are so certain of it."

"You swore to help me if you could, lady. Do you keep her imprisoned somewhere, as you mean to imprison me here?"

"You are not imprisoned, Alcestis. I wanted to speak to you, that is all."

Now I crossed my arms over my breasts and turned to look at her. "I cannot avoid hearing you. Speak."

"You are grown bold, girl," she said mildly. She wore only

a shift, plain as my own, and looked perfect and cool, no cloak covering her, no metal at her wrists or throat, no accoutrements of royalty. Virginal as one of her maidens. I don't know what made me more furious—the memory of her tryst with Hades or the fact that I could see no evidence of it on her now.

"Do not play with me," I said. "It's not fair sporting. Play with the lord Hades. He'll match you, I'm sure."

"Will he?"

"I saw you, and you saw me. You need not pretend, or forget, or whatever it is you do to put on such an innocent face." For her face was innocent and her expression injured, her gray eyes round and damp. I wavered. Could I believe the look she wore? Could I ever believe a god again?

"I do not understand you," she said, nearly in a whisper. There was a strange flavor in her voice, an accent I hadn't heard before—or had only half heard, listening behind doors to the soft sounds of my husband being kissed by his Olympian lover. She came closer to me, her shift dragging on the ground. The tips of her toes stuck out past the garment's hem; her feet were bare, the white lines of her toes like finely cut marble. She was shifting her weight from one foot to the other, nervous as a bride. Nervous!

"I do not understand you," I said. "But I know enough now to be cautious."

"You do not seem cautious to me. You are bold and brave."

"I am a daughter of Pelias. I am of his line."

"You are no part of a line, Alcestis. You are yourself alone and you have always been alone. That is what captures me."

Again she stepped closer and put one hand on my arm. Her lips were red, bitten looking, and when she looked down at her hand on my skin, her eyelashes lay golden as wheat against the plane of her cheek. I took a quick breath and the air cut sharply through my nostrils. "Let me out," I said, pulling away.

"That I shall not until you sit and listen to me."

"I don't want to sit. I want to go."

"Alcestis," she said, something curling beneath her voice. "You will sit. I do not ask much. Sit." And she pointed to the spot beneath the same tree, the curving ground where she had sat and eaten the pomegranate, where I knew the grass was soft and dead.

I sat, pulling my knees to my chest. She stood looking down at me for a long moment, that crease forming between her fine brows, her mouth tight.

"I saw you," she said, sounding worried. "Though I hardly knew you. I hardly know you now."

"I am changed."

"Yes." She looked at the ground. "You seek to know why."

"Of course I do," I said. "What did you think? That you could restore me to life in the underworld and receive a smile in thanks? I won't thank you for this."

"I did not think anything," she said, raising her head. Her gray eyes looked brackish. "This restoration, it is not my doing."

"I do not believe you."

"Alcestis," she said, then sighed. "No. It matters not."

She sat down beside me, less gracefully than I expected. She smelled of lightning and summer storms. I'd imagined sticky sweetness, but this scent was more honest and more terrifying. She bent her legs neatly before her, clasped her hands over her sharp knees. Her movements were oddly decorous; she still seemed nervous, and that made me believe her. I felt myself shift toward her, my legs going liquid and my balance tilting.

"Then you have not done this—to me."

She shook her head. "I did not. I—do not think I did. I told you, there is a thing about you that makes you different, interests me in you. It is not your eyes, though they are bright, nor your cheeks, though they are red. It is—a thing I cannot tell."

"Then—why?"

She was silent a moment. "I do not know," she said, and the words were quiet but wrenched. "You must not ask me."

"What may I ask then? Not how to find my sister, nor where, nor why I am breathing like a woman does."

She bent her head. Did she hide a blush beneath that spill of hair? I wanted to pull it back from her fair cheeks and tie it at her neck so she could not hide from me. She had nothing left to hide but the knowledge I wanted.

"You think there is some great meaning to this alteration?" I asked her, my words rushing out. My hands were sweating on my thighs. "You misunderstand me, goddess. If you did not do this, I don't care why I was restored, or what it means. That will be the choice of the Fates, and I submit to it. But you must tell me where my sister is. You must."

She raised her face, and her eyes shone.

"Do not call me goddess," she said. "I am Persephone. You are Alcestis. And I will tell you one thing about your sister."

I reached for her, and she held up her hand, blinking, the glisten of tears disappearing. The distressed twist of her mouth shifted, the corners of her lips curling up, and a sly light glinted in her eyes.

"In exchange for a story."

My hand dropped. "You cannot just give a thing, can you? You must demand."

"I cannot," she said, almost proudly. "It is not how I am made."

"But you have heard my—"

"No, you do not see." She let her legs fall sideways, knees toward me, and put her hand on the dry grass between us. "I do not ask you to tell me your story. I ask you to listen."

I fell back onto my palms. I could feel now how prickly the grass was. "I don't—"

"There is a story I have not told you, Alcestis," she whispered, leaning in so close that I could feel her breath flutter hot-cold upon my open lips. "Alcestis." Her lips moved the same way they had with Hades beneath her and her eyes on mine. She bent and kissed my knee, and I felt her mouth steaming through the fabric of my shift. I blushed, my face a sheet of flame, my chest burning. I was all heat. She put her hand on my shoulder and the touch of her warm palm seared me.

"What story? What do you mean?"

"The story of my marriage," she said, her thumb skimming my collarbone. "Of my wedding. The story no one knows, for the bards do not sing it and the painters do not smear it on their walls. It is not fit for such audiences. But it is fit for you, Alcestis."

She sprang toward me like a lion might, uncoiling in a burst. She knocked the air from me—I was still unused to breathing—and left me gasping. She pushed me onto my back and knelt over me as she had knelt over Hades, her skirt sliding up her bare white legs. Her thighs were hot around mine. I had my hands in the grass, my fingers pressing down toward its brown roots, and she picked up my right hand slowly, and curved it onto the flesh above her knee, just as Admetus had done a year ago. A life ago. I gasped. She bent down in a flash, faster than a mortal could, and pressed her soft mouth to mine.

Her kiss was like the first bite of fruit gone bitter—long wanted and terrible when possessed. I struggled under her hands, and she released me, our mouths slipping wetly as we parted. She murmured my name again, her lips soft on my cheek, the line of my jaw.

"This is how I was kissed when he wed me," she whispered. "Do you know what it is like, to be kissed this way when you are a virgin girl? It is worse than Elysium."

I thought Admetus had kissed me like this once, but I couldn't remember. Her fingers were warm and clever at the hem of my shift, twitching it upward.

"I do not think you know—what it is like for mortals—"

"I know," she said, her lips against my neck, kissing me until I went soft beneath her. "You keep your lightning within."

My stomach went cold. I tried to sit up, but she had pinned my hips to the ground, and when I tried to shove at her shoulders, she grabbed my hands hard.

"I am telling this story," she said, and pushed my wrists into the grass. When she lifted her hands away I couldn't move my arms; no roots seized me, but I was trapped. She did not need to command plants to capture me. She'd caught me by herself.

"What are you doing?" My voice came high pitched, a virgin girl's squeak of a plea. I struggled again but couldn't get free.

"Listen," she said, and pulled my shift up my body. Her gaze fell on my bare thighs, and I went feverish all over again, helpless and horrified, slick with want. "That is all I ask. It is a long story, but a sweet one in the end, and a bitter one too. You will like it."

"I don't care! I don't want to know your story," I cried. "Let me go, Persephone."

She sat back a little, startled, though her hands still clamped my wrists. "You do not want to know of my wedding? Truly?"

"Truly," I said, shaking beneath her. I should've stopped speaking then, but I could not. "I hate thinking of him wedding you. I hate to think of him having you. And to see it—" She'd broken into a canted smile, her eyelids low. The sight of it infuriated me and I writhed in her grasp, miserable and hot and alive in the dead garden.

"Oh, but again you do not see," she whispered, leaning in, pushing the whole hot length of her body against me. So like a woman she was, and so like me—both of us narrow and slim, our breasts soft and small, pressed together now. Her throat had gone scarlet, her cheeks flushed, her eyes storm green in contrast. I felt her heart striking against my chest like oncoming thunder. "He does not have me. He shall never have me, and that is why I may have him when I need him."

I gave in with an angry sigh. "And do you need me too?"

"How can you ask?" she whispered, and bent down again to kiss me. Her knees slid between mine, and her hands ran along my sides, sweeping, smoothing my shift across my ribs and over my belly. "You are for me. It is destined."

"That tells me nothing," I spat, broken words in a breaking voice. "You've told me nothing. How do—oh—how do I know I can trust you to tell me of Hippothoe after this?"

"Shall I swear? Choose a river." She buried her hands in my hair and pulled me into another kiss. With each taste her mouth grew sweeter, or I grew more accustomed to its taste. I couldn't help arching against her, pressing up into her hands. When the kiss broke, I had to breathe for a long moment before I could speak, my nose in the hot hollow under her jaw.

"Swear on the Phlegethon," I panted, trying to chill my voice. "I do not like the Styx."

"By the flame of the Phlegethon, I swear," she whispered into my skin. "I will tell you what I have promised."

"You will tell me of my sister Hippothoe—" I wanted to keep repeating her name—I was suddenly terrified that I would forget it forever, that Persephone would make me forget.

"I will tell you of your sister Hippothoe. So distrustful," she said sadly, and bit my ear. I cried out. The sound seemed to echo for a moment before the garden swallowed it and I wondered if Hades had heard it. He must know where Persephone had gone, I thought, if he had managed to rouse himself yet.

She was talking of him, but I was only half listening. My shift jerked higher on my legs and she spread her knees to push my legs apart. Every motion was just a little too fast, too sudden. "This is where he touched me, and how," and she touched the slickness between my legs in slow, knowing strokes. My hips followed her hand. I couldn't control my body, couldn't control myself. She would touch me like this and talk of her husband, and I could not make her stop.

"Do not say it," I hissed. "Oh, do not say it." My legs pulled her closer, my ankles hooked around hers. The back of my head rubbed hard on the ground, and I could imagine the disorder of my hair, brown blades of grass entwined in it rather than flowers. Just as ruined as she was, just as reduced. Was this to be my story now—a tryst with a goddess in a poisonous garden?

"But I promised."

"Why are you doing this?"

"Because I want to," she said, calm, and pulled my shift up over my hips and dropped kisses on my quivering stomach. I couldn't feel each kiss as a spark anymore—I was a pile of kindling already lit, and each brush of her mouth was like a breath on embers. In between kisses she spoke, and I, trapped, listened to her and cried out for her and seized beneath the power of her touch. I will not tell you what she did, for that is mine, not to be sung or painted. But this is what she said:

"He brought me to the castle after my mother left, and there was a bed in the throne chamber. He had created the bed for me in advance, as I have made this bed of grass for you, Alcestis, because he had thought of me and wanted me before he snatched me from the world. As I have been thinking of you in my arms. Alcestis. You do not believe me, I know—but I have. Oh, do not look at me so angrily. Do not, do not, please. Come here.

"He kissed me at the gate, and the gate sang, and I thought I was happy. I knew nothing. You would not have recognized me, Alcestis; I was so quiet and shy, and I obeyed him whenever he spoke. He did not order me about. He was too frightened. My dark uncle, afraid. But he showed me what he wanted. He took my hand, and he put it—here—yes. Alcestis, yes. And his mouth was on my throat and his teeth in my skin, and at once I thought I knew everything, and I felt like a wife, and I liked it. Oh, as you must have liked it some time, when it was new. The newness is enough. You like this, do you not? I see you do. I saw that you would when first I met you. The way you looked on me then— though you know I could appear as a man to you if you wished. I could appear as anything you like, and you would forget it was not my true shape. But I want to show you myself, Alcestis.

"In the mortal world I am sure they think he forced me, but he did not have to hurt me. I liked everything he did, and soon I found that I could make him do it whenever I wanted, and I could make him do other things as well. I could make him do my bidding. And now I am making you, but I do not want to make you, Alcestis. I want you to come to me of your own will, as a goddess might. I want you to come to me, Alcestis, come—"

Through the trees I saw that the barrier protecting the garden was crowded thick with shades. They were not watching us—the garden was hidden from their sight—but they'd thronged to its edges just as they gathered at the walls of Elysium or the palace. They had gathered to feed. I thought of the fiery light spreading through the palace walls, and I cried out—I felt as though I might crumble into ash under her fingers and lips.

But her damp fingers on my chin turned my face back to her, her slick lips pressed and opened mine. Her tongue was heavy with my taste. "Do not look," she said. "They cannot see. Only you can see, Alcestis, Alcestis."

The lightning she'd spoken of built in my belly. I fought it as I had fought despair when I was alive, for I was so furious that she was right—and yet I was grateful, so grateful, if only she would—

It was nothing like death. It was too-bright sunlight and whirlwinds and other things the gods control. I lay gasping on the grass, my hands in her golden hair, and thought that I hated her, and that I loved her, and that she had better keep her promise to tell me of my sister. But I said nothing. It was as if words had died within me.

She did not speak either. She slipped her head from beneath my hands and lay beside me, stretched out lionlike, propping herself on one slim arm, waiting to see what I would do. What did women usually do when taken by a god? Usually, I thought, they did not enjoy it so much. But our knees were almost touching, knocking together awkwardly when she moved, and she was watching me with a grave look in her eyes, and her cheeks were still pink and her chin shiny with my wetness. I wanted to kiss her. Instead I smoothed my shift down over my belly, trying not to notice how my thighs trembled. I looked down at my bare knees; looking at her for too long was unwise. She was lit with a scattery radiance, as if her very form were fragile, barely holding together.

"This is what I know of your sister," Persephone said. "She walks beside memories, on occasion."

I waited, as I had waited for the old seer to clarify his words, but she didn't unseal her lips again. "That is all you will tell me?"

"That is all I can tell you."

My body was still humming with the lightning of her touch. I'd thought I would feel betrayal as a stab to the gut, but it was only a dull surprise. "You are as bad as Tiresias. You are worse," I said, and pulled my legs away from hers.

She sat up and the lines of her body wavered. "You have spoken to Tiresias? But that is not right."

"It didn't help me, if that's what you fear. He said only confusing things. But he hadn't just—he wanted to tell me, and you do not."

"No, I do not," she said, and her voice became soft and maternal. Was it her mother's voice she mimicked? She was as maternal as a foaming river of rapids. "Alcestis, it is not something you can comprehend—"

"I'll make you tell me," I said, and pulled her to me, twining my arms around her and kissing her white neck, where she smelled of granite and of me and tasted like crushed flowers. A maiden Apollo loved had become a rooted tree to escape him; I could become a conqueror. I touched the winglike bones of her shoulder blades, the bumps of her spine. She twitched; the dark cloud I had seen when she was with Hades swept over her flesh once, like a traveling shiver. I pulled back to look in her eyes and her sun-colored eyelashes fluttered. Tears? I wanted her to cry. "Persephone," I said, and the little thrill of naming her familiarly ran through me, angry as I was.

"Alcestis," she said in a quiet, small voice.

"I swear by the Phlegethon, I will make you tell me."

She let out a soft cry, struggling in my arms. "Oh, you must not swear," she said, low. "You must not. You do not know what it shall mean."

"I told you," I said, "I don't care. Nothing means anything here. It doesn't matter."

She jerked out of my grasp and sprawled on the grass, and now she was panting, her chest heaving. I had wanted to see her upset, but now it made me feel sick. I reached for her, but she slipped away.

"I did not mean—"

"Yes, you did," she said. She rose and stood over me. She did not seem to tower; she was not terrifying, but she was a god and I her mortal. I put my hand on her ankle and she allowed it. "But it is no matter. I forgive you."

"Do you?" I said, the words spilling out. "It is kind of you. Then I shall forgive you for making me mortal once again."

"How cruel you are," she said wonderingly. "Are you angry? For I have kept my promise. And I will leave you now to search for that which you desire. It is not my search, after all."

I pushed myself up, thinking I would follow her, but she lifted one foot and pressed it to my shoulder, pushing me back against the dirt.

"Stay," she said, "if you like. If it means anything to you."

She left me on the grass as she swayed away in her shift, once again looking untouched and pure. I'd left no traces on her skin. She'd go out into the forest, among the shades, and none of them would know what she'd done, or what she'd done to me. She would go back to the palace, where Hades waited to greet her, and settle into her adamantine throne, spreading her unwrinkled shift over her unbruised knees.

I closed my eyes then, sure in my condemnation of her. But now I imagine that she raised her hand to her temple as she walked away, that she stopped to lean against the gate as if dizzy, collecting herself.

I lay on my back in the grass, my shift still rucked up around my legs and my thighs wet, and stared up at the gray ceiling of the underworld. Half of my mind was chattering about the sensation of Persephone's tongue against the crease of my hip, and the other half was numbed, silent, heavy with shock and distress. I felt as though she had opened me up and yanked the lightning from my belly. All that—all that, and I still did not know how to find Hippothoe.

She walks beside memories, I thought. Always riddles and half thoughts. Did the gods think the same way they spoke? When she remembered kissing me in the garden, would she think of that too in circular words and broken images? How would she tell this story, when she told it? *A mortal woman pressed into the ground like a new seed. Furrows in the soil. I gave her a bit of knowledge, left behind like sand melted into glass after Zeus throws his lightning, earth made sacred, and she scrabbled for it when I left her, eager, desperate, shameless, her fingers in the dirt.*

I would remember it wholly, I thought, no matter what befell me here.

And then I saw what she had meant: Lethe. Hippothoe walked by the bank of Lethe.

THE GATE ALLOWED me to pass. I had no energy for fighting, and I walked up to it slowly, still unsteady on my feet, but my outstretched hand passed right through its boundary and I stumbled out, shaky, into the woods. The mass of shades who had come to warm themselves with our sex milled about, a field of drooping flowers with no sun toward which to turn their hopeful faces. Persephone was not among them. Had they seen her as she passed? If so, she'd left as little mark on their faces as I had left on hers.

Behind me, both gate and garden had vanished. I swiveled to look for the best way out of the muddle, and in the crowd, I saw my father's mother, Tyro. I'd thought her so vibrant when I first saw her, so touched with life, but now she didn't look much different from the others to my mortal eyes. The dry mud cracking of her face had faded, and where she had been stippled with light she now seemed murky and worn, no marks of favor left in her countenance.

"Girl," she said. "Do you know where the queen has gone?"

Stricken, I stared at her. "The queen of the underworld?"

"What queen of the underworld?" She laughed, her voice a

crackling mess. "The underworld is no place for a woman. No, I seek the queen of Iolcus. The one—the one who died." She was looking about the crowd as if she might see the face she wanted, leaning forward to peer over my shoulder. I reached for her arm to steady her, and my hand passed through the amorphous stalk of her forearm. She looked down at my fingers in her arm as one might glance at a fly that had landed on one's skin. I took my hand away.

"Do you know the lady I seek?" she asked me.

I said gently, "Lady Tyro—you are the queen of Iolcus. You were. You left when I was young."

The other shades swirled about us.

"And what are you now?" She squinted at me, then turned slowly, as if rotating on a spit, to look over her shoulder.

It was a fair question. I found it hard to answer. "I am your son's child, Pelias's girl. Alcestis." Here I choked a bit. "Admetus's wife."

"Alcestis," she said, considering, then shook her head. "No, not that one. He had girls, though—one died. Name like a horse. Face like a horse too."

"Hippothoe," I said. "Yes. I'm looking for her, Tyro. I am—I am told she walks by the river Lethe sometimes."

"Better for her if she swam in it," Tyro said. "Takes away the pain, you know, the water does."

"I've heard that." I felt light-headed, thinking of Hippothoe rising from the water, her hair wet and her eyes quiet.

"It is true. One of the few things you will hear that is. Have you gone yet?"

I shook my head and said, lying, "I have nothing I need to forget."

"You are the lucky one then."

I pushed my hand through my disheveled hair, fingers catching on tangles and bits of the garden entwined in it. "Lady Tyro, there's something I must ask you."

"Ask, child," she said. "I must seek this woman, the queen. You should not detain me so long. It is important, you know. She has things to tell me."

"When you met my grandsire—"

"Who, girl?"

"The lord Poseidon," I said as patiently as I could. "When you met him, did he know you? Did he already know who you were? Had he sought you out?"

"Oh, yes, he knew," she said. "He knew, all right. Laid his plans well. Or maybe he had no plan, maybe just took me, but no one likes to think that. Not such an honor as the men say, inciting lust in Olympian loins."

"No," I said slowly.

"They will trick you. He was a clever one. Tricked me that night—I had not gone out to meet him, not him. But, you see—I fell asleep." She said this conspiratorially, as if it explained everything she had previously said, and she didn't want this private truth spread. "On the bank, fell asleep. I was waiting for my lover, but he came instead, and what could I do? Resist him?"

My body went still, almost as still as death had left it, except for the pounding of blood in my head. Her lover? She had not loved the god? "You were not—you were not waiting for Poseidon?"

"Had never seen him before, not once in my life. Never saw him again. Never wanted to."

"But you bore his children."

"Many thanks they gave me for it too," she said. "Bad as

their father. Bad as both their fathers. It is not good, having so many men. We will need the war to kill them off."

"War?" I asked her absently. There were skirmishes at the barriers between kingdoms, messy encounters at sea, but Iolcus had known no war while I lived. Pelias had always ascribed this to Poseidon's protection, had talked of the love the god held for our land, the love for his children and their worthy mother. We had built our lives on the tale of their love.

She was silent. Then her eyes suddenly focused on me and she said: "What?"

"Never mind, lady," I said, my voice as rough as hers.

She nodded sharply and then turned her head. "It is an old story. An old story. Always repeating." The energy had gone out of her voice, and she raised one spectral hand to her face, patting at her chin as if to be sure she hadn't crumbled away. When she turned back to me, she blinked in surprise, seized by a new confusion.

"But you, girl, you smell like the sea." She looked at me suspiciously. "Do you come from him? From that god?"

I smelled like a storm over water, like shellfish cracked against rock. "I suppose I do," I said.

She turned away from me, then turned back, unsure. "And you do not—you are sure you have not seen the Iolcan queen? None of you?" Her voice rose as she spoke, and the other shades watched us curiously and said nothing.

"No," I said. "Goodbye, mother of my father."

She tottered away without bidding me farewell, the curve of her spine like a bent bow, never to be released.

The other shades too began to drift away. I was not enough to hold their attention.

There was a pattern to these events, an accepted path. A

god saw a beautiful woman, desired her, raped her, and left her alone except for the half-Olympian children in her belly. The lucky ones perhaps were wed and didn't die in the bearing of children or the breaking of oaths or the collapse of ruling houses, and the luckiest were forgotten by the gods and never visited again. And yet a god had desired my husband and disregarded me, and there would be no children from that union, no curse haunting my line. In the eyes of men I was a virtuous wife. Had I not died a chaste woman?

But now I'd stepped into the embrace of a goddess, sunk into her dizzying kisses. That wouldn't fit the story; it could not be neatly slotted into a line of poetry. Out of rhythm, out of tune, as I'd always been. Now I was the lover of the queen of the dead, alive in the underworld, and I could taste her dusty sweetness when I ran my tongue over my lips.

I turned from the vanished garden gate and stalked away through the forest, away from the place where the goddess had pinned me to the ground. Shades scattered around me, then fell in behind me as I pushed through the trees. Finally I emerged from the forest onto the bank of the river Lethe.

I'd known of this river forever, or at least since childhood, when I'd haunted the kitchens and listened to the servants and the slaves complain of their lot. They'd talked of Lethe with longing; they said they wanted to forget their lives, the families they'd lost or hadn't lost, the mistreatment at my father's hands or at the hands of his men. They spoke of this river the way Acastus's young friends spoke of Elysium, like a god who would swoop down to save them, a name to invoke whenever they felt that they couldn't go on.

I had expected a crowd, a flock, some herding mass struggling for the riverbank, but instead I found slow-moving lines of shades waiting to sip the waters in turn. They didn't shove or push—they didn't even fidget as a group of the living would have, didn't lift hands to touch their hair or adjust their shifts. They merely stood, sometimes looking incuriously at one another, sometimes staring at some point in the distance, thinking of the living perhaps, of lost families and beatings and oatcakes and songs. Which of you were servants, which warriors? I wanted to ask them. Which among you have dreamed of this since your birth?

Down the line I walked, ducking amongst them when I had to, peering into their faces. I looked into the soft eyes of old men, and strong boys gone transparent and sad, and women. Many women. I walked along the entire line. None of the waiting shades were Hippothoe.

I began to ask them if they had seen her. A little girl, I said, about this tall, big mess of hair, skinny, noisy laugh.

"Laugh?" said the shade of a young man faintly.

I came to the river's edge. The shades fanned out when they reached it, each one finding his or her own place at the bank. I knelt beside them and waited as they drank, watched the water run from their cupped hands. Some of them braced their palms on the bank and bent to lap at the river like dogs, blurry, hunched shapes. Servants and warriors, all single-minded and dumb and thirsty. As I watched them drink, the shades still waiting in line watched me, wondering, perhaps, why I did not take the water myself.

I didn't want the water. I was terrified of forgetting and terrified of being forgotten. What if Hippothoe had already knelt at this bank, already lifted this water in her spidery hands and drunk it?

I followed a long swoop of the river down into the asphodel

fields, looking at every shade, and Hippothoe was not there. My face felt hot again and I was fisting the cloth of my skirt in twitching fingers. I was worried, but also I was angry, and it was a god's anger, boiling and immediate. I'd walked far enough that I could see the roof of the palace beyond the fields. "Let me think," I snapped, as if the queen could hear me, as if she were listening for my voice. I couldn't think. I was scattered as chaff. Each thought was swallowed at once by another; I couldn't even hold my sister's face in my mind. Yet if I loved my sister, wouldn't I wait by the riverbank until she wandered past? For Hippothoe would come, if I trusted what Persephone had told me; if I believed that she had traded knowledge for my assent; if I believed that my assent mattered; if I believed that she wanted me enough to barter with me like an equal.

I did not want to wait. I wanted to go to the palace. I wanted Persephone.

I looked at the dead lined up to receive oblivion, the water sluicing down the pale arms of those who drank. When they rose, they looked like children just awakened from anxious dreams, their faces nearly slack, still clinging to the slightest remnants of fear and worry. I'd stepped back from the river only a few paces, only the length of a body. By the time they'd walked as far from the bank, those traces had vanished, leaving their faces stripped of shadows, their foreheads the flat gray of winter skies.

My stomach stirred, unsettled, and I averted my eyes from the shade nearest me—only to find another an arm's length away, watching me. Calm. No smile, no grimace, no fear. Her wet shift hung damp over dark breasts and a gray mass that had once been a gravid belly.

I backed away, and her gaze slid off me; I was no longer interesting because I was no longer in her path. She still walked like a woman with child, her feet turned out and her hand at her hip for support, carrying her forgotten loss before her. I wanted to ask if she'd given the child a name, but I knew without uttering a word that she would not remember the name, or the child, or the father. She knew the path through the asphodel and she knew the river. That was all.

I was beginning to see. But then I knew only that I couldn't bear to watch the shades any longer. I turned and bolted into the fields, left the path, and ran through the spiny asphodel, my hair whipping against my back and my shift flapping open over my breastbone. I slipped on the sloping hill to the royal road, catching myself hard on my palms. The gravelly dirt stuck to my hands, and sweat slicked the back of my neck and under my breasts—the places she had touched.

My chest began to ache and I wanted to cry with joy at the feeling of air whistling in my lungs. I remembered chasing Hippothoe up the stairs to the women's quarters, giddy, our skirts bunched around our knees and our fingers scraping the stone walls. The adamantine gate gave a dissonant grumble as I ran beneath it.

I burst into the palace, all sense of decorum forgotten, and the spatter of my footsteps echoed in the dim, silent entrance hall. Panting, I ducked into the long hallway that led to the megaron—but then I stopped. Beneath the golden curtain I could see a circle of light swimming on the floor at the far end of the hall, like the aureole of a lamp. I took a hesitant step toward it, and the light shivered and pulsed, rolling sideways and back through the filtered gloom.

Then came a noise like a dragon sighing, a long purr of

violent contentment. I was frozen, my chest all thunder, one hand on the wall. The noise—I heard it again, this time followed by a quiet and slippery sound, like a strigil on oil-covered flesh. Whispery. Or was it actually a whisper?

I crept down the hall, grazing the cool crystal with my fingertips, until I reached the hanging curtain. I put out my hand, mesmerized by the light glinting on the jewels, and pushed the curtain aside. Then I saw Persephone—and Hades. The gods stood in the middle of the room, arms slung around each other's waists, Persephone's head on her husband's shoulder and her crown tilting slightly toward the floor. She was still wearing the same thin shift. Just above them hung a small globe of coppery light, a lamp with no oil and no base, its rays slanting like the long reach of the sun on a summer afternoon. They had captured that light just as they had the brilliance of the stars, tamed it and confined it here, where it would please them most. The radiant, lazy circle I had seen was the glow of the miniature sun, reflected by Persephone's slipping crown. She lifted her hand and touched the back of Hades' head, her fingertips disappearing into his dark curls. Her eyes were closed. That was merciful.

I'd hated it when she whispered his name into the crease below my earlobe. This was worse. This made me ill. The way she talked of him, even when she spoke into my hair, was not loving—not tender, not equal. She'd spoken of him as an adversary, perhaps worthy but never trusted, and certainly never to be touched with affection. Never to serve as a sanctuary. But again she'd deceived me. Perhaps the garden was her retreat, but this was her home.

I stared at the back of Hades' head. I'd thought that he was like the surface of a river, throwing her reflection back, shining dully as armor does in the sun. She was so much brighter than he. But I could see her face, and he was reflected in it, like the sun circle on the floor. Her fingers were still in his hair, and she was humming—the dragon murmur of happiness.

I'd thought I understood her. Such a stupid mortal way to think—I had been more blind than the seer. She was not a human. She was not to be understood. Layers of her came off like sunburnt skin. If I touched her, I would be left with a sheath, an impression, a lie.

I stumbled and caught myself against the wall. My skin was white against the smoke-colored stone. Then my breath stopped: for behind my fingers sat the hand of a shade, pressed to the translucent side of the palace. Wondering, I lifted my fingers slowly from the wall and stared at the smudge dark fingertips, the lighter gray of the tapering fingers, the dense darkness of the palm, the evidence of some tiny bit of fumbling mortal life.

Hippothoe, I thought. I shot one last desperate glance toward the throne room. Behind the sparkling curtain they still stood entwined, eyes closed, uncaring. Bronze-green ripples crossed the surface of the ball of light, slow as shallow waves.

I ran, my feet slapping on the stone floor. I felt the moment when Persephone heard me—it was as if the building took a breath—and I felt it when she realized that I had seen her.

"Alcestis, no," she cried. Her feet were silent on the stone, but I knew she was following me. I thudded against the broad door, my forearms bruising on wood. It wouldn't move. I pounded on it with fists still sore from hitting the garden gate.

She came into the entry hall with a rush of wind, blowing my hair up around my face. She didn't speak; she waited in the doorway, expecting me to confront her. Wanting me to address her as a supplicant might. I was suddenly exhausted by the gods and their stubborn doors and their hidden motives and their incomprehensible loves. Slumping, I turned to face her.

She looked breathless; that was clever, and maddening.

"Stay out of my mind," I told her.

Now she looked displeased. "Where are you going?"

"Outside," I said. "It's my sister. She's come to find me. Will you not let me *go*?"

"It is not your sister," she said.

"How do you know? Oh, don't look at me like that. I don't care if you are a god. You don't know my sister. Let me out!"

She looked at me impassively for a moment, then flicked her fingers at the door, which swung open. I hurried through it.

"Go," she said to my back, "you will see—"

But I didn't hear the rest. I raced around the side of the palace, my breath stinging in my chest, to find the shade whose hand had almost touched mine. It still stood there at the wall, its hand pressed against the crystal. It was small, nearly the right size—and hooded; that was strange—and I threw myself toward it, as much a tackle as a greeting.

My hands went through the cloak, through the shade's thin shoulders. "Hippothoe," I cried, and the hooded face lifted. The eyes were soft, unfocused, and the smile simple. Persephone was right, of course: those were not my sister's eyes. That was not my sister's smile. This shade had been a boy once, some anonymous shepherd or stablehand, clothed for a journey it had never completed. It had been mesmerized by my shadow, like a baby or a sheep or a horse might be. Now it lifted its small hand to touch my face. Stunned, I stood and let the hand breach my cheek, cold as a splash of water from the river where memories sink.

The shade's smile dripped away.

"I'm sorry," I said. "I'm sorry." I turned and walked back to the front of the palace, stumbling a little on nothing, my heart gone quiet.

Persephone stood in the open doorway. I think she expected me to slink back in, chastened and apologetic, to curl up at her feet like a hound and raise my face to be petted. I walked away from her.

She caught me at the gate, flashing into substance in front of me with a soft pop of air. I knocked into her and reached up instinctively to steady myself—that made her smile and raise her hands to my arms. But I shook her hands away and shouldered past her, bumping my knee against the gate, which chirped curiously at the contact.

"Alcestis, this is madness," she said. "Come back. You will find her when you must. There is no sense in making yourself upset."

I would not be provoked.

"You will come back," she said then, with certainty. But it was a mortal-sounding certainty, not the prophesying voice of a god; it was the certainty a wife had in her husband's fidelity, the certainty a father had in his daughter's love. I twisted to look at her over my shoulder. She stood with her arms crossed over her chest.

"And what do I have to come back for?" I asked.

She was silent, but she fixed her eyes on me, blue hot, and I knew what she would say. I swallowed a surge of fury.

"Go back to your husband," I told her, and just then her husband appeared behind her, watching from the doorway to the palace. He didn't look angry. Mild, vaguely curious, bemused. Did they have no expressions between fury and boredom? They'd watched mortals live and die for years. Could they not have studied our reactions a bit more closely, made some attempt to speak with their faces as we did? Could he not show a little hate for me, a little envy, some twitch of the lips to reassure me that I had not imagined her love for me?

"Leave me be, both of you," I said. "I don't want to be your plaything. I want my sister."

I meant to sound strong, but the last words came out plaintive and young, barely above a whimper. My hair was hanging in my eyes, and when I pushed at the strands, my fingers snagged in grass-furred knots. Persephone watched; I wanted to see her fingers twitch or her teeth sink into her lip with wanting, but her face was marble smooth. Then she lifted a hand and swept it through the air between us, and I was neatened, my shift dry and straight, my hair hanging smooth, no longer tangled by her touch.

"Do you deny it then?" I said to her. "You can't unmake the past so easily."

"I do not seek to."

"I do not believe you. You lied to me about my sister. I searched, and she was not there. I think I will not ever find her," I said. "I think I am in Tartarus, and this is my eternal duty, to look for her."

"No, that is not the case," she said. "You place yourself too high, Alcestis. The underworld changes for no man and no woman either. What I told you was truth."

"You placed me high. I didn't ask to be chosen as your pet. And still you keep lying," I said. "I've seen it change. I've been to the river Lethe, and I saw what happens to them when they drink. What would you call that?"

"Mercy," Hades said from the doorway.

"You would," I said to him. He shrugged. I turned away

again, tired of arguing, but Persephone grabbed me and would
not let me slip free of her grip.

"What will you do now? Wait and hide forever?" she said.
Her cheeks were streaked with red, and her voice trembled, as
if she were on the verge of tears. "There is nothing to do here,
Alcestis. Nothing ever happens."

"I don't care—"

Her fingers dug into my arms, crackling around my bones.

"But you happened," she said. "You came. You are here, and
you shall be mine, as was destined."

"I'll be no one's," I said. "And you'll go to see your mother
in a few months and forget me entirely, and all the pleading in
the world will not change that."

Her fingers unclamped. "No. But that is why you must not
go now. You must stay here with me."

"To entertain you?"

"To *love* me," she moaned.

"You have maidens for that," I said. "Now let me go."

She fell back against the adamantine gate, bracing herself
there as if I had shoved her. Now she bit her lip; now she stared
at me with wounded desire. I did want to go to her, to pull
her against me and press my hands into the small of her back.
I wanted to sit beside her in the palace, ensconced in a smaller
throne, her consort forever. I wanted her to stop my breath. But
I left.

15

I EXPECTED HER to follow—and then I expected her to curse me—and then I expected her to kill me—but she did not. I walked down the road slowly as a sick old woman and tried to believe that I was free. I'd never heard a story of a woman abandoning a god. Fleeing, yes—and the transformations that followed—but I would not run from her now. I walked out of the palace courtyard, and my fingers didn't lengthen into branches, nor did my limbs sprout feathers or my heels harden into hooves.

I left the road and crossed into the asphodel field, slipping in among the shades there, then looked back at the palace. Persephone and Hades had vanished and the gate stood empty. I was safe, for the moment, whatever that meant. And I was tired. There were no stones on which to perch, so I crossed my legs beneath me and sat on the dirt.

My stomach clenched and rumbled, and I pressed my hands to it, startled: I was hungry. I hadn't eaten for—for as long as I'd been dead, but now my body remembered its emptiness and want.

Once I began thinking about eating I could hardly stop. I

could tear into a pomegranate, pluck the webbing apart and pop the seeds free, and even one seed split between my teeth would render me doubly hers. How happy Persephone would be when she found me sprawled under that tree in the garden, my mouth stained and my fingers sticky. I could almost feel the squirt of juice on my tongue—the juice, and then the kiss. I lost myself in thinking of it, my fingers falling away from my belly, skimming across my thighs.

But my hands stilled. I thought of the platters spread on the gods' table and how she'd swept them to the ground (for I knew she had done it) to spread Hades on that table too, for her consumption. She was the serpent Tiresias had prophesied, the snake coiled within the fruit, and still I would eat. It was useless to pretend otherwise. It wouldn't matter, in the end, if I waited until the arches of my ribs pressed against the thin cloth of my shift before I took the fruit. The stories told of me in the world above would be the same.

The shades had thinned around me. I looked up to the road and saw a banner of dust moving down it—Hades on a black chariot pulled by four dark horses, ghost horses, beasts of wind. Was the wrath I thought I had escaped coming to meet me?

The chariot approached. I looked around frantically for a clump of souls to screen me, hoping to hide until the horses had passed, but I heard the chariot murmur to a stop on the road beside me.

Hades called my name. I stood slowly and brushed dirt from my shift. The god towered above me, looking more imposing than he had in his own palace. He appeared more powerful when Persephone was not around.

"Alcestis," he said again. "You halt like a startled deer."

"I will not go," I told him. A brave little noise, for he could force me to do whatever he liked, just as Persephone could.

But he shook his head—choosing not to force me. Choosing to let me choose. And that made him even more incomprehensible, for what god, when his blood floated with such a surfeit of power, would restrain it? "You are going to the river Lethe. I am going. I will take you." He spoke as a woman might speak to a child, with slight impatience, slight fondness. Not a bit of wrath. Even his dark horses stood uncannily still, not stamping or tossing their bridled heads.

I hadn't decided to go back to Lethe, but when he said it I knew he was right. I could think of nowhere else to go. "No, you shall not," I said.

"You are contrary. Why?"

"I'll share nothing with you, not even your chariot."

"Ah, so you are jealous," he said. "It is charming how you lack all sense of proportion."

"What do you mean?"

"She is my wife, Alcestis, and you, dead though you may be, belong to a mortal."

"I belong to death."

"Then you belong to me," he said. "So you will listen. You are walking to the river Lethe. I will take you there in my chariot. Do you understand?"

"No," I said. Then: "I'll go with you to the Lethe."

"Was that so difficult?" His voice was flat.

"Perhaps not for you."

"How little you know," he said. "The world is always startling to mortals. Every day new."

"Do not mock me."

"Oh, I do not," said Hades, and a darkness stole over his face, like the traveling cloud that had swept Persephone's skin. "I forget, that is all. The ones I see no longer suffer mortality, and they have no more new days to startle them. We have few enough ourselves."

"You have thousands of days," I whispered, thinking: thousands of days with her.

"Yes, precisely. And the days must be marked. She has her fancies, and they do not trouble me. But this is not a fancy."

"No, this is a selfish desire. She wants to keep me from my sister."

"Yes, she does."

"Then you'll admit it, that you have kept me from Hippothoe."

Hades raised his hand, and the ground before me shifted into a smooth ramp from field to road. "I have done nothing," he said. "Poor mortal, do not think of it. Come and seek your sister. I tire of shouting to you from this height."

I glared at him. He waited. I walked up the ramp and took his outstretched hand, and he pulled me up onto the chariot, his grip a hot vise. I thought I ought to say something, some mixture of thanks and apology and curse, but I could not imagine what words might suit. Hades urged the horses on.

Shades clustered along the edges of the road, staring up at him as the villagers had stared at my father during his infrequent tours of the Iolcan town. The same fear, the same dull thrall. I couldn't survey their faces quickly enough to see them all, but I couldn't stop myself from looking. I suppose I still possessed a little hope, or it possessed me. First I thought I saw a slave girl who had worked in Pelias's kitchens. I thought for a moment that I saw Pelias, but it was another man, tall and heavy shouldered, slumped like a bear at rest. No Hippothoe. Never Hippothoe.

We crossed the Phlegethon on a bridge of black wood that hardly seemed sturdy enough to bear the weight of chariot and horses. Between the gaps in the bridge's floor, I saw blue flame only cubits below the horses' hooves, but they trotted on, unbothered by the bright river. Where had Hades gotten these horses? Had he dragged them from the world above as well, dead in their prime, and trained them with his own hands so they could serve him here? Horses that never tired, never spooked, never grew swaybacked from age.

Beyond the river the road sloped toward a great swallowing pit, then circled its edge. From the depths came a long, grating sigh that smothered the horses' hoofbeats. The pit was Tartarus—the sigh the sound of eternal torment.

Hades halted the chariot at the lip of the pit. On its terraced floor lay more cells than I could count, cells bounded not by walls but by glowing envelopes like the barrier that sealed Elysium. The cavern glowed with a light from which no shade could escape. Shades packed into some of the cells, dark clots of cloud, while other cells held single prisoners. The cells seemed to breathe as a flopping fish breathed, expanding and contracting in fast, shuddery jerks.

I saw the hill and the stone, and the receding water; I watched the tree lift its fruit out of reach; I saw beasts besetting shades, spiders crawling upon their cloudy forms. From above, they resembled mural figures, and I felt no more sorrow for them than I would have felt for paint and plaster. I knew their stories—stories enacted for the lord Hades whenever he desired to view them and now enacted for me. Yet if my sister had been among them, I would've thrown myself into the pit to rescue her, would've sprawled prostrate before Hades for his mercy and help.

Still I watched them calmly, and after a long moment, the chariot rolled on.

Soon we came to a hill over the Lethe's bank, just by the edge of the forest. Hades stopped the chariot there, and the dust stirred by the horses' hooves overtook us, billowing like a sail. I coughed and wiped at my eyes, but Hades stood unmoving as the cloud swirled past him, waiting for me to breathe again.

"My thanks," I said when the dust had passed, "for the ride."

He nodded.

"Lord Hades," I said, and he waited again, stone still. "Why do you not punish me?"

"I do not punish." He looked out over the souls gathered by the riverbank. "I have the judges for that, if punishment must be done. But any punishment can be forgotten here by those who suffer it. The mortals can forget."

"And you cannot," I said, thinking of Persephone's hands on my arms, the low echo of her plaint as I left her. He would always remember it.

"The marks of life cannot be erased from my sight. But there are many here, and their lives are indistinct." He looked at me sidelong, and I began to mistrust what he had said about not punishing me, for he looked as though he were judging some element of my nature. Appraising me. I lifted my chin and stared back at him, and he smiled, though his eyes did not soften.

"Here, I will show you," he said, and touched my temple. A film slid over my vision, like the finest linen waxed for transparency. I closed my eyes to blink the film away, but Hades said, "No. You must look. You have wanted to see what we see."

I opened my eyes and looked out at the shades—they seemed to stand in two layers, their dark bodies the same, but a new brightness swarming around their heads and shoulders, like a sheet of clouds around hilltops. It cast a delicate and smothering radiance upon their faces, a light that flattened their features and made them look alike as soldiers in their faceplates looked alike, unnamed, interchangeable. This was how I'd seen them at first, but I had never seen this light.

"What is that?" I breathed. "That—light."

The chariot lurched forward and the sudden motion made me clutch at the rail. Hades' fingertips pressed hard against my skull. "Look now," he said.

It was not one cloud, but hundreds, thousands. Over each shade's head hung an enveloping mass of light, knotty and pulsating, stuck about with images too small to see clearly, like tiny figures tied to a warp, woven together. Spangled strings of memory and life. And all trailing loose at the edges, where they had been cut out of some greater fabric—each shade a patch of life, removed.

I peered at the closest shade: his tangled strings of light looked like a net draped over his shoulders. Fish swung in the net, and lightning, and a curved bronze knife; and an image of a boy, slim and smiling, his brown hair haloed by sun. Death had eroded the shade's features, and I couldn't tell whether the boy was his son or his brother or his favorite lover, but I saw now that it did not matter. The ties were still there.

The shade beside him had been a girl, and her cloud was studded with baby faces, smiling or sleeping or screwed up in furious tears; not her own children, I guessed, but siblings or a mistress's brood. She'd just come from the river, wiping her mouth and still swallowing the last of the water, and I watched to see if her cloud would wither as her memories disappeared. Her face smoothed; the cloud didn't fade, but slipped back a little, like a loosely moored ship bobbing away on slackening ropes. The babies kept on crying or beaming or squalling;

beside her cloud, the pretty brown-haired boy whom the man had loved ducked his head and grinned.

All so similar—the men and the women, the slaves and the sailors. Lives reduced to images and the images all equally bright, though some were of family and some of objects, some of sunrises or of a tree branch loaded with snow. It was a misleading simplicity, but I felt it nonetheless—how alike we were, mortals, and how easy to understand. We were made of pieces. I was not whole as Persephone was whole; I was what Pelias and Hippothoe and Phylomache and Admetus had made me. I tried to twist, to see what mess of fate hung over my head, but it seemed to hover just at the edge of my vision, a bright cloud swerving away when I shifted. "I can't see," I said, turning to Hades, and gasped at the sight of him.

Hades was stone and earth in the shape of a man, his muscles rough and massive like worn hills, his eyes black as the gloom of caverns, untouched by Apollo's or Selene's light. He was not merely hard—he was bedrock, the great heaviness of the stone that lies beneath the world, the immovable mass of death.

I jerked away from his touch, and he slipped into a man's form again, not shrinking but lessening. I could see a faint remnant of his granite heart, but I saw it as if through the crystal walls of the palace, dull and obscured. I had thought him beautiful before; I had feared him in this mortal-looking form, while the truth of his nature had waited, hidden from me. How could I have seen what he meant to Persephone when I could not see him? It struck me how unfair it was, as a mortal, to love a god. A fly might as well love the horse whose tail swatted it to death.

"What do you see upon me?" I asked Hades, unsure what answer would please or frighten me most. Did I want to think of a tiny image of Persephone's face shimmering among my sisters and brothers, my husband, my life?

"Uncut knots," he said. "Straight threads. Your sister." And there he stopped, studying me again.

"My sister—"

"You love her. That is all I can see. I do not lie to you," he said, to my obvious distrust. "You are not like the others. Do not be angry at me because I cannot see."

But he could see, even if he didn't see my whole life shrouding me, and I envied him his sight.

"What does Persephone look like?" I whispered.

For a long time he did not answer. I stared out at the shades, at their simple gray bodies, and I didn't know if I wished to see their lives or if I was relieved not to see them. Did the clouds knock into each other as the shades walked—brush and tangle and leave strands behind, like a lock of wool caught on a bush?

"Like sun," he said, "sun that punishes, first blushes, then burns. Breezes that sting. Flowers that smell sweet and kill the bee that sucks at them. Vines. With thorns, and soothing sap, and more thorns. Fruit gone soft and fermenting and gaseous in the belly." He looked at me closely, and I thought he might touch me again, but I didn't shrink back. He seemed to reconsider; his hand, fisted by his side, uncurled. "You cannot see it."

I shook my head. I couldn't see what he had described, but I knew that his words were true. Persephone contained those things. She'd ruined me with her envenomed touch. I couldn't blame her for acting as her nature required. I could've resisted her; I could've fought. But I didn't want to fight. I would have swallowed poison from her mouth to feel the slickness of her lips once more.

"Unfair," he said, and I started at the sound of my own thoughts coming from his lips. "She ought not to destroy you."

"I cannot be destroyed," I said softly, growing frightened. "I am living in the world of the dead."

"That is why—," he began, then stopped, shook his head and laughed, a scoured sound. "I will leave you here. You know that she will find you."

I knew. But I thanked him and took his hand when he offered it and stepped down to the ground with a lightness I had not previously felt. It was the sort of lightness I recalled from my wedding day, a dizzy frothing like a swirl of foaming water closing over my head. The world for me was ending, and a new world coming, as it had when I left my father's house and wed. She would find me and Hades would not stop her.

Hades looked down at me once more from the chariot, swiveling as he turned the horses around, then stopped them again. "You will be punished enough," he said, so quietly that the slow lapping of the river Lethe nearly drowned his words. The horses stirred uneasily in their harnesses, their heavy black bodies coiling with lifelike distress.

Hades slapped the reins down on the horses' rumps. They bolted, rattling the chariot wheels, which were not made to shake, against the hard surface of the road. Shades stared as the chariot flew by; they were probably used to seeing the chariot, but I doubted they had ever seen it shudder as if it might break apart. As if Hades himself might break apart.

I too was staring, almost against my will, as I had done so many things in the underworld. I watched the chariot shrink, Hades dark and the horses darker, rounding the curve that would lead them back to the palace. Even he could not resist her.

As the chariot passed out of sight, a paler figure appeared, coming slowly up the road.

Persephone? My belly clenched. Could she have come to find me already, walking on foot as a mortal would? That would be her kind of penance, misdirected and irrelevant. But the figure was not stalk slender, upright, or lovely. It was crooked and hunched; it shuffled.

So came Tiresias, leaning on his staff, to usher me into my next new world.

16 I DIDN'T KNOW then what he wanted, but I knew he sought me. Another godlike thought, full of my own importance. As it happened, I was right. He slowed as I ran to meet him and lifted his ugly gray head in greeting. His wrinkles and radiance were unchanged since I'd last seen him. I tried to guess what images studded the cloud hanging invisibly over his slumped shoulders: visions of future life, scenes yet unplayed? Murder and doom?

Worry made me brusque, and I didn't welcome him by name, only asked, "What have you to tell me now?"

"Lady Alcestis," the old seer said. Though I knew it unlikely, he seemed short of breath. "The end of the journey."

"Yes, you have found me," I said. "What news, Grandsire?"

His blank eyes rolled toward me and I stepped back just slightly, startled. I had the sudden sense that he knew everything I'd done with Persephone, each word and touch and thought, that he knew everything to come, and that it mattered little to him except as a cause of frustration.

Tiresias leaned toward me, gripping his staff, tilting perilously.

He said, "When two leaves fall together, one must still land on the bottom."

"My sister," I said, my worry receding a bit. His voice was kind. I convinced myself that he must care for my welfare, or he would not have come to speak to me again. "I'm waiting for her here. Do you know where she's fallen?"

"It is not the dirt that matters, but the seed. The growth," he said.

I looked to the asphodel across the road. "Am I to seek her in the field?"

He shook his head fiercely. "No. The roots do not grow."

"I shouldn't seek her in the field." Again his head shook. "All right. I shall not stray. I shall wait for her here. But that's what I intended. There was no need for you to come, Grandsire." I put my hands out toward him, looking around for some rock I could usher him toward, some place where he could rest.

Tiresias turned his head toward the river. "No," he said clearly.

The dread returned. I felt it first in my hands—my palms tingled and then went numb—then in my feet and calves, as if a coat of ice or a slick of molten bronze were forming on the inner surface of my skin. The dread seized my stomach and choked my throat.

"You came to tell me something," I said, and each word felt as if it were covered in burrs.

He turned his blind eyes to me again. He blinked slowly, as if he were as reluctant to speak as I was to hear him. As if he could forestall whatever he saw by forcing me to wait.

"Say it," I told him. "Say it now."

"You will not like," he ground out, and had to pause to collect himself. "You will not—"

"Slowly, old man, if you must," I said, trying to keep my breath even. "I listen."

"What you find," he said. "You will not like it."

The look he wore was horrible. I screwed my eyes shut. Better to see darkness than to see that I was pitied by a shade. Better to think my fear might be unjustified. Better to think of Persephone—or Hippothoe—

My eyes opened. "Go on," I said.

"The lions are tamed and spread beneath the hero's feet. When the horses stamp their feet in the stable, their hooves ring on rock."

"The lions? There are no lions here. What hero?"

"The man with poisoned blood. The snake in the vein. The trophy borne up. Betrayed, but forgiving. There is too much to see," he said, suddenly angry, his mouth working as if he tasted something bitter. "Too much. The way is blocked. I cannot say."

"I do not understand," I said. "I am trying. But I don't understand. Is there anything you can say? Any piece you can give me? I'll take anything."

Tiresias was rocking now, swaying from toe to heel, the end of his staff boring a hole in the soil.

"Please, Grandsire," I whispered. "There must be something."

He stopped swaying abruptly enough that I thought he might topple. "Yes," he said. "Yes." But then he fell silent again, and I despaired of ever knowing what he meant. Out of habit, I turned to look at the shades now lining the banks of the Lethe—I was so close to knowledge. How strange it would be if I found her now; I had grown used to looking. But still I had to look.

Tiresias's mouth hung open and his eyes had closed, their milk swirls hidden. He looked like an old man drifting to sleep in late afternoon. I will learn nothing here, I thought, and my gut constricted in rage.

But as I turned away from him, the old seer's eyelids snapped open, and his blurry stare caught me.

"He—is coming—for you," he said in a strangled growl, and his hand fell away from his staff. I moved to catch him before I remembered that my arms would pass through him, that I could not hold him up. He fell away from my grasp and crumpled to the ground like a folding cloud. His eyes roved in his head, twisting as if he would see, somehow, if only he found the right place to look.

I knelt beside him, grit pressing against my knees through my thin shift. "Who, Grandsire? Who comes here?"

His chest heaved as if with mortal breath. He wheezed, "I cannot. It is—"

"You must tell me. Please, you must."

"The hero," he said. Then, gusting against my cheek like a real breath: "Heracles."

He went limp; had he been alive, I would've said that he had fainted, his senses taken by the gods. But I think he was simply drained, nothing left, all his tiny store of energy used in fighting to speak.

I tried to touch him, tried to shake him, but my fingers closed on chilly air.

"Tiresias," I said, "Tiresias, Grandsire." My voice came out flat, smooth, like the road that led to the palace. He didn't respond, and after a long moment I stood, wiping my hands on my thighs mechanically. Heracles? My husband's friend? He was hardly a hero. I'd seen him drunk and drooling on the floor of our hall, and though I could imagine him in battle, I could also imagine him stumbling over his own huge feet when the charge was called. And yet he was loyal and senseless and strong. If any mortal could cross the barrier between the world above and the underworld, it would be Heracles, favored child of Zeus.

There was only one reason for a mortal hero to venture into the underworld: to retrieve what had been taken. I'd been taken. He was coming for me, Tiresias had said. Coming to take me back. I felt no joy at this, no bursting of brightness in my chest. I felt bronze heavy and cold and I couldn't think. Heracles. Here. To take me back. To take me from her.

The ferryman will refuse him passage, I told myself. He'll drown in the river Styx, fall face-first into the marsh. If he does cross, the hound at the gate will catch him, sink its teeth into his thighs, herd him back to the boats. He'll lose his way among the asphodel flowers and find himself in Elysium, and he will never wish to leave.

I will tell him, I thought, that I do not wish to leave.

I stood over the fallen seer and watched the shades meandering in their pathless ways, unaware. The happy dead, the forgetful dead, dripping with Lethe water. For the first time, I looked to the river with a kind of desperate hope. Heracles wouldn't want to return me to Admetus a blank-faced and blank-minded wanderer; if I drank from the Lethe, he might leave me. But I wouldn't remember why I had drunk—I wouldn't be able to argue my case, or to recall why I wanted to stay. I would forget even the taste of her skin. I would never find my sister.

"He cannot have me," I said aloud. "I will stay. There is nothing for me in life."

"Nothing," mumbled Tiresias from where he lay. "The circle on the ground. The grip." His eyes were closed, and he spoke as an idol speaks, his mouth hardly moving.

I bent again, and asked, "How long before he comes?"

"How long?" the seer echoed. "How long?" He repeated the question again and again, chanting it like a prayer, until the words ran down to senselessness. How long? It didn't matter. Heracles was coming, had probably already left my husband's house to make his awful journey, and I was to wait until he arrived and then allow myself to be led, docile, to the surface world.

I felt a chill on my ankle. Tiresias had struggled up enough to wrap his insubstantial hand around it, his fingers hovering over my skin, threatening to pass through me.

"Go," he said in that broken growl, and released me, his arm falling back to the dirt.

Go.

I ran, following the tracks of the chariot on the road. When I looked back over my shoulder, Tiresias still lay supine by the river, other shades gathering around him, staring down like the servants had stared at Hippothoe the night she died. I couldn't stay with him—I had to get to the palace, to tell Persephone what I had learned and to beg her aid. Heracles wouldn't listen to me if I pleaded with him to be left behind, but he would listen to a goddess. He'd listen when her voice rose up in echo after mine, when she told him that I was hers.

My feet pounded on the packed dirt. The road curved and I raced across the shallowest part of the curve, slipping on the crumbling bank. My hair flew around my face, bits of it sticking to my eyes and mouth and smacking against my sweaty neck. I was tiring when I saw the palace and the adamantine gate rise up before me. The chariot stood empty in front of the gate, the horses gone. One of its wheels sat crooked. I ran past it, touched the dark wood with my fingertips, touched the gate beyond it.

The gate chimed at my touch, like the sound of perfect blades striking. The tone rang in my ears as I pushed the doors open and ran through the entrance hall and toward the draped golden curtain. I heard nothing from the throne room, and I didn't know what sort of scene I might burst in on—Persephone naked? Hades naked? The two of them sitting and smiling, playing at the dotage of an old king and queen? It didn't matter. I needed them now, and I would see them.

The throne room was dim, the golden ball of light vanished and the room lit only by the gray seep from moving windows. No thrones, only the table—and there, the gods, sitting opposite me. Persephone had her hands in her lap as if she had been waiting; Hades sat beside her, his back straight and his eyes lowered to the empty surface of the table.

They looked up when I came in, observed my disordered shift and my sweat-stuck hair.

"Sit," Persephone said. Her eyes were pink rimmed, the irises azure gray. She nodded to the bench on my side of the table, pulled back just far enough to allow me to slide in gracefully. But I wouldn't sit. There was no time for a civilized discussion about Heracles' arrival—there was no time at all.

"I have seen Tiresias," I said. "He came to find me, to tell me that Heracles is coming."

They watched me. Hades nodded. Persephone's mouth trembled, I thought, but she did not speak.

"He is coming to take me. For my husband. He is my husband's friend, and he comes here to take me away, back to the mortal world." Persephone didn't react, so I kept talking, waiting for her to speak and anguished by every moment that she remained silent. "He is a hero. He will come soon."

"Yes," Hades said. "He plans to wrestle death for you. It is a little sweet."

All the air went out of me. "You know?" Persephone had cast her eyes down, and I wanted to dive across the table and yank her chin up, force her to look at me. "*You* knew?" I asked her, my voice sharp.

"Only just—," she said faintly, but she was lying.

"You knew that he was coming, and that means you knew that I wouldn't stay. You let me think I was dead when you knew I was not."

"I was not sure," she said, raising her face. Her cheeks were pale. "I did not know what the Fates would decide. They are capricious, Alcestis. They are not to be relied upon."

"I relied upon you!" I cried. "I would curse you by the gods if you weren't a god yourself."

"Do not say such things—"

"Why not? Why did you not tell me of this?"

"I did not want to," she said.

I stared at her. This girl-woman, this goddess. She sat watching me, slim and gilded and sharp as a blade, just as cruel as her husband had promised. I'd thought she must have been angling for some new destiny for me, some trick for the Fates, but I had been wrong. She did not want to, and so she did not.

"Sit down," Hades said to me. He was leaning forward, elbows on the table. For a moment I saw him as that mass of rock, as if he'd tapped a finger against my temple and given me a god's sight again. Then he was Hades, the husband, carefully not looking at his wife.

I wouldn't have sat down if Persephone had ordered me, but

Hades I obeyed. I went numbly to the bench and sat before them. "You will fight him," I said to Hades. "When he comes to fight for me, you will defend me."

"I will do what I must."

My stomach sank. But what more could I demand? He was not my husband. If Persephone wouldn't force him to help me, I could not either. But surely she would help me. She would keep me. She couldn't have seduced me intending to let me go now.

"Then you'll entrap him." I turned to Persephone. "Show him Elysium. You would teach me to stay—teach him. Don't let him take me."

"Oh, I would not," she said, her voice rich and sad. "Were it in my power to prevent."

"You are a god. It must be in your power. He will listen to you, to both of you. Tell him that I do not want to leave. I don't want to go back to the world of mortals. He came alone, he can return alone. You will not have to hurt him."

"No," Hades said.

"No, you will not hurt him? Or no, you will not help?"

"No," he said again, "it is not in her power, nor is it in mine."

I wished he had never shown me the world through a god's sight, for I wanted to argue with him, to shout that he was wrong. But I couldn't argue with what I knew to be true. Had he given me that burst of vision so I would be quiet and pliable now? When she kissed me, had she thought of kissing me farewell? They had both known Heracles would come for me; I could trust nothing they had said or done.

"Then I must leave with Heracles, for you will not save me." I said it as much to punish Persephone as to hear their reactions. Hades nodded, and though I was expecting that nod, I choked on the breath I'd drawn. Persephone lifted her hand, reaching across the table as if to stroke my brow.

"Do not touch me," I hissed at her. "Do not come near me. You should've told me, Persephone, and you said nothing. You tempted me as you were tempted."

"But I love you," Persephone said, sounding anguished. Her cool face had gone flushed and splotchy, as if she were the one who had just run from the river to the palace. "I wanted you to stay, though I knew you must go. What good would it have done for me to tell you of this when I could not stop it?"

"If you had known the seeds would bind you here, would you have eaten them?"

She didn't pretend to be confused. "Yes," she said, the word soft as breath. "So you see. It would not have mattered."

I began to say that I was not like her: I wouldn't have eaten. But with her cheeks red as if they had been rubbed, her mouth thin and tight with distress, and her eyes shifting from gray to green like the sky before a storm, I could not lie. It was unthinkable that I might not have wanted her, that I might have been offered her fresh-swollen kiss, turned her down, and walked chastely away. Now I would not leave her for anything. But neither would I forget Hippothoe.

"I must find my sister before he comes," I said.

"I wish you would give up this search," Persephone said, fretful. "It will do you no good. You do not see, Alcestis, why I worry for you."

"You won't have to worry for me much longer if Heracles crosses the river and passes the beast at the gate."

"I know that," she said. "Do not be cruel."

A fine instruction from you, I thought, but I said: "Then you will tell me now."

"It does not matter," she said sadly, "whether I tell you or not."

"You lie."

"No, Alcestis. I do not. All you must do is wait."

I loved her. I had been waiting long enough. I put my hand on the table, palm up, and lifted my eyes to her face. Her smile fell apart. She reached out and slipped her hand into mine, her fingers curling over the rise of my thumb, the bones of her wrist light atop my fingers. My knuckles pressed against the table's surface.

Hades sat, watching us, silent, smiling a little.

A wail broke in through the windows, a low sound at first, then growing louder. I opened my mouth to ask what it was, but just then the sound split and split again, resolving into a chilling tripartite howl, each throat open on a different tone. It was the hound Cerberus, crying out against the invasion of his home, calling to Hades to announce the presence of an intruder. Heracles had come.

WE SAT, THREE silent figures, as the great room echoed with the sound. The dog's howl made the crystal walls hum, and Persephone clutched at my hand but did not speak. She looked like a frightened maiden, and I felt another flash of fury—I seemed always to cycle between adoration and anger with her. She had no reason to fear him.

"Will you wait then?" I asked her, my voice taut. "Will you sit and wait for him to come?"

"What else ought we to do?" she said.

I pulled my hand from hers, ignoring the way she clutched at me, the hot scratch of her nails across my palm. I couldn't wait. Not to find Hippothoe, not to face Heracles.

"I will go to him and meet him in the fields," I said. "You know he must be coming here. He will know where I am."

"Yes," said Hades. "It is good that you go."

He spoke as if to drown out his wife's objection, but Persephone was silent, her eyes downcast. I looked at the slope of her eyelids, the sad flutter of her lashes against her carven cheeks.

"I will bring him to you," I said, and stood, and turned my back on the gods.

The adamantine gate sang to me as I passed beneath it. I paused and looked out over the plain, at the moving clumps of shades and the distant rivers. He'd passed the guarding hound, and now he would be coming toward the palace, for in the underworld as in life, the first thing one must do in a new territory is visit its royal house.

A shade brushed by me. I saw tangled hair and turned, but it was a boy with a long braid half loose from its tie. Was I to leave this place without ever seeing my sister? Wait, Persephone had said. You only have to wait.

I walked down the road toward the river Styx and the hound Cerberus, looking for my husband's friend, the son of Zeus.

I saw him in the distance, striding toward the palace and me, his arms up and tensed, prepared to strike at any assailant. A pack of shades floated after him, dully curious, and he glanced back at them every few moments. It seemed he thought they might attack him, and his steps grew quicker until he was half trotting down the road. His curls bounced on his shoulders and his tanned skin seemed to twitch like that of a horse beset by flies. Heracles, the hero.

A noise came out of my mouth: a snort of angry laughter, stinging in my nostrils. He was only a chariot length from me now, perhaps two, and he faltered at the sound of the laugh, his eyes slipping over the shades moving on the road until he saw me standing still in the center of it.

"Lady Alcestis," he said, disbelieving. "Is it indeed you?"

I didn't acknowledge him, though I met his eyes. Let him see the answer he wanted there, I thought. It was the only thing he would see in my eyes, after all, no matter what I said.

"I did not expect to find you so easily," he said. "The way from the world above was long and dangerous, and the underworld is full of shades. I had not thought it so full."

He looked at me with expectation, still believing that I would answer him as a polite girl of a royal family would, that I would make approving noises and then be silent until spoken to again, as I had in the world above. He didn't know that women too could choose different types of silence.

"You look almost as one alive, lady," he said, though with little wonder. I imagine that he was used to extraordinary treatment and saw my lively appearance as just another instance of his deserved luck. "Will you not speak?"

He didn't look frightened of me at all. I wished I could frighten him—wished I could appear to him as Hades looked to me, with a face of thunder and doom. Instead I must have looked tired, and worried, and angry, and none of those were expressions likely to surprise him when seen on a woman's face.

Heracles gestured to me, making pulling motions in the air as if he could haul me in like a ship. He came closer, slowly, approaching me as he might a spooked horse, his hands out before him.

"I will lead you home, Lady Alcestis."

It is not my home, I thought fiercely. When he reached for me I slipped back, and his arms closed in the air before me. Three times he sought to embrace me, and three times I evaded him, though his hands did not pass through me as mine had through Tiresias and Tyro. I just stepped back. But he didn't understand my reluctance—his eyebrows twisted up and his mouth puckered.

"What is this enchantment?" he muttered. "She cannot speak, and she escapes me."

So he thought that death had bound my tongue? I wanted to speak then, to tell him precisely what sort of enchantment lay upon me and what sort of torture he deserved for breaking it. But he wasn't speaking to me, and he wouldn't have listened if I had spoken honestly. He expected this, I saw, to be a transaction between men—he intended to fight Hades for me, win me, and return to the mortal world in a glow of triumph and loyal friendship.

"Come then," he said, trying to calm me. "I will lead you out of this place. Come." And when I would not move, and could not be grasped, he said again, "Will you not speak?"

I watched him for a moment longer. Then I said roughly: "Give me the blood sacrifice. You'd do it if I were a man."

"What?"

"The blood sacrifice. Bleed for me, and I will speak."

"But you speak now," he said, perplexed.

I glared at him for a moment. Then I took a step toward him, opened my mouth, and screamed. He jerked, startled, and raised a hand to hit me before he remembered that I was a woman, and a wife, and the object of his search. His hand lowered.

"If it will please you," he said stiffly; pleasing a woman was something he could understand. He drew the bronze dagger from his belt—a tiny thing, snub and harmless looking in his big hand—raised it to his forearm, and cut.

The blood made a red runnel on his rough skin, skipping down his arm, around the bone of his wrist, and across the back of his hand. I came toward him and bent, reaching for his hand, reaching for the sacrifice. He shuddered when I touched him, shuddered again when I opened my mouth. I lapped at the blood dripping from his knuckles: it tasted like blood always does, metallic and blunt. I let him go and stood, wiping my mouth on the back of my hand. I could feel his blood smudged hot around my lips, its half-dilute Olympian power. I looked at the stain on my hand, then turned it over and looked at the scratches still raised pink on my palm, the marks of Persephone's nails as she'd tried to hold onto me.

"Speak, speak," Heracles said, a little unnnerved. Still not frightened enough. "Are you well? Did you eat anything? Did you? Did he make you drink—make you do anything that would keep you from returning to your husband?"

"I ate my life for him," I said.

I could see him growing angrier and less uneasy.

"Not Hades," I said, "or Persephone. For Admetus I ate my life. Let me be. I do not want to go. I am done with life." As I spoke, I felt a small wild hope, a tiny flame flickering in my chest: that he might hear me, might comprehend. I watched his face, and I saw him hear my words, understand them, then reject them in the length of a moment.

I danced back, in case he tried to seize me. I wasn't ready to be forcibly taken. And he did reach out for me, but only half-heartedly, staring at me as he did, the look in his eyes curiously flat. Blood still ran sluggishly down his arm, drops falling from his fingertips, and other shades, smelling it, had drifted into a half circle around us.

"You should not be here," he said. "You belong with Admetus, and I will bring you to him. I came to fight death for you. You are under some thrall, and I will break it. Lead me to the lord Hades and let me challenge him."

I suppose I could've tried to mislead him, directed him on curling paths through the fields and the forests, taken him to the banks of the rivers and told him he had to cross. But it was hopeless. If Persephone and Hades thought he was meant to take me, if Tiresias knew of his journey, then a detour along the Phlegethon would make no difference in the end. I'd bring him to the palace and let him speak with Persephone and Hades, as they sat silent at the great table, holding hands.

I stood back and crossed my arms. "All right. But you must walk behind me once we reach the adamantine gate, and you must let me go into the palace to announce you first. You wouldn't go into a royal home unannounced, whatever your errand."

"My errand—," he said, indignant, then subsided. "You are right. I follow."

And he did follow, meek and ponderous as a cow. I looked back at him as we walked, just as he'd looked at the crowd of shades shadowing his path. I didn't trust him, though that was silly, for if Heracles was anything, he was worthy of trust.

I led him up the slanting road to the palace, but my steps were short and slow. I couldn't have made my feet move quickly if I'd wanted to; my legs were heavy, my body resistant. Even my knees did not want to leave.

I felt Heracles stirring restlessly behind me. He didn't like this pace, nor did he like the shades that thronged behind us as village children might follow a caravan of warriors. I forgot how I too had sometimes disliked them; I gave them fond looks as we walked. I'd almost grown used to their quietness, their smooth or cracked faces, their lack of feeling and lack of want. Everything that frightened Heracles about the underworld now seemed familiar to me, in the way that absence becomes familiar, or the loss of what one values. Heracles feared death as a woman fears marriage—in uncertainty and trembling.

We came to the gate, and I turned on him like a dog might,

with a half snarl. "You must wait. I will call for you when the king and queen have agreed to receive you."

He didn't like being told to wait, but he was too polite to argue with me, a woman, his object. I left him at the gate and went into the dark palace, down the long hall, and past the golden curtain, which twinkled only faintly as I pushed it aside.

The table was gone, replaced by the thrones of jet and obsidian. Persephone and Hades wore lush gray robes and adamantine jewelry, draped in finery as if armed with it for battle. They looked like statues adorned for a feast day, their faces remote and perfect, unmarred by mortal distress. But they stood when I entered, stood as one, and when I came stumbling toward their thrones, they came to me with their arms open and pressed me between their bodies. It was like being lifted by eagles, their wings enfolding me. But Hades and Persephone had no wings to bear me away.

I sobbed out two bursts of sorrow on Persephone's shoulder. Then I pulled back, sniveling, and looked at their solemn faces.

"He's outside," I said. "He is waiting. I said I would call him in. But I don't want to."

"I know," Persephone said, and kissed my damp brow.

"And still you will not help?" I grew tearful again. "Still you will not aid me?"

"We cannot," said Hades, his arm strong around my back. I wriggled against his touch, wanting him to leave us, to stand by his throne and wait. And, strangely, he did. I burrowed against Persephone, pressing my hot face against her neck. Her necklace dug a cool line into my cheek, and I knotted my hands in the thick fabric of her robe, searching out the firmness of her flesh beneath the cloth.

She took my face in her slim white hands and kissed me. Her lips quivered on mine.

"He awaits us," Hades said, though not impatiently.

"Let him wait," Persephone said, and kissed me again, soft and clinging. "He has time."

"But she does not."

Persephone lifted her head, and I saw that her cheeks too were tear streaked. "I know that," she said, forceful. "You and he and all the world can wait." She slid her arms around me again and leaned down to rest her temple against mine. Her breath puffed unsteadily on my jaw.

"It's all right," I murmured to her. "Let him come."

"I am not yet ready to receive him." This time her voice carried a hint of panic. "He must wait until we call. I am not ready."

But he would not wait. Persephone and I, entwined, hadn't heard his footfalls in the corridor—Hades, if he heard, said nothing. The jeweled curtains sang gently in the doorway, and Heracles, the hero, entered the throne room of the palace of Hades, eager to wrest me from the grasp of death.

HE WAS NOT prepared, however, to see me in the grasp of the crying queen. He gave a little gasp like a girl and stepped back, brushing the golden curtain and making it chime again. I turned in Persephone's arms, leaning against her. Her breasts were soft and warm against my back.

Hades, now sitting regal on his throne of jet, nodded to Heracles. That was his only greeting, bare by the standards of Achaean grace. Heracles returned the nod and stood with his hands hanging awkwardly at his sides, as if he wanted to reach for a weapon but felt it would be rude.

"Lord Hades," he said, confusion making him bold, "I have come to fight for this woman and to restore her to life and to her husband, the lord Admetus."

Hades waited, calm as granite, as he spoke. I had never loved Hades, but I began to love him a little then for his stony silence and his imperturbable manner. I tightened my fingers in the cloth of Persephone's robe and watched.

"I challenge you," said Heracles, sputtering into uncertainty under Hades' gaze, "to fight me, for the right to the lady Alcestis' life."

"No need to grapple like beasts," Hades said. "She is not a brood cow."

Heracles flicked a look at me, at Persephone; his eyes rested upon us for a moment, then flicked away. His cheeks had grown ruddy with heat, and he cleared his throat before he spoke to Hades again.

"Then you will not answer my challenge? You give up without even a fight?"

"Without even a fight," said the lord Hades.

This bemused Heracles. He looked around anxiously, twitching when a window opened in the palace wall behind him, as if he were expecting an ambush—an army of shades swarming through the hall.

"So I may take her to the surface without harm," he said.

"You may."

Heracles looked at me again.

"Why does your queen coddle Alcestis so?" he asked softly.

"That," said Hades, "you had better ask my queen."

But Heracles did not dare. I saw him shrink under the suggestion, paling.

"I will ask," I said, and relished his open-mouthed stare. Now he feared me. I twisted in her embrace again and put my hands on her cheeks, framing her face as she had mine. I studied the wide line of her lips, the rounds of her eyes, felt the edges of her cheekbones under my thumbs. She had tiny freckles below her left eye, like sprinkles of kohl—I hadn't noticed them before. Such a little time to grow a love.

"Alcestis," she murmured, and I leaned up to kiss her. Then I asked: "Why do you coddle me so, Persephone?"

"Because I want to," she said. "I did not want you to know—what it means to be among the dead."

"But I do know."

She smiled. Her fingers dug into my arms, and she shook her head once, quickly, as if shaking away tears.

"You," she said sharply to Heracles, "can wait a moment longer." She turned back to me, eyes brimming. "I must tell you."

"Yes."

"You shall bear two children, Alcestis, a boy and a girl. The boy shall be his father's son." She spoke hurriedly, as if the boy did not matter, and I listened in disbelief. "But the daughter shall be mine, and yours. She shall marry a king as you did, and she shall seem to live in seasons, bright one day and gloomy the next, and you shall love her but never understand her. And that way you shall always remember me." The last words came in a ringing tone, the clear, terrible voice I had always imagined gods to have, and her eyes were nearly unrecognizable beneath their film of tears.

"I shall always remember you," I said fiercely, and though I had distrusted her words before, I believed this prediction. I knew I would not forget her, knew it more purely and concretely than I had ever known anything else.

"I shall see you in years and years. Die in your bed an old woman, and come to meet me," she whispered, and kissed me again. Her tears tasted strong and hot, like unmixed wine.

"Farewell, Alcestis," she said. "You will find her now." Her voice did not sound as strong as it should have, but she smiled again as we stepped apart and brushed a loose piece of hair from her eyes as if it were the sole reason they watered.

My heart spun in my chest. I knew what she meant, and as much as I loved her, a small part of me wanted to race out through the halls into the fields right then, finally to find my sister. But I chose to trust her and to wait a moment longer. I wrapped her in my arms and crushed her to me—she felt as thin as Hippothoe, all bird bones and heat. "Farewell," I said into the curl of her ear. "Farewell, Persephone."

Then I turned to Heracles, unsmiling. "You may lead me."

He looked uneasily at Hades, at Persephone, and finally at me.

"I speak for myself," I said. "And I will follow."

Heracles turned and pushed the curtain aside.

I looked my last. I saw her beauty, saw Hades', saw the way her hand lifted and stretched toward him before I'd even turned away. That was right. And I had been wrong, wrongly placed and wrongly killed, and now I must leave.

"Come," said Heracles, more quietly than I would have expected. I went.

The courtyard was empty, but beneath the adamantine gate stood a small figure, sapling slim.

As soon as I saw her, I knew her as Hippothoe. She was dressed in the shift she had worn the night she died, her knotty hair hanging down around her thin face, hiding her eyes. She was looking at the ground, at her own bare gray feet on the dirt, and she didn't look up as I followed Heracles out of the palace.

"Hippothoe," I cried, breaking into a run. "Hippothoe!" I stumbled to a halt beside her. She was so short, the tangled crown of her head only reaching my collarbone. I reached out and stopped, my hand hovering over her bony shoulder; I wanted to touch her, but I was struck with sudden fear, recalling how my fingers had sunk into Tiresias's misty form.

She did not raise her head.

"Hippothoe," I said as gently as I could, "it is Alcestis, your sister. I've been looking for you everywhere. Where have you been? I have searched for you."

"Sister?" she mumbled to the ground. The warmth had bled out of her voice, though it was still gravel rough, the mess of her throat and chest unmended by death.

My hands fluttered above her shoulders—I couldn't seem to control them. I wanted to put my fingers beneath her pointed little chin, lift her face to me to see if she would know me, even grown, a woman and a wife, but again that creeping fear gave me pause. "Yes, your sister, as you are mine. And I've found you. Look at me, Hippothoe—will you not look at me?"

She blinked once, twice. I could see the slow dip of eyelashes beneath her veil of hair. "Look?"

"Look," I said, desperate, and put my hands to her cool, crumbling cheeks. Her pale mouth fell open, and inside there was darkness like the darkness of an empty room, and I thought of the empty room in which our mother had died, in which I had lain as a child, waiting: waiting for Hippothoe, waiting for this moment, waiting for death.

Her eyes were closed, her lashes dark gray smudges against her pale gray face. Unlined skin, no cracks for light to creep through. No light beyond the smallest flicker, the glow that remains in the eye after a tiny flame has guttered out.

"Look at me," I whispered. "Hippothoe."

Her eyelids lifted, and her mouth closed, and the corners of her pale lips twitched toward a smile. I thought—I thought I saw her work to form a name, and I thought it was my name, and I thought I could save her, take her with me, if I had to leave, and bring her back to life.

"Hippothoe?" she murmured, and her voice, her dear, rough, ugly voice, held as little knowledge as a baby's wail.

"No," I breathed, but I knew as I spoke that the denial was useless. Her eyes held nothing. No wit, no reassurance, and no recognition. She did not know me, and she did not know herself. Speaking to her grave had given me more hope, for then I could at least imagine my words sinking into the soil, finding their way to her ears. Now I saw that my words went into her like pebbles into an empty vessel, rattling as they fell and then settling, silent and heavy. She had become an empty vessel. She was exactly like the others. I had been wrong to hope.

For years she had languished here, walking amongst the asphodel flowers and weaving between the trees. She had drunk the Lethe water, had cupped it in her palms and gulped it down as I remembered her gulping hot honeyed wine to soothe her throat. And she had forgotten me—forgotten everything she knew, but especially me.

This was why Persephone had kept her from me: to keep from me the truth of death. I had only been stopped, hovering, waiting to return to life. But death was the land Persephone ruled, and to this land I would come, an old woman, to be her subject. And I too would become exactly like the others. I wouldn't know Hippothoe or Tyro or Tiresias; I wouldn't know Persephone. She would look on me as I looked on Hippothoe now, her love absorbed and reflected as blankness. She would know me as I had been and see me as I was. That was the nature of a god's sight.

The shade of my sister was still waiting, her face lifted, though the faint questioning look had disappeared from her eyes. She had probably forgotten the question.

"Hippothoe," I said softly. Not even a blink answered me. "Sister. Hippothoe."

Was this the girl I had known and loved, who had let me curl around her skinny body in the night and stroked my hair when I pressed, whimpering, into her arms? The nightmare soother, the undimmable light?

She was not. But she smiled again, just slightly, when I touched the crackling mass of her hair. Death had rendered it transparent as spider silk, and I smiled too to think of the head maid's great grievance with Hippothoe finally settled. When I tried to stop smiling, I could not—my face felt frozen as a statue's, my lips hard in that little curve that indicated life. And so I was smiling as I watched her leave, her small feet shuffling on the dirt and her head sinking down, down, to see the mesmerizing pattern of her own steps. Always forward. Always wandering.

When Heracles took me by the wrist to lead me away, I did not fight him.

I said nothing, saw nothing, until we approached the bank of the Styx. I didn't know how he expected to cross it, nor did I care. He stopped just before we reached the river, and I waited in numb patience. After a moment he turned to me with a look of confused concern.

"Was that—was that someone you knew?" he asked. It took me a moment to understand that he was talking about Hippothoe. Had he not been listening? Perhaps he'd found it easier not to listen.

"No," I said. "Not any longer."

"But you said—"

"She was my sister. She's not my sister now. She is a shade like the others." He still looked uncertain. "Have you seen nothing here?" I asked in sudden frustration.

"I have seen many shades," he said. "But you do not fade as they do."

"No," I said. "I do not. And that is why you have come to retrieve me."

He nodded but slowly, as if unsure whether I should be allowed to describe his quest so lightly. Then he turned, and I thought he meant to lead me to the river, but again he stopped and shifted and looked back at me with a shadow of compassion in his eyes.

"What about the river?" he asked.

"It is just there," I said.

"The river Lethe." He looked away when my gaze sharpened. "If you were to drink, perhaps—perhaps it would go easier for you. Upon your return."

The kindness of his suggestion startled me, but I thought of the shades lining the banks, the water running from their hands like blood, and wrapped my arms around myself. "No," I said. "I don't want to forget."

He stood, silent. He didn't pretend to understand, but he didn't rail at me or growl like my lion-father either. His mother too had been tricked by and beloved of a god. It seemed that those two acts went together, that a god's loving could not be had without tricks.

"We must go," said Heracles, the son of Zeus, and he marched toward the river Styx as if he believed its waters would part. Again I followed.

Even the hound Cerberus did not try to stop the hero, but slunk instead into his cave. His six eyes glistened like wet coins as we passed.

Charon took us over the marsh, having accepted the bronze dagger from Heracles with a look of childish pleasure. The boat-man hummed as he lifted the pole and pushed it through the water into the muck on the bottom of the marsh; hummed as he guided the boat toward the shore crowded with shades waiting for passage. It was a tuneless song, a little joyous, a little sad.

Heracles leapt off the boat when it touched the shore, and turned to help me, impatient. I looked back once toward the distant palace and saw the edges of its walls gleam sharp.

Refusing his hand, I stepped down onto the living dirt.

WITH HERMES, I had flown from life to death; with Heracles, I walked away from death with trudging steps. The path was long and gray, with indeterminate edges beyond which it fell away into dark confusion. Heracles walked in the precise middle of the road, talking.

When I died, he told me, Admetus did all the right things. He cut the throats of young beasts and spilled their blood on the altars and burnt the meat in hot towering piles until the palace smelt of roasted offal. He dedicated all to the gods, not only the best cuts, and the villagers, upon hearing of this wasteful piety, had thought to riot until informed that the sacrifices were for the honor of my soul. (I had not thought the villagers knew my face, much less cared for my soul, but this touched me in a distant way.)

Admetus had called on Apollo, but the god had not appeared to him. Nor had fleet Hermes, nor strict Artemis, and by their absence, Admetus knew that his sacrifices were not large enough. These things Heracles told me as we walked from the underworld to the surface world above. He didn't tell me all—indeed he didn't tell me most of it, for he was not garrulous as some warriors are, but I could imagine the rest as he spoke. I knew enough of poems to fill in the expected phrases, finish out the lines.

He said that Admetus had sworn great oaths—of celibacy, of devoted love. Since I was dead and Apollo did not come, no one present could have known how easily those oaths came to his lips. We were the only two Admetus had ever loved. He went about the palace in mourning wear, suited in a gray tunic as if he were the shade, and had a slave girl shear off his lovely hair, leaving his head rough and pitted with stubble.

He had been wearing this tunic when Heracles first arrived at the palace, barely three days after my death, on the eve of the funeral games planned to mark my departure. Admetus had invited him to stay—my husband was always hospitable, no matter the circumstances. (Three days—I was shocked to hear it. I had been in the underworld, owned by Hades, in thrall to Persephone, for just three days of mortal life? It had taken her only three days to split me open, to pluck me apart as easily as peeling a pomegranate. In the timeless underworld, I couldn't have known how days were passing in the world above—but still I felt the first stirrings of shame when I learned this.) Heracles soon discovered the source of Admetus's misery and declared that he would travel to the underworld, fight death for me, and bring me home to my husband that very day. For this brave boast, the best portion of the next cow slaughtered was reserved for him, rather than being burned in honor of the still-absent gods.

Heracles' story was about Heracles, who found the cause of his friend's woe and sought to make all right. His was a narrow and particular kind of right: it demanded that I be found and captured (though he would say rescued) and returned whole (which meant unraped). He had gone bravely to a cave that held an entrance to the underworld, and he had not turned back at the threshold. He had steeled himself and walked inside. Entering the underworld had not hurt him, though he had grimaced as if it did. (I am sure of this.)

About his struggles in the underworld, there was not much to tell: he bribed the ferryman, tamed the hound at the gates, which he had subdued before on an earlier journey to the realm of the dead, and met me on the road. He had not gone astray; he had encountered no monsters other than Cerberus. (Though here he gave me a sidelong glance, as if he suddenly doubted.) He did not see Elysium, but if he had seen it, he would have thought its glow calming and pretty—if such a man could think anything pretty but a boy's smooth thigh or a woman's curling hair or the arc of light from an axe as it is swung.

We had been walking for several hours. I could tell that now—my sense of time was returning faintly, like a scent. (Three days. I couldn't stop thinking of it.) The landscape, what there was of it, had not changed, though the cloudiness surrounding the road seemed brighter. Heracles had stopped talking. I did not mind the silence at first, for I had grown unused to the manner of living men, and when he began to walk faster and pulled ahead of me, I trudged along behind him. But soon I began to feel weary, dragged down, as if my grief were growing heavier, binding my throat and weighing on my shoulders. With each step I grew more solid. I looked down at my white ankles, my thin wrists with their twin pulses of blood, channels just beneath the surface. Life did not feel sweet.

"I cannot go on," I said quietly. Heracles didn't hear, but I hadn't spoken for him. I slowed and stopped, turning to look over my shoulder. The Styx, the shades, the ferry—all had receded into distance and obscurity.

Heracles noticed that I wasn't trailing at his heels like a puppy any longer. He ran back to me, seized my arms, and shook me once sharply. I turned my face to him and he let me go. "What is it?" he asked, and his voice was surprisingly mild.

"I cannot go on," I repeated. "I've grown too heavy."

"You can," he said. "You must go on. It was not your time to die. And now you are saved. The gods have shown their agreement by allowing me to rescue you."

"Do not call this a rescue. I wanted you to leave me. I was happy there."

"You are upset, and disordered in your mind," he said. "The gods of the underworld have put mighty spells upon you. But I will lead you home nonetheless, and there you will heal, and heal your husband, who is lost without you."

"Three days of being lost," I said, "how miserable."

Heracles shook his head. He spoke to me now as if speaking to a child, all caution and patience. "Forget the darkling gods, the lord Hades, and the—the queen Persephone. Admetus loves you and will honor you."

I looked away.

"And I will not dishonor him with—what I have seen," he said.

"What dishonor? How can it matter to anyone alive what happened when I was dead?"

"You must keep your shame to yourself," Heracles commanded me.

"I will not tell him anything," I said bitterly, and pushed past Heracles toward the waiting world.

The road, which had been flat and broad and nondescript, grew rocky. At first there were only small stones mixed into the dry dirt, pebbles that bruised but did not sting my bare feet. Then finger-sized rocks, then palm-sized, tumbling down from the lifting sides of the road. It became a narrow valley, damp and lichen crusted, through which we had to walk with gingerly steps. Soon my feet began to bleed, leaving red prints on the green-gray lichen. I bent down to peer at the growth, and Heracles stopped, and saw my bloody feet.

"Come, I will carry you," he said, and wobbled toward me over the rocky ground.

"No, I shall walk."

"Your feet bleed."

"I don't care. I shall walk."

He let me be. I'd thought he might sling me over his shoulder like an overeager bridegroom, but he seemed to have a sense of embarrassment, of some unheroic dignity, that kept him from handling me violently. He walked, and I walked, and the air grew fresher and lighter around us. I thought I felt the smallest suggestion of a breeze, though I could not identify its origin.

"There," said Heracles, halting, and pointed above our heads.

I hadn't looked up once as we walked—I'd grown used to the dull ceiling of the underworld and had forgotten the sky. This was just a patch of sky: a roughly round hole punched through from one world to the next, bare rimmed, vacant. No one was looking over the edge.

"There?" I whispered.

He leapt, arrowing up from the dirt, his arms spread to seize some purchase on the rim. I watched him struggle and wondered if he would fall and die. If Hermes came to take him down, could I clutch the hem of the god's cloak and beg him to take me too?

Heracles hung from the edge, his fingers whitening at the knuckles, his grip on the rock tenuous. "Take my hand," he said. "I will pull you up."

I didn't reach for him. I raised my hand, but I couldn't stretch out my arm to be taken from the underworld, even though I knew I could not go back to Persephone. With a grunt of frustration, he swung down and caught my arm, wrenching me up off the road. I thrust my other hand toward him and he seized it—the pain in my shoulder lessened, and Heracles lifted me into the world.

I felt both alive and dead. The breath seemed to reverse in my chest, air rushing out of my lungs, then flooding back as the underworld relinquished me. The sun stabbed at my eyes—I had forgotten its white-gold fury, the color of Olympian beauty and Olympian wrath. My eyelids squeezed shut involuntarily and my lashes prickled with water. My body felt terribly heavy.

"Sit, lady," said Heracles, and his hand curled warm around mine. He led me to a rock and pressed me down until I sat. "I will bind your feet."

In the sunlight my cut soles looked worse. I let him wipe the blood from my skin, barely heeding the sting. He tore strips from his own robe and wound them around my ankles and my arches. He treated me as I expected he might treat a young wounded soldier, as if we were compatriots, brothers in arms. Perhaps he sensed the similarity between us: the hero and the sacrifice, both marked for death, both marked by it.

"This will need water and wine, but I have neither," he said, in the brusque tone of the head maid in Iolcus. "But you will be well looked after, lady, when you are brought home."

He stood and looked me over, seeming satisfied. I looked down: my shift was clean. I was pristine as a virgin, except for the heat in the skin around my eyes, the feeling of tears spent and tears waiting. I supposed I would suit for a wife brought back from the dead.

For the first time I looked beyond the rock on which I sat to the small scrubby trees around us and the ocean thundering cubits away. I knew this place vaguely—a rocky cove I could see from the higher rooms in the palace at Pherae. Heracles saw me looking about and spoke. "Your husband is only a short way away. I can carry you, if you are too tired or footsore."

I was tired, but I shook my head.

"Wait," he said, and bent to tear a wider strip from his robe. He handed me the cloth—it was worn thin but not transparent.

"What is this?"

"For a veil," he said. "That you may pass along the road unmolested, and that even Admetus may not know you by sight."

"Why should—my husband—not know me?" I choked on the words.

"That you may know his loyalty and be received with perfect truth." He said this perplexedly. "Do you not wish it?"

I did not wish it. I needed no proofs of Admetus's devotion; I knew he cared for me, but devotion would change nothing now, when I'd had love. So he had been alone, without me, without Apollo, for a short time. So he had suffered to think of me wandering in the underworld. I could summon no sympathy for him—he hadn't been separated from his god forever. He did not know what it would mean to die.

I looked back through the cave's entrance at the waiting

chasm within. I could see the rocks faintly and the gray enveloping light of the underworld.

"This pathway," I said, "has it always been here?"

His face darkened. He shook his head once angrily. "It appeared for me. It will vanish when I leave it."

He insisted that I wear the veil, and I didn't argue. As we left, climbing over rocks, I lifted an edge of it and looked back toward the entrance to the underworld. He was right. I was trapped here, alive.

THE GUARDS LET us through with no trouble. They didn't recognize me; no one on the road had, though they had regarded me with curiosity, unused to seeing veiled women led by heroes. I wouldn't have expected the veil to conceal me so well, but it seemed that few here knew me. They did know Heracles, and they admired him, their worship clear in their wide-stretched smiles.

He didn't stop to speak to them, but nodded curtly and led me on. I'd been trailing behind him as we walked along the road, keeping a respectful distance. After the rocks, the pounded dirt felt soft under my torn feet, though the cuts gave out little jags of pain that made my eyes water.

The fragment of Heracles' robe rubbed against the end of my nose, and I could see through it, though it gave the world a blurred look and made the faces of the people we passed seem as smudged as the faces of shades. I could watch them without their knowledge, without their recognition. I thought they might appear different to me now that I knew how they would look when they were dead, but they looked like villagers and guards and slaves. Like Pheraeans. My people.

I hadn't looked at the palace yet. I didn't want to. Around us were all the marks of my death—the scorched piles of bones, the tents of guests come to attend the funeral games. But it was late in the day, the sun lowering in the west, and the courtyard was quiet, the slaves and guests having retired to doze in the afternoon sun. The palace would be quiet too, except for the kitchens; my bedchamber would be quiet, the stars on the ceiling silent and still. And where was Admetus? What would he do when Heracles brought me to him? Did he sit now on his throne, gazing at my empty place beside him? I imagined Apollo installed in my smaller throne, his golden haze drifting over the faces of the slaves, drying their tears like sunlight. I wondered if Admetus was imagining this too.

Soon I would know.

We came to the base of the stairs to the great hall. I paused, staring up them with resignation. Heracles stood me there, his hands on my shoulders, moving me as if I were a solid mass, carved from wood or stone. "Stay here," he said, "and I shall call your husband." He waited a moment, watching me cautiously, and then he turned and mounted the broad stairs, taking them two at a time, his legs pumping.

I thought of running but I did not. I waited, as he had ordered. But I didn't know how to stand unnoticed in my own courtyard. I wasn't sure what to do with my hands. I clasped them before me, then behind my back. My feet throbbed. I felt terrifically, miserably alive.

A slave hurried past me, not looking at my veiled face. I lifted my chin; it was habit, to tilt my face up, seeking attention from those I ruled. I was standing in that manner, bold as any queen, when Admetus emerged from the palace, hand shading his eyes as he crossed into the sunlight.

He lowered his hand. He had been weeping, and his fine golden-brown skin looked weathered, like old cloth. He had shaved off his beard too, and he had a growth of stubble on his soft cheeks. I imagined putting my hand on the curve of his cheekbone, then thought of the sharpness of Persephone's face, the silky glide of her skin.

Heracles stood behind him like a silent mountain.

Admetus saw me at once. "What is this, Heracles?" he said with surprising fury in his voice and surprising restraint. "I will have no wife. I told you that when you arrived. My wife is dead."

"Listen, I beg you, to her tale." Heracles passed Admetus and came down the stairs to stand beside me, his hand hovering over my shoulder as if he were afraid it would pass through my flesh. "She has traveled far to come to you."

Admetus's eyes flickered to my wrapped feet, then back to the veil. Men could not keep their eyes from it; the cloth made me a mysterious blank, and I suppose that appealed to them. I wondered if they would find the smoothed face of a shade as compelling. "I will have none of her," he said. There was strength in his voice, and the ruin of tears. "I am married yet, and I will not break the bond."

I looked on my faithful husband, who had feared death more than dishonor, who had been willing to sacrifice me to save himself. I wanted to tell him that he had nothing to fear, that death wasn't terrible for the dead, and that he would have no fear when he died. Death was terrible only for the living and for me.

"Speak, lady," Heracles urged. "Tell him your story."

The veil stirred over my mouth, for I was breathing heavily as if winded from a run, but I didn't speak.

"Lady—"

"Do not force her," said Admetus, ever gentle. "You have brought me a mute bride, Heracles? Take her away, please. You may give her to the maids to house and take her when you leave after the games."

Heracles stared at me, frustrated. He wanted to help Admetus; he wanted to be honored, and I wouldn't submit. I smiled beneath the veil; the cloth was a freedom like death. I waited to see what he would do.

Admetus turned away and Heracles bounded up the stairs to stop him, putting a hand on his arm and turning him back. I watched Admetus's familiar profile, the noble line of his nose, his beautiful boyish face grown sad.

"Wait," Heracles said, "wait. You will wrong her if you do not take her."

"How can I wrong her? I wrong myself if I betray my wife."

"Do you not know her then, after so short a time?"

"What—," Admetus began, and then he closed his mouth. He began to realize what Heracles meant. The wrinkles around his eyes relaxed and his dark eyelashes fluttered. His hands, which he had raised to fend off Heracles, fell to his sides. He looked as shocked as the shades waiting for Charon, but his eyes were not blank. I saw joy, relief, and fear there, mingled.

Heracles descended the stairs and tugged the veil from my head. It caught on my hair, and then the torn edges of the cloth brushed over my skin like wind. I was revealed. There was no general hush in the courtyard, no strike of a far-off gong to mark the moment. I heard Admetus take a short breath, a swallow of stabbing air.

"It is she," said the hero. "Your wife, Admetus. The lady Alcestis. I have brought her back to you, living. Will you not welcome her?"

"My wife—" Admetus put a hand to his mouth, then lowered it. He came down the stairs slowly, falteringly, as if they were shifting beneath him. "My wife?" He paused. "Alcestis?"

I lifted my head a little, but still I said nothing. I could not imagine what to say. I am come home, though I did not want to come?

"You are Alcestis," he said wonderingly, "though you are silent. How can this be? How did you do it?" He looked at Heracles, not at me, when he asked.

"I won her back from death."

That might have tempted me to open my lips. But why should I ruin a hero's tale? I looked at the ground and thought of Hades on his black throne, smiling to hear Heracles celebrated for my rescue.

Admetus's fingers grazed my cheek, and I jerked my head up, surprised. His eyes seemed alight as they never had before my death—touched with a fire directed only at me. I didn't like it. I wanted to squirm away, but I stayed still. "You fought death to save her?"

"He did surrender her to me, and I have brought her to you, to her home," said Heracles. "You will not refuse her?"

"What kind of man do you think me to be?" Admetus said to Heracles, but he spoke distractedly, without heat. He stared at me: the willing sacrifice. He didn't seem to consider that I might've been an unwilling prize. "Alcestis," he said again, as if testing the word.

I was silent. My silence comforted me; it felt like the numb wrapping of the underworld, the endless calm. If I determined to be silent, then I didn't have to think about what to say, or how to say it, or where to direct my eyes while I spoke. I did not have to address the growing crowd of onlookers. The slaves and servants had begun to notice Admetus's distraction, his interest in the woman brought by Heracles, and when my veil was removed, they gathered as the shades had gathered, curious, feeding on the energy of royal distress.

"Still she does not speak," Admetus said, concerned—and nervous. "What has happened to her?" He touched my cheek again and I didn't flinch away. His fingers were cold. They didn't strike fire under my skin.

"Why, she died." Heracles gave me a desperate look. "It is the shock of it, Admetus, the strain of death. She may not speak for several days, until she is recovered. You must be careful with her. Do not startle her or excite her too much. And do not let her leave the palace walls."

"Why not?" Admetus asked absently. He lifted my hand and examined it, with an air half of love and half of curiosity.

"The business of the village will overtax her," said Heracles, but he was looking at me as he spoke, and I knew that he had seen me look back toward the chasm in the earth. "Until she is healed."

"Is she ill then? Does she need care? I can send for the maid." Admetus's voice was still uneven, heightened with elation and terror. He was not entirely eager to be alone with me, then. I was glad.

"Only a husband's care," Heracles said. "You must touch her, speak to her, as your wife. It will remind her of her earlier life."

"Remind her? Does she not remember?" Admetus looked stricken. I wondered at this. We had shared some affection, many habits, and a fair amount of desperation. Did he truly think that losing my memory of our short marriage would be a terrible blow? But I would once have thought it so, I remembered suddenly. I would've wept his loss as if I loved him true.

"No. She remembers all."

I looked to Heracles, whose face was all fury, though he tore his eyes away when I met his stare.

Admetus touched the center of my palm. The callus on his thumb scraped at my skin, and I felt sweat rising in the tiny creases of his fingerprints, chill as the touch of a shade.

"I shall leave you now." Heracles backed away; only two steps or three, but it was a clear abandonment.

"Now?" my husband cried. "Heracles, what is this sudden retreat?"

"I've done you the service I could, and I must go back to my home. I must—I want to see my wife."

Admetus released me and stepped toward Heracles. "But you must stay. You must stay and be celebrated. We'll have the games already planned, but we shall honor you as well, good Heracles. You can't simply leave us after such a feat."

"I'm wanted elsewhere." Heracles spoke gently. "I have other duties. As do you, Admetus, king of Pherae. The games are a worthy and a pleasant rite to honor your wife's homecoming, but you must not draw the attention of the envious gods with too much celebration. Keep her safe and rejoice in her return, but do not make spectacular shows of your good fortune. Be quiet and careful."

Admetus looked back at me. The flame in his eyes had cooled. What had we that was worthy of envy? What had I to tempt the jealousy of a god? A little mortal life, a little mortal marriage. A quiet bed, unstirred by the furor of Olympian love.

Heracles looked to the stables, then to the gaping arched

door of the great hall. "Take your wife into your home," he said. "I will call my servants and take my leave."

Admetus could not argue: to refuse a guest the right to leave was nearly as inhospitable as denying shelter. But he looked at Heracles with obvious longing, wishing for a friend to support him—he seemed as nervous as he had when we wed, the skin around his mouth gone pale and his hands trembling. They embraced once, fiercely. Heracles stretched out his arms exactly as he had when trying to capture me.

"Be thankful," said Heracles, in a voice meant for my husband's ears. "She who was lost has come back to you. You lose no honor in this, Admetus."

Admetus's dark head lowered. It was a kindness, what Heracles had said—but it was not true, and we all knew it.

"May the gods protect you." Heracles clapped Admetus on the arm, flexed his fingers around the muscle. Then he turned to me.

"Farewell, lady," he said. The manners of my birth and his dictated that he ought to have knelt before me, taken my hand, and spoken to me without meeting my eyes. Then I ought to have dipped to my knees, covered his hand with mine, and spoken just as obliquely. But I didn't mind his gruffness; we had no politeness between us. I looked into his troubled eyes, and then I looked away. That was my farewell to Heracles.

The hero left the courtyard speedily, as if pursued. The crowd of silent watchers parted to let him through, then turned their faces back to us, waiting for the story's end.

Admetus stood, watching Heracles go, and I watched Admetus. I saw that he wanted to call out to Heracles, to call him back, to ask what he ought to do next. But then Heracles passed through the gate, nodding to the guards, and Admetus straightened, as if Heracles had actually vanished, as if the gate were a barrier to another world.

We stood, side by side but hardly together, before the entrance to the palace we ruled, the village we owned, the life we had traded, and sundered, and now shared again.

My husband looked at me, still uncertain.

"Will you come in, Alcestis?"

He reached out for me, his fingers vibrating slightly in the air, as if the whole world were trembling. All the courtyard seemed to quiet: the slaves, the guests, all were waiting and expecting me to lift my tender white hand and place it on my husband's open palm. I looked at his palm, at the lines I had once thought to memorize, patterns I had traced with the edge of my fingernail, patterns that now looked as incomprehensible to me as writing.

A breath of wind stirred in the courtyard, lifting my freed hair. Some god inhaling in anticipation or poignant pleasure. For were we not a picture, his hand outstretched and his face open and me standing pure in my slip of cloth? Was this not the moment in which I ought to return, fully, to life?

21

Outside was revelry and drunkenness and the sound of joy. The athletes had been told that the funeral games were canceled, due to my sudden return from the underworld. To soften this disagreeable news, they'd been given sacks of wine and allowed to stay for one more night before departing. They'd set about celebrating my freedom from death with vigor, and their shouts and songs echoed in the courtyard and tumbled in through the open window of my bedchamber. The songs were dirty—lyrics to sing to a prostitute rather than a queen—and I liked them, though I was sure that Admetus, wherever he was, was blushing to hear me feted so.

I had not lifted my hand to let my husband lead me to the royal bedchamber. I had stood wordless until Admetus, finding the wait unbearable, had grasped my hand and raised it with a brave smile, as if he'd caught me just before the moment when I would have taken his hand.

He'd led me into the palace accompanied by the cheers of the assembled slaves, the prayers and cries of the now-unneeded funeral guests. They'd pressed around us as we climbed the stairs, hot bodies smelling of oil and sweat and garlic, hot breath weaving around us like a fog. So many bodies! So much life. And their brief touches, fluttering on my arm, my hip, my ankle—liberties they would never have dared before I rose from the dead—felt pleasant, harmless, like the nudging of children. But Admetus had spun and snapped at them, ordered them away from me. I was delicate yet, he said, and they might damage my health. So it was that we'd come into the palace alone, passed through the great hall, and gone to our chamber, where the bed waited, and the starred ceiling waited, and the stone windowsill waited. Then my husband had walked me to the bed, sat me down upon it, and fled, saying that he would fetch the head maid to care for my feet.

He had not yet returned. After an hour had passed—a numb hour, dull with disbelief—I limped over to the windowsill to look out on the world below.

The slaves hadn't cleaned the bedchamber since I'd died. The windowsill bore a thin layer of dust, stirred by the travelers' arrival in the courtyard, and beneath that a thinner but darker layer of burnt sacrificial grime. I licked the tip of my finger and touched it to the dust-smeared stone, looked at my stained skin. I could skim my fingertips around my eyes, mark out tears in char, darken my lips until they looked swollen, press my thumb into the dirt and smudge my throat to record each touch of Persephone's mouth. I could tell my story with dust, never needing a word.

If I had been dead, captured, never to return, Admetus would've kept troth: pledged his life to me, pledged never to accept another bride. When he'd needed a son, he might have adopted a boy, some promising child from the village, perhaps, with golden hair and golden skin and a charming downturned smile like the curve of the sun cresting the horizon. I knew these things about him, as I knew that his denials to Heracles had been heartfelt. He had missed me. He did honor me. In my absence he'd slipped into misery, and his sorrow marked our chamber still. There were clothes dangling from the headboard of the bed, sandals lying tangled by the door. He had dropped a cloak on the floor, and it pooled there, dusty, like the ghost of a billowing cloud. He didn't like disarray. Had my death truly caused this minor chaos? Was this the grief of a widowed husband, or of an abandoned lover?

I couldn't smell Apollo in the room at all. Only smoke, and the sea, and the dustiness of drying grain.

The harvest had been finished just before I died, the stalks of grain sliced through and tumbled on the ground, the fields cut to stubble. All the air had been full of chaff before Admetus had filled it with smoke. Beyond the bonfires in the courtyard, beyond the heat of wine in young men's veins, the villagers would be cold in their small houses. The air was already crisp. Soon would come fall apples, their red skins covering flesh with only a pale sweet crunch, no succulence, no seeds that burst like joy on the tongue. Persephone would remain under the earth for months to come, shining at the heart of the palace beside her shining husband, cut off from the rest of their kind, twin thunderstorms raging unseen. She was as distant from me now as the floating islands of the north or the backward-flowing rivers of the south, distant as the road outside the palace gates.

I sat on the dusty windowsill, glad to dirty my pristine pale shift, glad that I was still wearing the cloth she'd touched. I tried to pay attention to the men below, but I couldn't stop thinking of her, and under the muffling blanket of shock I felt sadness rise. Persephone! I mourned for her, my heart beating like a funeral drum against my ribs. But also I mourned for myself, who had found death and love together. I'd never loved life, but it was all I had now.

When the door opened, I was still perched on the sill, my hands in my lap, my face unstreaked by tears. I knew at once that it was Admetus, finally having gathered the courage to speak to me, as a hero might prepare for battle with a deadly beast. In the same instant I thought of how Persephone would've entered: the sweep of her skirt, the slow spread of her gentle and insinuating smile, the white hand floating in readiness to touch my skin. Admetus came in carrying cloth, a jug of wine, a pitcher of water. He'd slopped water over his hands and onto his tunic. When he saw me sitting by the window, he nearly dropped the pitcher and another wave of water sloshed from its wide mouth. Dripping, he put the water and wine and cloth on the trunk at the end of the bed, then looked up at me. His face was white.

"Alcestis," he whispered, and winced at a prolonged yell from the men below. "Are you all right?"

I looked out the window again. Fires leapt in the courtyard pits, and men danced around them, their shadowy bodies blocking out the light.

"I know you," Admetus said, "and I know what Heracles said to be true. You are my wife. But you are changed. I cannot quite believe it, seeing you here. I went to find the maid, and—I half thought I'd come back to find the room empty."

I turned back to him. He had come nearer, though not close enough to touch. Afraid of frightening me, probably. As if I would kick or snap like a startled animal. I did not ask if he had wanted to find the room empty.

He said, "I do not know what I would have done, if you had vanished again. I do not know what I have done in your absence. I did what was expected. That was all I knew how to do. But Heracles did more than that. He took my place. He did what I should have done.

"And now you are—here. Rescued. And I still do not know what to do. I cannot quite—" Here he looked away, just a flash of his eyes, as if distracted. I think he was embarrassed. If I hadn't been absorbed in my own sorrow, I might've been embarrassed too. We did not speak this way, my husband and I. "I cannot believe it, without your voice."

I waited, letting the sound of his own hoarse voice sit in the air. I couldn't speak.

He took one step closer. "I will not ask again after this. But I must ask once more. Are you my Alcestis?"

I was his Alcestis. Returned and owned. Alive and married. And he was waiting. His eyes, in the dim light, were as dark as Hades', as round and tear powered as Persephone's. He was filled with fear, as he had been when the god arrived at the feast, filled with anticipation, waiting for me to speak.

I didn't speak. But I let him take my hand again, and when he'd waited nearly long enough (for it would never be truly long enough) I bent my head forward, just slightly, so that my hair slipped over my cheeks, and then I looked up at him. It was not quite a nod, but I knew he would interpret it as assent; he was interpreting all my actions now, ascribing meaning to the barest motion of my hand or mouth. He read me as an augur reads the skies, as a woman reads the face of her father to know when the time for marriage has come. My silence made me remote as a god. It gave me a distance I had never been allowed. But I could not keep it forever.

Three days. I would take three days of silence to mark the change in me. Three days for Persephone. Three days for

Hippothoe, silent now in her wanderings, with no one to echo. Three days for death in life. I made this decision as I'd done everything since I returned to the world above: wordlessly, giving no sign. Unaware, Admetus lifted my hand to his lips. They were rough and dry and scraped against my knuckles.

"I will take the answer you give me now," he said hesitantly. "Still you do not speak. But I will not press you. I trust that when you are healthy, you will speak again." There was a little relief in his voice, as if he feared what I might say to him. I felt a grim certainty of the power I had over him, the thrall in which I held him, and with that knowledge came a rush of sympathy, unwanted. I would've taken his hand then, if only I could have pressed it into Apollo's.

He released my hand. I flexed my fingers instinctively, and he stared at the small movements with wonder, as Phylomache used to watch her babies. I folded my fingers into my palms, out of his sight. I wasn't ready to be cherished in that way—not by him. He pulled his hand away and looked down at my feet. The paleness had left him; he was flushed now, like a youth alone with a woman for the first time. Death had reduced us to this, the formal dance of the newly married. I took a small amount of pity on him and lifted my bound feet.

At once he knelt before me and touched an ankle gently. "Of course," he said, still flushed. "I will do it." He rose, went to the end of the bed to fetch the wine and water and cloth, and came back to sit before me again.

I don't know if he had ever seen my blood before; I hadn't bled the first time, after all my subterfuge with the sheets to please the servants. I'd passed through a year of married life uninjured. Now he peeled back the strips of Heracles' robe binding my cut feet and sucked in a sharp breath as if the mere sight hurt him.

I imagine that it did. This was the only sign of my sacrifice that he could see: the real sacrifice, not my resignation at the feast.

"Does it hurt?" he said, looking into my eyes. I closed them, just for a moment, and when I opened them, I saw that he had looked down again—embarrassed or perhaps ashamed—as if he had been answered.

⚜

ON THE FIRST night I lay stiff and silent beside Admetus, unwilling to sleep. I feared I might talk in my slumber and release some secret of my death. I couldn't tell him about Persephone; I knew that. But I suppose I could have told him of Hippothoe, in vague terms that would not have revealed to him the truth of death. I could've said: I met my sister in my last moments in the underworld, and I had to leave her. I could've cried. Tears he might have understood. But I lay in the dark with my dry eyes open, unable to call them up. The bedchamber seemed so small and familiar, so enclosed, so ringing with life. I listened to the rustling of animals in the courtyard, to slaves moving about as the night shaded toward gray morning, awake hours before we were meant to rise. How had I slept through these sounds before?

But finally I slept through them again. I woke to an empty bed, my muscles aching from the effort of holding myself apart. I hadn't moved since nightfall.

I spent the day in my chamber. The servants refused to enter—neither the slave girl nor the Cretan women arrived to dress me, and my meals were delivered with a timorous tap on the door. I left the food sitting in the hallway, an offering to the local gods, but even they hardly touched it.

In the evening I heard my husband shouting at the slave

girls in the courtyard. He came back still angry, slamming the chamber doors and breathing like a warrior, ferocious huffs through his nose. I was sitting on the bed, my bandaged feet on the cool stone floor, and when he saw me, the anger seeped out of him at once. He came to me, halting barely an arm's length away, unsure.

"They're just silly girls," he said, his words strangled and gruff, as if he were trying to speak in my father's voice. I bent my head. After a long moment he put a hand on my hair, his touch light as the veil I'd worn. But I leaned away from him and lay down again, pulling the bedclothes up to cover my face, my breath heating and thickening the air. I heard him move, heard the clank and shift of his scabbard on his hips, the sigh he let out when he realized I still would not speak.

I fell asleep under the covers. In the middle of the night I thrashed awake in the grip of dreams that didn't wake Admetus, dreams of shades and goddesses. I studied him in the darkness, hovered a hand's length away from his calm face and tried to remember how I'd felt on the day I married him, how I'd lain awake alone and wished for him to touch me, wished for him to want me, my entire body clenching in misery and desire. There had been a time, I remembered, when all I wanted was his love and the physical mark of it, the round of a swollen belly that would prove me a good wife.

I sat up for the rest of the night, my back against the wall, staring at the ceiling's flat, immobile stars.

Admetus shouted at the servants on the second day as well, and halfway through that afternoon, the slaves came to clean the chamber, hesitant as children. Most of them ignored me, but I saw that they wished me gone, though some of them looked sorry for it. They moved in skittering groups like shades, the slower ones trailing after. The chamber had never been neatened so quickly or so poorly. They too kept silent as they cleaned, as if my reticence had spread to them, but I heard them whispering outside the door when they left and hushing each other at the slightest sound from within my chamber. After they were gone, scuttling off down the hall to the kitchens, I limped to the door and waited, waited for some sound to stir the quiet. I wanted to call them back, those soot-marked girls, the quick ones and the slow ones, to tell them they had nothing to fear from me—for if I couldn't say it to my husband, not without knowing that I lied, at least I could reassure someone.

One of the girls had brought a tray of food when they came. It was almost all sweet things, dates and crumbled nuts and honey, dried figs like wrinkled little heads, flatbread wrapped around chunks of cheese. After the girls were gone I sat on the bed and stared at the food, my chin on my knees, wary, as if I expected a viper to uncoil from beneath a platter and strike me. I was so hungry that I felt malleable and shimmery like pounded gold. And it did not matter if I ate this fruit; Admetus would not appear to count the date pits, and I would be kept here whether I sickened myself or not. The cords of my fate had been cut.

I ate the bread and cheese and honey and left the fruit behind. Then I curled up to sleep again; I wanted to be deep in slumber when Admetus returned. And I was. But again the dreams came, and in them came Persephone. In the dreams she said, *I am yours, Alcestis, believe me*—but her face was blurred, as if I were seeing her through tears. The rest of the dream held a predictable misery: easy to guess how many times I reached for her, at what distance my arms seemed to dissolve into smoke.

I woke in the rosy dawn, crying. Admetus stirred a little

but did not wake. I pressed my hands over my mouth and shook, my shoulders heaving, hot all over with the horror of missing her. Spring would come and she would be freed— but I would watch the trees green from this chamber, feel the warm breeze only in the hallways, the courtyard, the frame of the window. Every year I would watch, and I would know that she had come among us again, in the world above, come to live with her lonely mother. She would leave Hades behind, but she would not spend her springs and summers locked in my arms or lazing in my bed. The men would not allow it, not for two women watched as carefully as we would be. They would hold us to our promises, keep us in our marriages, the places we were given as girls and must sorrow in as women. And I would miss her in every fruit and every flower, every pain and every poison, every bit of rot.

I spent the beginning of my last day of silence watching my husband, who didn't know how soon I would speak to him, who had only Heracles' promise for comfort. He still lay asleep beside me; he smelled of smoke again, not of sunshine or laurel. I wondered what sacrifices he had been burning since I returned, to which god, to what purpose.

He blushed when he woke to find me looking at him. I saw the blood travel up from his chest. I lay beside him with my cold cheeks, my newly imperturbable body, and wished I could feel his excitement and anxiety. Wished I could think that the act of speaking to him would make new my story, reshape my world, change my return into a triumph and my heart into a clear and joyful thing.

"Good morning, Alcestis," he said. His voice was wistful. Then he rolled away.

I let him go.

After he dressed and left me, a slave girl came to braid my hair. Her fingers trembled as she combed it out, and when I turned to look out the window, she cried out and dropped my wooden comb. It rattled on the floor, unbroken. I bent to retrieve it and offered it to the girl; she snatched it from my hand jerkily and ran out the door.

I reached up and felt the half-finished plaits around my head. The braids she'd completed seemed uncommonly tight. I had grown used to the sweep of my loose hair across my cheek, tangling in my eyelashes or brushing at the corner of my mouth. But I was a wife again and needed a wife's containing braids. I finished the rest of the braids myself and submitted to be dressed when the Cretan women finally appeared. They stripped my pale shift over my head like removing a skin and wrapped me in bright, living fabric, yellow as a sun.

Then I sat down by the window and waited. Admetus insisted that I not walk on my wounded feet, but he would not let a male slave carry me, would not stay during the day to carry me himself. And yet he returned throughout the day—I'd hear a soft knock at the door and then the sound of his breath as he waited, fruitlessly, for me to call him in. With each visit the wait shortened, and when he knocked not long before sunset, he hardly waited at all.

He smiled at the sight of me in my simple robe. "Alcestis," he said, on a breath of recognition. I lowered my eyes.

But he had grown bolder. He went to the jug and poured water and wine into the empty bowl beside it, carrying it over to set at my feet. He crouched before me, looked up into my face.

"The guests have left," he said. "The courtyard must be cleared and the leavings burnt. The servants are all occupied, but I know how to change a wrapping." He sounded cheerful, confident, but the edges of his smile looked fragile.

"May I?" he asked, reaching out, and I let him lift my foot.

My soles were healing well—indeed, almost too quickly, and the maids had whispered about it when they left my chamber. Admetus tended to my feet wordlessly, his hands gentle. His eyes were dark and lonely in a manner that made me think of Hades. I looked down at his bent head while he worked, at the pale skin usually hidden beneath his curls, now visible, vulnerable. I might have leaned down to kiss his hair—but I could not.

The cuts were still bright red, some of the skin puffy, but they were not much poisoned with dirt. My flesh would knit together, and in time only tiny white scars would remain, like the lines that had crossed my dead grandmother's face. While Admetus worked, I sat on the windowsill and rubbed my fingers in the layer of ash. The servants had still not wiped it clean.

Admetus glanced up at me as he covered my feet with fresh bandages. He seemed nervous in the way Pelias had been nervous before Phylomache gave birth, as if he knew I might change, unexpectedly, and didn't want to miss the moment. This was what awaited me: Admetus and his guilt, this new solicitousness, the blushes that traveled his skin. The children would come, and his concern for me would only grow, for I would then be a true Achaean woman, a producer of heirs. I'd spend long nights staring at the painted stars. It would be, in every outward sense, as if I had never chosen the underworld over the feasting table. I would grow old as Persephone had prophesied, delayed long in this world before I came to death at last.

But still I waited to speak until sunset. I didn't want Admetus to think of Apollo, even indirectly, when I spoke. I wanted him to hear me. I wanted his attention, selfishly, as Persephone had wanted mine. I would never be able to act like this again—to act like a god or a child. This was my last day to try on either role, and I felt furious and almost relieved to have my freedom stripped from me like my pale, thin shift. Life was simpler than death; I would again know how to behave. There were, after all, some rules of Achaean life that I never could give up.

At sunset I put my hands on the sill and leaned out into the air. The window did not snap shut upon me. I watched the heavy way the sun slid below the mountains and thought of the skin stretching on my belly, the springlike promise of life. The horizon darkened.

Someone tapped at the door.

Admetus, startled, rose to collect our dinner from the slave girl and returned with a platter piled with bread and meat and red, polished apples balanced on the edge of the plate and looking as though they might tumble to the floor at any moment. I watched from the window, half hoping that the fruit would fall. I was afraid. I knew what to say, but I did not want to say it.

I waited for him to set down the platter. I could not look at him now; I cast down my eyes, thinking of the goddess's lowered eyelids, thinking of the world hidden beneath the stone floor of our palace, beneath and beyond the earth. Then I asked him hoarsely the words scraping up my throat: "Have you learned to believe that I am Alcestis?"

I'd thought of speaking first to a slave or a maid or to the uncomprehending walls of our bedchamber. Had I not been kept penned in our chamber, I might have spoken to the dirt, hoping my words would travel through the soil to reach

Persephone. But I knew I must speak to him before anyone else. I owed him this much, whatever he thought of me now, whatever he would think of me privately in quiet moments throughout the rest of his long life and mine.

I looked up. He was staring at me—at my mouth—as if he wanted to pry me open and seek out the source of that sound, my voice. He'd spent three days waiting for me to speak and he didn't know what to think. There had been no living men to watch me in the underworld, to shame or honor me, and no one could tell him what had happened to me when I died, not even Heracles. He would have to accept what I said. He would have to take my word, as if I were a man, as if my word were worth taking.

"Alcestis," he said slowly. And then: "Of course. Yes, of course I believe."

[EPILOGUE]

THEY REMEMBERED HER name for centuries, and more than centuries. Poems and songs, plays and dreams of plays, translations. Yet whatever the structure of the verse or the pattern of the chorus, the story remained the same.

She was the wife of Admetus, who so loved him that she gave her life to save his.

She was returned to her husband silent, tainted, as Heracles said, by her time in the underworld. She did not speak for three days. And after that, what? There is no record but the stories of her heroic son, of her murderous half sisters, of her husband's Olympian lover.

She bore two children, a boy and a girl, and lived to raise them; the boy grew to become a bold Achaean warrior, and then he grew old. When the war came, he led the Pheraeans and Iolcans into battle at Troy. He crouched in the dank confines of the horse his brother-in-law had built, his aching arms braced against the walls, listening to the Trojans sing praise to the gods for his army's surrender. He thought of his own wife and his wife's sister, both waiting husbandless at home, no doubt besieged by suitors—for they were daughters of a naiad, and quite beautiful—and reassured himself by thinking that

Ipthime and Penelope had inherited their father's stubborn-
ness. He thought that his wife would sacrifice herself before
allowing another man to take her husband's place, and as he
sweated in the hot wooden gullet of the horse, in the center of
the Trojan city, he was proud.

About her daughter nothing is written. She is blank as a
shade. One could assume that the goddess was correct about
her, as she had been correct about the son—but then one must
also assume that Alcestis died in bed, faint with age, and never
saw the underworld again until she crossed it on Charon's raft,
clinging to the shade beside her, swaying slightly with each
push of the old man's pole in the swampy water.

Her half sisters, Phylomache's children, earned a place in
lyric through the spilling of blood. They grew up bitter and
sharp. When Jason, rightful heir of the king whom Pelias had
long ago deposed, returned to Iolcus and brought with him
the golden fleece and his whispering Eastern wife, Medea,
Phylomache's girls needed little encouragement to turn their
sharpness on their father. No man wants to remember being
bested by his daughter, and so it was fortunate, perhaps, that
Pelias did not have to suffer that injustice for long. They cut
him up and boiled him in a bronze pot—the same pot the head
maid had used to boil water for Hippothoe when she coughed
and coughed in the night.

But even these are not Alcestis' stories—they are stories that
circle around her, draw some energy from her as the shades
in the underworld did, reflect a little of her light. However
incomplete the tales may be, they illuminate her, pick her out
of history and set her in words, shining, as an example for
womankind. Sometimes she seems so bright, so exemplary, so
morally necessary, that words are not enough to describe her.

Her image is carved into sarcophagi, rendered in oil on canvas. In one painting, Alcestis looks toward the sky—or toward the ceiling, perhaps, with its painted stars. Light pours down on her, cool as milk. Her hand splays on her breast. Her other hand, extended, fades into darkness as she reaches toward her stricken husband. She will never touch him. He is not looking at her, anyway; the god Hermes has bent to murmur in his ear. Others have crowded around, trying to touch her, to speak to her, to hold her in the mortal world—but still she looks up, away. She is waiting for death to come and claim her; she's been waiting all her life.